LANGBOURNE'S

Evolution

ALAN P. LANDAU

NATIONAL
LIBRARY
OF AUSTRALIA

A catalogue record for this
book is available from the
National Library of Australia

ISBN: 978-0-9953628-6-4 (Paperback)
ISBN: 978-0-9953628-7-1 (Ebook)
ISBN: 978-0-9953628-8-8 (Audio Book)

Contact details for the author can be found at
www.landaubooks.com

First Edit : Cindy Kramer, South Africa
Final Edit : Mike Kantey, Watercourse Plettenberg Bay
Audio Book Production : AudioShelf
Narrated by : Adrian Galley
First published 2018

To my lovely wife, Sharon,
without whom I would never have written these books.

Chapter One

Bulawayo, Rhodesia 1898

Morris walked briskly along the earthen street into the gloom of their warehouse with a brown folder clutched tightly under his left arm. Wearing a light grey day suit and an ominous frown, he ignored everyone he passed, as his thoughts were all-consuming. David's brow creased as he took in his brother's mood and stole a quick glance at Harry, who merely shrugged in silence. Gently closing the drawer of the cash register, David quietly followed Morris into his office.

"What's wrong?" David asked as he entered the dingy room with some concern in his voice.

"I hate those meetings," Morris snapped as he tossed the folder onto his desk. The sheets of paper inside fanned out slightly, exposing some of Morris' illegible scrawl, doodles and ink blotches.

"Now I have to write up the minutes as the Secretary didn't attend, and you know how I feel about that!"

David was about to offer to write up the minutes for him, but a momentary glance at the illegible scribbles that the brown folder exposed made him change his mind abruptly. "Well, that's what happens when they hold you in such high regard," said David, trying to ease the atmosphere with a compliment.

About seven months earlier, in mid-November 1897, three distinguished elderly gentlemen had approached Morris as he enjoyed a family meal with his brothers at the Charter Hotel, and asked if they might have a private word with him. They introduced themselves as representatives of the Jewish community of Bulawayo, an introduction which had taken Morris by surprise. He had realised, though, that it would have been just a matter of time before his Jewish heritage had been discovered, hard as he had tried to conceal it. They informed him that they had received word that a gentleman overseas called Theodore Herzl had formed a group called the Zionist Organisation, and their first congress had just been held in Basel, Switzerland. The three men had been tasked to establish a branch of the group in Rhodesia, as had other Jews scattered around the world. They didn't have many details of what the organisation was about, or what it stood for, but it had something to do with uniting all Jews around the globe as one voice, possibly because of the persecution they had endured over many decades. They wanted Morris to be the Chairman of the inaugural meeting in Rhodesia and to form the association officially.

Morris had agreed, and so it was that, at the age of 22, he chaired the first meeting of the Rhodesian Zionist Movement just three months after it was formally established in Switzerland. Twenty-four people attended, and it was a most awkward gathering as almost every attendee had a strongly-held personal opinion on what exactly the purpose of the movement was. In the end, Morris dismissed the meeting with only one resolution; the Rhodesian Chapter would just be called the "Friends of Zion Society" and nothing more. It was a perfect solution to a sensitive situation, and the delegates were so well pleased with Morris and his conduct that they immediately appointed him as their President for the future meetings.

"I've decided to resign at the next meeting. I have better things to spend my time on," Morris grumbled as he removed his jacket and hung it on a nail on the wall. He looked at his pocket watch and noticed it had stopped; he had forgotten to wind it that morning, as he was wont to do, which made him even more irritated with the way the day was going.

"What's the time?" he shot at David as he fumbled with the minuscule winding mechanism, giving up almost immediately in frustration.

Right on cue, Harry's muffled voice filtered through to the office, "Time please, ladies and gentlemen."

"Five o'clock precisely, Morris," David announced with a wink.

"Good!" Morris reached for the ledger that stood on its end on a shelf, and sat down at his desk, placing it heavily on top of the committee meeting notes and opening the sturdy leather cover. "Cash up and bring me the figures."

There was very little diplomacy from Morris when he was in a bad mood - even when he was in a good mood for that matter. 'Please' and 'thank you' were rare expressions in Morris' vocabulary, but David understood his brother's ways and didn't expect any extraneous pleasantries from him. Without complaint, David left the room to tally up the daily takings and balance the antiquated cash register that they had acquired at great expense. He had now mastered it and relied heavily on its accuracy. Although Morris was practically a genius at numbers, David preferred the written word, his flamboyant handwriting complementing his literacy skills.

The routine of the end of the trading day was simple; David would cash up and balance the till, while Harry would proudly man the main door and bid their lingering customers a polite farewell as they exited, before bolting the door shut and calling out his traditional thanks to his brothers. David would take the cash and cheques to Morris' office, and Harry would saunter down to the rear of the warehouse to unlatch the back door in anticipation of Louis' arrival. Louis was running the retail branch of Langbourne Brothers on Fife Street, just a couple of blocks away. After Louis arrived, he would likewise give Morris the takings, and then they would all sit in the office discussing the day's events while Morris entered the financials into his ledger, which he guarded with an almost obsessive jealousy.

"Your sales could have been better," Morris griped at Louis.

"It was quiet today, Morris. Tomorrow will be good, though. I have a large sale put aside for Mr Naidoo from that settlement in the east, Um-ti, or whatever it is called."

"Umtali," David interjected. "It's in the mountains, where the Manica tribe lives."

"Yes, that's the one. Mr Naidoo will collect and pay tomorrow morning, so I will get off to a marvellous start."

"Splendid!" Morris' mood seemed to lift momentarily. "He's bought from us before, hasn't he?"

"Yes," Louis confirmed with a decided nod. "He has asked for a credit account this time as he believes he has proven his worth to us now. Is it acceptable if I grant him our usual terms?"

"Agreed?" Morris glanced at David and Harry who nodded their response. "The usual, then. Is he still buying fabric?" Morris asked curiously.

"Indeed," Louis smiled and straightened up slightly. "Material for gentlemen's attire; business suits in particular. I hear that Mr Naidoo has a reputation for being one of the best gentlemen's outfitters in the country. It seems he has even made a business suit for Mr Rhodes, no less!"

"Perhaps you should ask him to fit you out for a suit," said Harry. He looked down at Louis' ankles and nodded at his exposed socks. "You've outgrown your suit already."

"I have already placed my order, actually," Louis grinned. "If any of you brothers would like a fitting, he will be back at Fife Street with his tape measure at eight o'clock sharp. That reminds me, David, please have the document for credit ready for him to sign by then."

"Certainly," David responded.

"Right!" Morris exclaimed, startling his brothers. "We move on. I have decided it is time to move our business to the next level." He paused to make sure he had his three brothers' full attention; the scowl that had slipped away returned with a vengeance.

"Here we go again," David sighed, causing his brothers to look at him curiously.

For the next hour-and-a-quarter, Morris detailed his plans for the immediate future to his brothers. Their business had been brisk, and profits exceptional, but he believed more could be achieved - much more. He was going to go back to Ireland, firstly to see the family and fill them in on all the news from Africa, and then he would be opening a purchasing and shipping business to supply their warehouse in Bulawayo. He knew what had to be done and how he was going to do it.

It had become abundantly clear to the brothers that their primary wholesale supplier, Julian Weil, in Mafeking, had been starting to take advantage of them, increasing prices when there was no necessity to do so by artificially causing shortages of essential commodities, and tweaking interest rates on credit accounts. Morris wanted to become more independent as soon as possible and believed they could make far more profit if they could control their purchases, and the negotiations that went with them, as well as their shipping needs. Indeed, Langbourne Brothers were big enough now to enable these scales of economies to work in their favour.

Another deep concern for Morris was the political climate within the colonies to the south of them. Because of the gold rush to the Witwatersrand in the area that became known as Johannesburg, thousands of mostly new immigrants from abroad had come to seek their fortunes. These new arrivals, known as "Uitlanders", or "Outlanders", by the mostly Dutch-speaking Republicans, or "Boers", had increased so much in number that the Boers began to feel their culture and language identity might become lost, and therefore preferred a tighter authority. The Uitlanders appeared to be contributing far more to the Transvaal economy than the Boers, yet the Boers refused to give them a vote or any say in the running of the economy. The government brought out a law that forced the Uitlanders to relinquish their birthright, and then wait seven years as a stateless person before they would even consider their application for citizenship in the Transvaal. The Uitlanders understandably felt they were disenfranchised and the rule of law was not in their favour either.

In retrospect, Morris and David now understood why Dr Jameson had gathered a force of men from Bulawayo, and, taking off from Mafeking, launched the doomed Jameson Raid. The intention had been to foster an uprising between the Uitlanders and the Boers. Of course, that failed dismally as the Boers had mysteriously learned of his plans before he got there and waited in ambush. Those raiders who were not killed were captured and imprisoned, and the President of the Cape Colony, Mr Cecil John Rhodes, was implicated in sanctioning this raid, forcing him to resign his position as a result. Whatever the true causes might have been, tensions in the Transvaal were at breaking point.

"One of the reasons David and I named our Johannesburg company 'Langbourne Coetsee' is because, if there is another Boer War, whoever wins will hopefully think we are either English, Dutch or both. This will, we theorise, let the business continue without some exorbitant tax or restriction hindering it. Having Danie Coetsee as our silent partner has some very significant hidden advantages for us, and, for this reason, our company in Ireland will also be called Langbourne Coetsee. It should confuse the average Boer or Englishman who has to deal with our shipping papers."

"Is Danie Coetsee Dutch?" Louis asked.

"I don't know," Morris shrugged. "I would assume so as he speaks Afrikaans equally as well as English. He's a capitalist, a businessman, and a good friend. David and I trust him implicitly, which is all that matters."

Part of Morris' plan was to place Louis in the Johannesburg warehouse, where he would work with Danie if necessary. David would control the Bulawayo warehouse, and Harry would run the retail shop on Fife Street. Because travel was so much more convenient now that a train service had been established between Cape Town and Bulawayo, David, being a founder member of the business, would have the added responsibility of supervising all three African companies. Morris would establish and control the Ireland office and keep Africa supplied – on his terms.

"So, when will all this happen?" Harry ventured hesitantly.

Morris leaned forward and placed his elbows on the desk, an aura of authority and command naturally emanating from him as he outlined his plan. "In about one year from now, I will catch that train and start my journey to Ireland. It will take me a good two or three months to get there and set up shop. David, closer to my arrival time in Ireland, I want you and Louis to go down to Johannesburg and prepare our warehouse at 9 Railway Road. Danie kept the rentals up; warehouse availability in Johannesburg is acute at the moment. While you two are doing that," Morris looked Harry in the eye, "you, Harry, will have to run both Fife Street and the warehouse, including our wagon trading arm."

"I can do that," Harry readily agreed. He was confident he could manage, even though it would mean a lot of extra hard work. The necessary systems were in place, and they worked exceptionally well. Further, he was fully competent in all aspects of their business. "I'm assuming we will start employing staff?"

"Yes," Morris nodded and leant back in his seat again, satisfied that his brothers were accepting his visions without objection, "but not until I leave for Ireland. David, you will take care of engaging staff." As usual, there was no 'please', or 'if you will'. Morris didn't expect to pander to his siblings, nor did they expect it from him; it was just the way he was.

David broke the short silence that had descended on the four brothers as they considered this significant change to their way of life. "It will be sad to see you go, Brother. We have made a good team."

"Indeed we have," Morris smiled for the first time that day. "But, time marches on and we must march with it."

Suddenly Morris became very serious again, his brief smile vanishing as if it had never surfaced, and a determined scowl creased his forehead. "Once I have set up the Irish office, I want us to rotate every five years, to manage each branch of our business so that there is always one of us, knowledgeable and in control, in whichever country we may be. Never, and I repeat this, never must we allow anyone outside our family to control our business. Do you understand?"

His question was so venomous that all three brothers, including the placid and calm David, were somewhat taken aback.

David looked Morris in the eye, his head cocked, slightly confused by this statement. "At the rate you are thinking of expanding, we will run out of brothers very smartly. Surely we will need managers who have some form of autonomy or authority to conduct business?"

"Ahh... You misunderstand me," said Morris, rocking back in his seat. "Yes, we will have managers and staff, but only we four brothers will hold the cheque book, sign legal documents, or make corporate or business decisions, and always in conjunction with each other. Managers and the like can run the day-to-day operation of our outlets."

"Alright, I can agree with that," David said slowly, nodding his acceptance. The younger brothers cautiously replicated his nod, somewhat nervous to do anything else.

"Good!" Morris exclaimed. "Now for something important I want to discuss with you."

"Heavens, Morris," David sighed, "what could be more important than that?"

"Oh, this is important, mark my words," he said, the smile returning to his face fleetingly. "Our company is called Langbourne Brothers, and that is because David and I, brothers, started the business in Port Elizabeth before you two even set foot in Africa. As you know, there are two shareholders and two directors of this company: David and myself, brothers," he repeated. "We are the founder members, so to speak."

David realised where this conversation was going and began to relax and smile a little, but noticed Harry and Louis still looked concerned, and unsure.

"Right now," Morris continued, keeping his gaze fixed on his two younger siblings, "you two gentlemen are nothing but unpaid workers in the business. You have never asked for anything, and have shown nothing but true loyalty to our family and our business." Morris looked at David and smiled broadly. "What do you say we formally include these two scoundrels into the firm and give them a wage?"

David allowed a chuckle to escape. "I think that's a sterling idea, Brother."

Louis and Harry began to smile, and visibly relaxed. Morris could be very unpredictable, and all three brothers were fully aware of his blunt mannerisms. Only David had an uncanny ability to control Morris, to calm him down or take what he threw at him on the chin, never letting his unusual character get to him personally. Harry, the youngest, was very similar to Morris in personality and looks, but also found him hard to deal with on occasions, and secretly preferred to be in David's company when things got a little hot under Morris' collar.

"Right-oh," Morris beamed, "David and I would like to officially invite you into the business, as equal shareholders, and to be eligible for an equal wage and trading dividend if and when one is declared. However, there is one condition that you both need to accept before we formalise this decision."

David held his breath momentarily as he was expecting the next condition from Morris to be either calmly accepted, or cause a massive argument to erupt. He and Morris had discussed this issue the previous week during one of their walks around the pavements of Bulawayo. Morris was convinced the younger brothers would not object in the slightest, but David wasn't as confident.

Morris took a deep breath and continued. "Our cigarette business in Port Elizabeth grossed us about £75 000 profit, which we invested into the Bulawayo business, and subsequently lost it all during the Matabele wars and the Rinderpest plague."

"Well, I would say that the Rinderpest was a blessing, not a curse," Harry surprisingly interrupted, which caught Morris entirely off guard.

David laughed. "I think Harry might have a point there, Brother!"

Although Morris' volatile and embarrassing behaviour resulted in a vast quantity of their stock to be lost in the Rhodesian bush for over a year, almost sending them into bankruptcy, the change in the commercial environment after the wagons had been located made the family a lot of money with the massive increases in local prices.

Morris smiled thinly, his eyes conveying that he was not impressed by the interruption. "Nevertheless,' he continued, 'before we induct you into our business, I want to make it clear that the first £75 000 profit our company made will be distributed between David and myself in equal shares. That money, because of the risks we took to get it, belongs to us. After that, all profits we make will be distributed equally among the four of us."

For a brief moment, it looked like Louis and Harry would object to all their hard work for the company going unrewarded.

"I trust you two have no objections to that?" David asked quickly; he knew his brothers regarded his opinions very highly, and if he were in agreement with Morris, they would probably not question him.

"Absolutely," Louis smiled back, quickly realising it would be pointless to argue the matter.

"We would be honoured to be equal partners of Langbourne Brothers," Harry added his concurrence.

Morris winked at David, a secret smile hooked at one corner of his lips as if to say 'I told you so!'

"Splendid!" Morris rocked back and clapped his hands in the air, showing his delight.

Louis raised his hand slightly to interject politely. "If I may, Brother Morris?" he asked, "when do you anticipate the business making £75 000 profit?"

"I'm glad you asked," Morris beamed as he opened the leather-bound ledger that was on his desk. He ran his finger down the last column of numbers on the page and stopped at a figure that was scrawled in his sloppy handwriting. "Behold!" he proudly announced as if he were a magician who had just performed a miraculous trick.

The two younger brothers leant forward and scrutinised the final figure on the page: £74 997 with a few shillings and pence after the numbers, but no one was looking at the small stuff.

"Unless you put less than £3 in the tills today, then..."

"My first sale this morning was for £12," Harry said with a smirk.

"Then, today is the day! Remember this date, gentlemen." Morris smiled openly and closed the journal. "The 8th of June 1898."

A gentle round of banter took over as the brothers congratulated each other. It was indeed a memorable day, and they all took a brief moment, in their own unique way, to reflect on what had happened in the last six months or so.

"Mr Secretary," Morris suddenly became serious and addressed David, slipping into his usual stern business mode, "We need to record this meeting formally. Do we have a quorum?"

"Yes Mr Chairman," David announced, cocking an eyebrow with a sly smile.

Morris was pedantic about business etiquette and formalities. When he called a meeting, even with his brothers, he conducted himself, and the meeting, in a most formal manner. He did it for two reasons. Firstly because he believed business was a very essential and vital part of their lives, and all seriousness must be given when conducting these affairs. Secondly, Morris felt it was good practice and training for the young entrepreneurs for future meetings, be it corporate, committee or association matters.

When members of good standing in the community came across his antics in various situations, they would at first mock him behind his back, but very soon the tide would swing, and they came to respect and admire his dedication and professionalism. This was one of the reasons why the Jewish community approached him to Chair the first meeting of this new Zionist movement.

Since everything Morris wanted to discuss had already been covered, and none of the brothers wished to add anything, Morris moved the meeting to a close in record time and then quickly suggested they go to the Charter Hotel to have a well-deserved meal.

"We also have some celebrating to do, now that Louis and Harry are fully-fledged members of the business." Morris stood abruptly and reached for his jacket. "David, you will attend to the minutes of this meeting, won't you?"

David nodded as the boys donned their jackets before leaving through the big wooden doors at the back of the warehouse.

During the short walk to the Charter Hotel, the conversation flowed freely among the boys. Even as early as six o'clock in the evening, the streets were all but deserted, and the businesses closed up for the night. Only the dining rooms of the few established hotels remained open, as well as the officer's mess in the camp of the British South Africa Company. The company had been reconstituted lately from a paramilitary unit into a new and independent entity, called the British South Africa Police, or BSAP, which was rapidly gaining respect in the community.

"You must be excited about returning home to Ireland," Louis said to Morris, who smiled inwardly.

"Yes, indeed," he said. He was keen to reconnect with his family and to start the purchasing office. He was sure that this new development would further streamline an already efficient operation, enabling them to earn yet more money than they were currently receiving.

As the younger boys strolled along on Morris' left and right, David drifted slightly behind them, preferring not to take part in this aspect of the conversation. He was aching inside, knowing that his brother, mentor, and business partner was leaving him. They had always been a close-knit pair, but now, suddenly, distance would play a significant part in their relationship. It was going to be tough for him, but he couldn't show it. As much as he had wished that this day would never come, he had known it most certainly would.

"And you'll be able to meet your new brother and sister at last!" Harry piped in excitedly.

"Hang on, hang on!" Morris threw his arms in the air without breaking his stride, "I don't have a new brother or sister. Those children father had with his marriage to Aunt Helena are not my siblings."

"But..." Louis tried to object.

"No, wait a minute," Morris stopped suddenly and turned to face his brothers; this subject irritated him. "Mother had seven children, Bloomy, me, David, and May, who died at birth," Morris counted the children on his fingers in order of age, "then Louis, Harry and Sally. That's all! We are her family. Aunt Helena came to help Bloomy raise you two before Mother passed away from her illness. Aunt Helena is not your mother; she is your aunt."

"Father told us to call her Mother, so we do." Harry objected.

"Fair enough, I accept that you respect our father's wishes, but I'm not calling her 'Mother'!" Morris exclaimed, thumping his finger hard on his chest. "Heavens! It's bad enough that Father married our Mother's niece, and then went on to have two children with her, but she is only a little older than me. No, I'm not calling her 'Mother'!" Morris' tirade continued after a short pause, "and let me tell you something else: as far as I am concerned, these two children they have had are neither my brother nor my sister; and don't contemplate for even a moment that they will have a share in my business." He thumped his finger on his chest again to enforce his point. "Langbourne Brothers is only for us four brothers, standing here tonight: Mother's only four sons."

There was an uncomfortable silence as the younger boys looked sheepishly at each other.

"In reality," Louis ventured cautiously, "Mother – I beg your pardon – Aunt Helena, is your step-mother. And Rachel and Erin are your half-sister and half-brother."

"Yes," Morris said dejectedly, "I cannot argue that, but they are not my siblings, let's get that clear. Up until now, I have not even met them."

"Well, Rachel is quite cute, actually," Harry smiled as he cast his memory back to Ireland, "but Erin is just an infant. They say he looks like our father."

"Harry!" Morris put his hand up to stop him. "That's enough on that subject. We will discuss it no further. Now, let's get something to eat before I lose my appetite." Morris spun on his heel and marched on.

As the four boys strode off to the Charter Hotel in a strained silence, David, who was still at the rear of the group, suddenly started giggling.

"What's so funny, David?" Morris called brusquely over his shoulder, not looking back.

"I've got some bad news for you, Morris," he replied, starting to chuckle louder. "If Aunt Helena is Mother's niece, and if she has married Father, then Aunt Helena is both our step-mother and our first cousin. It seems that their children are well and truly related to you."

Morris continued walking without missing a step, totally ignoring what David had said. After about twenty paces he slowly lifted his arms to the heavens and looked into the pristine night sky, shaking his head resignedly from side to side.

David could no longer contain himself and burst into raucous laughter.

MINUTES OF AN EXTRAORDINARY GENERAL MEETING
OF LANGBOURNE BROTHERS
Held at Langbourne Brothers, Abercorn Street, Bulawayo, Rhodesia.
On 8th June 1898 at 5:20pm

Present:
M Langbourne (Chairman)
D Langbourne (Secretary)
L Langbourne (Treasurer)
H Langbourne (Member)

Chairman's Address:

The Chairman welcomed those present to the meeting and expressed his gratitude for the help with the business.

ML confirmed that all debts to the business had been settled.

With the advent of international telegraph wires, and the arrival of a railway line, the company was ready to expand internationally.

The new retail store on Fife Street was performing exceptionally well under LL's management, and he was heartily congratulated.

HL to proceed to Johannesburg and command Langbourne Coetzee. DL to oversee Jbh and both Byo stores. DL tasked to reward Nguni and Daluxolo for their loyalty.

Dividend: The first dividend of the business was unanimously approved and distributed equally between ML and DL.

Shareholders: LL and HL invited to become equal shareholders of Langbourne Bros. They accepted and were warmly welcomed by ML & DL. Future dividends to be shared equally between ML, DL, LL and HL.

All matters were unanimously agreed upon.

There being no further business, the meeting closed at 5:26pm with a vote of thanks to the Chair.

Signed:

Secretary   Chairman/Treasurer

Chapter Two

England 1899

Slipping over the greasy waters, the ship crept silently towards her dock, her horn bellowing mournfully over the grey, soot-stained apartments that lined Southampton's harbour. The responding echo was nearly as loud. It was 4 o'clock in the morning on a very calm sea with hardly a whisper of a breeze to unsettle one's hair. Most dockside residents were still fast asleep, wrapped up in the warmth of their blankets, but the ship's captain did not care for that; he had a vessel to dock, and nothing else mattered.

As early as the hour was, with barely a hint of the morning sun penetrating the gloomy skies above, Morris stood on the bow in his thick, pure-wool overcoat, watching the shoreline approach far too slowly. Forever impatient, he had been confined to the cabins of the steamship for nearly three weeks and was desperate to disembark.

The slight chill in the air forced Morris to pull his collar up roughly around his neck, before plunging his hands back into the warmth of his pockets. It was taking far too long to reach the land, but as the buildings became more visible through the light fog, he reflected on the day he had departed from this port for the southern tip of Africa.

He had been away from his original home and family for about eight years. It had been a most incredible time, but to Morris, this was just part of life, part of growing up; it was nothing unusual. He had been 16 when he had run away with his younger brother David, leaving the poverty, hunger, and cold of Ireland behind. Travelling first to London with some money that he found hidden between the pages of books, both he and David had consciously bought some quality, stylish garments to improve their image. Their purchases had included felt Derby hats, suspenders, and expensive-leather brogue shoes. They had then boarded the first available ship to Southern Africa. That was in 1891.

Almost immediately, Morris silently acknowledged to himself, they had enjoyed some success, and they had made good money in the process, but it was not without risk to life. In fact, thinking about it now, the hazards had at times been extreme. In the heart of Africa, though, the dangers both man and beast had to endure were necessary, almost commonplace. Morris gave a barely noticeable shrug as he stared unblinkingly at the shoreline. Walking through the African bush in one direction for three months among wild and ferocious animals was accepted as a requirement at the time. Of course, now that a railway line stood completed, one would be insane to attempt that again. "No," Morris thought aloud, "we did the right thing, the necessary thing, at the time, and it has paid off."

The ship's offensive horn bellowed across the harbour once more, long and low. The occasional window on the shoreline began to show signs of candlelight, and Morris could not bear the suspense any longer. He turned on his heel and made his way to the dining hall in the hopes of finding a cup of hot coffee. "Maybe by the time I have had some coffee, we will be on that damn shore..." he muttered quietly to himself.

Once on shore, Morris didn't waste any time arranging a passage to Dublin, where his family lived. Unlike the day he had left the country eight years previously, carefully protecting the money he had in his pockets, he now travelled first class - whether by rail, ferry, or carriage. Having had some reasonable success, Morris booked overnight accommodation in expensive hotels and only dined in their top restaurants. It soon struck him, however, that he was by far the youngest person in these establishments and that he appeared to attract some strange stares and raised eyebrows from the fellow gentry, who were all, in Morris' opinion, old men.

Guests and staff of the hotels Morris stayed in were civil enough to doff their hat, or nod a courteous greeting at him, which he readily reciprocated, but that was as far as the politeness would go. They would happily stop and chat with fellow residents, but when he approached they would quietly turn a shoulder or tactfully move away. It confused Morris, but he didn't dwell on it much as his attention always focused on finding his father. In any case, it thrilled him to enjoy the new tastes and flavours at meal times, undisturbed and on his own.

When he disembarked from the train in Dublin, he did not recognise any of the buildings or streets. Nevertheless, everyone he approached for directions to St. Kevin's Parade in Wood Quay was more than delighted to point him in the right direction. The Irish, he thought, were far more hospitable than the people in England!

With their red-brick walls and slate-roof tiles, the double-storey apartments in St. Kevin's Parade were not too difficult to locate. It was a fairly lengthy walk, but, with only one tote bag to his name, Morris had no trouble covering the distance; he was used to far more significant journeys, anyhow. He stopped at the top of the street and looked at the row of buildings on both sides - all the same colour and all devoid of any plant life.

"Excuse me, sir," Morris asked a man who was walking past him at a plodding pace, pushing a barrow, "I'm seeking the Langbourne residence. I believe the family lives on this street. Would you know..?"

"Aye," the man said slowly cutting Morris off. "He'd be the Rabbi what lives haaf way down the street."

Both Morris and the old man stared down the row of houses in silent anticipation, almost expecting a man in a flowing black robe to appear from a doorway. The street was empty, apart from two young girls who were playing contentedly on the pavement.

"The Rabbi?" Morris tore his perplexed stare from the street and addressed the barrow-pushing man squarely.

"Aye," the man responded dreamily, as though something equally as uninteresting had crossed his mind, distracting him.

"Langbourne?" Morris tried to pull the gent's attention back. "The Rabbi? He lives down this street, does he? Which house?"

"Aye," the man repeated, and putting down the barrow, painstakingly lifted one arm and pointed to where he was looking. "'Bout haaf way down, on yer rayt, perhups, or maybe the left."

"Halfway down?" Morris had become impatient and wanted to keep moving; this man was not very helpful. "Right oh, thank you, sir," he snapped and strode off before the old man could even acknowledge his thanks, or lower his arm.

"Good Lord," Morris mumbled to himself, "there must be fifty doors on each side of the street. Halfway down? And the Rabbi? Has father become a Rabbi? That wouldn't surprise me. Good Lord...!"

He was still mumbling irritably to himself when he stopped to look at the closest set of four doors on his right. "Can you believe it?" Morris burst out, dropping his tote bag unceremoniously at his feet and folding his arms in disgust. "There's not a single number on any of the doors!"

"Are you lost, Mister?" the older of the two girls who had been playing in the street asked when she saw him standing indignantly, looking decidedly annoyed and casting sharp glances at all the doors up and down the road.

"Well, I hope not," Morris replied, his scowl softening at her innocent face and curious smile. She looked to be nine or ten years' old with porcelain-smooth skin and jet-black hair that hung loosely down to the small of her back. She also wore a bright, floral dress that further reached to her ankles.

The younger child, whom Morris thought could be no more than four years old, was carrying a ginger tabby cat and sidled up to the older girl. "Hello," she smiled happily, "this is my cat, Toffie!"

Morris' couldn't help but smile now. "That's nice. And how old are you?"

"I'm four years old," she said proudly. "How old are you, Mister?" she asked, thrusting her cat at Morris.

Morris cleared his throat. "I'm... I mean, I've just turned 24," he stammered, pleasantly caught by surprise at her forthright and youthful innocence, but stepping back ever so slightly to keep out of reach of the cat.

"What's your name, Mister?" she pressed.

"Morris," he obliged.

"My eldest brother is also called Morris," the ten-year-old said, matter-of-factly.

"Is that so? Is he here?" Morris asked hopefully. "He might know the man I am looking for."

"No," she almost sang out casually. "He's not here, but my father is here," she smiled as she cast a quick glance at the black wooden door to her left.

"Please, would you kindly ask him to come out and perhaps give me some directions?"

"Certainly, Mister Morris. Come." She took the little girl's free hand, "let's go find Abba."

As the two children walked inside with Toffie slumped miserably over the crook of the younger girl's arm, tail flicking in irritation, Morris tapped the toe of his shoe against his duffle bag to reassure himself that it was still there, then started to scan the row of houses in his view. He was now the only person on the street and began to feel a little isolated. Morris tried to calculate how long it would take to walk back into town to a somewhat prestigious hotel he had passed earlier, the name of which now escaped him. If he didn't find his family in the next two hours, he would abandon the exercise for the day and head back into Dublin. His thoughts were interrupted when the two girls came out the house babbling excitedly, each holding a hand of a big man, immaculately dressed, but in his shirtsleeves. He had a full beard that he had perfectly groomed and presented the distinct image of a well-respected statesman.

The moment the man saw Morris, however, he froze in disbelief.

"Father?" Morris addressed the man calmly, but he wanted to dance for joy. The head of his family had not changed one iota.

Jacob didn't hold back his emotions; he let go of the young girls' hands and leapt down the two steps to the pavement, embracing Morris in a robust, fatherly hug. It caught Morris off guard, and he had to quickly rescue the Derby hat that had almost been knocked off his head in the process.

"My son, my son!" Jacob blubbered, as tears of joy began to roll down his cheeks. He let go of his grip and instantly held Morris' shoulders, shaking him slightly, almost as if to prove to himself that this was not an illusion, but his first-born son in the flesh.

"It has been a long time, Father," said Morris calmly.

"Is it really you, Morris? Look how you have grown!" Jacob almost shouted, and then, glancing up at the sky thanked his Lord in Hebrew. Morris didn't quite catch what he had said; it had been a very long time since he had heard the Hebrew language, and he had been quite young at the time, but he understood his father's elation, and gratitude for prayers answered.

Morris wanted to break free of Jacob's grip and attempted to reach down for his duffel bag as a means to do so, but it was hopeless. Jacob's joy would not be interrupted, and Morris couldn't get a word in at all. Secretly, he enjoyed the attention, but it was getting a bit much, and he was concerned at what bystanders might think. Thankfully, a quick glance around his father's torso showed the street was still devoid of human population.

Suddenly a look of concern came over Jacob's face, and he looked Morris in the eye. "Your brothers? Are they alright?"

"Yes, yes, Father," Morris smiled openly, "they send their love. I have much news to tell you."

"Praise our Lord God Almighty!" Jacob boomed. "Come inside Morris, come inside and meet your family." He took Morris by the arm, allowing him to quickly snatch his tote bag off the pavement before turning on his heel, heavily bumping into the ten-year-old girl, who had crept up close behind him, curiosity getting the better of her.

"Oh, Sarah! I'm sorry, I didn't see you there," Jacob apologised, gripping her gently by the shoulder too. "Sarah, this is…"

"Sarah?!" Morris exclaimed, his eyebrows arched high. "Is that you? Sarah Sally? My sister?" There was almost a look of disbelief and confusion on Morris' face.

"Yes!" Jacob shouted, perhaps a little too loudly. "She has grown up since you left, Morris, don't you think?"

"He's not my brother, Abba. Brother Morris doesn't look like him."

"No?" Jacob chuckled and put another reassuring hand on her shoulder. "He is your brother, I promise you."

Morris carefully dropped to one knee to bring himself down to her level. "When I last saw you, you were only three years old, and I was sixteen," he said gently. "I am the same person, only I have also grown up, just like you have. I can't believe you are ten years old. You look so different - such a big girl now. I didn't recognise you."

"But I have other brothers. Do you know them?" There was a slight tremble in her voice as she tried to comprehend that this stranger, this adult, was the almost unknown brother she had believed she loved and missed so dearly her entire life. He was different now, very different to what she remembered. He had a masculine shadow on his cheeks and chin and wore a rich man's clothing. He was broader around the shoulders, and the colour of his skin had deepened; yet he looked somewhat similar to the brother she recalled when he had been so thin, undernourished, pale and dressed like a pauper.

"Yes, I know them, they are my brothers, too." Morris cast a quick glance up at his father, whose tears were flowing freely down his face. "David, and Louis, and Harry. They were all with me in Africa when I left them just three weeks ago. They send their love to you."

"Are they in Dublin, too? I miss them."

"No," Morris said sadly and squeezed her hand. "Not this time; but they will come back and visit you. That is a promise. Harry especially misses you; he told me to tell you that."

Sarah began to smile, then wrapped her arms around Morris' neck as realisation settled in. "I missed you, my brother. You have changed so much, but you are my brother, and I love you."

"I missed you, too, Sarah," Morris spoke gently, before breaking their embrace to stand up. "Come on, take me inside, and show me your home."

"Come, come!" Jacob enthused, as he proudly ushered everyone inside. "Give me your bag, son. We have much to discuss; we will prepare your room; you must eat."

Jacob babbled endlessly until they were well inside the home, Sarah skipping excitedly ahead as she took the lead.

Once inside, Morris hung his hat on a crude hook that protruded from the wall, out of reach of the children (and any inquisitive felines), then quickly observed the décor of the interior. It was modest but comfortable, a far cry from the home he had left when he stole off to Africa. It had been more of a cottage in an open field on a farmstead. It had consisted of two rooms, one of which he had shared with his brothers, while his father had slept in the living area on a small bed that had doubled as a couch, or a bench by the kitchen table during daylight hours. The cottage had been draughty and cold, had leaked in the rain, and the kitchen fire had struggled in vain to keep them warm.

This new flat, however, was solid, warm and cosy. An old painting of an Irish landscape hung on one wall of the lounge in a tacky frame, the glue at the bottom right-hand corner of which had failed and was coming loose. A vase stood on the dining table with nothing in it, and a bookcase leant against the wall with several old books. It was apparent to Morris that the reading matter belonged to his father, as the books all seemed to centre on religious subjects.

Morris was more concerned about the state of the building, though, than the décor, as it was he, or rather his business in Africa, that was paying the rent. He turned his back to the fireplace, even though there was no fire burning, and put his hands in his pockets, unconsciously jingling two coins together. He carefully observed the ceilings, window frames, and wooden finishes, and was somewhat satisfied that at least his family was living comfortably, protected from the harsh elements that would so often descend upon the people of Ireland. Morris then looked towards the kitchen where his father was excitedly putting a blackened kettle on the fire and instructing Sarah to find the best crockery. His attention was distracted when the four-year-old child walked up to him and thrust her cat at him again.

"Hold Toffie," she boldly instructed him.

"Go see if you can help Sarah." Without taking his hands out of his pockets, Morris jerked his head towards the kitchen. He was not interested in cats, and in any case, he didn't want any dirt or hair on his new business suit.

"She doesn't need any help," the child retorted indignantly. "Here: say 'hello' to Toffie."

Just at that moment, Sarah entered the room with two teacups on mismatched saucers. "What's your friend's name?" Morris asked Sarah, trying to divert all attention away from the unwanted bundle of fur.

"That's Rachel," Sarah answered sweetly with a coy smile. "She's not my friend; she's my sister."

"Your sister?" Morris repeated, cocking his head in trying to understand what she said.

"So she is your sister, too," Sarah beamed, setting the teacups down on the dining table with a gentle clink.

"My sister? No, my sister... our sister is Bloomy."

"Yes, Bloomy is my older sister, and..."

"Of course!" Jacob thundered in from the kitchen, holding an enamel teapot in one hand and a bowl of sugar in the other. "You don't know your new family; it's been such a long time. Morris, this is Rachel Raie, my first born from my second wife." He quickly placed the kettle on the table and put his hand on Rachel's head.

"Ahh, yes, you did mention it some years back, I remember. I must congratulate you and Aunt Helena on your marriage."

"Thank you, son." Jacob accepted the comment with a nod, but the veiled sarcastic reference to 'the aunt' did not escape him. "With the advent of our marriage, Helena became your step-mother. Perhaps you might like to address her as 'Mother' from now on?"

"No," Morris stated firmly. He was not one for beating around the bush, and diplomacy was not his strong point, even towards his father. "She is first and foremost my cousin, Father. Before we left for Africa I was much younger, and as a mark of respect, we addressed her as 'Aunt' - also because she took the role of the matron of the house. I feel that, because she is both cousin and step-mother, it will be appropriate for me to call her by her first name only."

Jacob took a breath and nodded his agreement. He remembered Morris' forthright and somewhat abrupt demeanour. He had hoped Morris' character had softened with age but feared Africa might have hardened him instead. And now his son was standing in his lounge, in a very expensive suit, oozing confidence and importance, and it was evident that he was well-moneyed.

"As you wish, Son." Jacob returned to the teapot. "I am sure she will be agreeable to that." To his slight relief, he noticed a small smile begin at the corners of Morris' mouth, and he was pleased that they could now move past this issue, something he had correctly suspected would be a bone of contention with his first-born son. Jacob understood that his marriage to Helena had nothing to do with Morris, it was just that he felt acceptance within the family, all members of the family, bode well for a close family unit, something that was extremely important to him.

The tea, having been poured, both father and son took seats near the window, while the children played quietly on the floor at their feet. Morris settled into the old chair and crossed his ankles, ready to fill his father in on the eight years of news, when the front door opened down the hallway, causing the young girls to leap to their feet and run to meet the visitor, shouting "Ima!" in excitement.

"Helena has returned from the grocery store," Jacob told Morris as the big man stood up to greet her in the corridor. "Wait here, Son, I will bring her through."

Morris stood up politely and waited by his seat, all the time listening to his father's excited voice as he told Helena that Morris has returned. She sounded thrilled to hear this news and came bustling into the lounge, followed closely by Jacob. She held a young child on her hip.

"Morris!" she almost squealed. "I can't believe this! Look at you. How wonderful to see you, welcome home." She embraced Morris with her free hand and kissed him once on each cheek.

"Helena," Morris responded politely. She was looking radiant and healthy; her face a picture of happiness. He also could not help noticing how Helena had blossomed into a most beautiful woman. When Morris had last seen her, she had been so thin it looked as if a gust of wind might have done her some damage.

Now her dress fitted her well, while the skirt billowed out copiously from her waist. Morris' anxious feelings about her subsided slightly; he was pleased to see her, despite the fact that she had married into his family. If he were totally honest with himself, he was actually quite happy about this now.

Morris thought back to the day he had departed for Africa. He had resented that his father had lost all interest in supporting his family and that he had failed to provide for them and had led them into a dangerous state of hunger and poverty. It had been left to him and his brother, David – no more than 16 and 15 years old at the time – to be forced to work in appalling conditions and earn a subsistence wage as labourers. He had loved his close-knit family, including his father, but these polar sentiments about him were most confusing. Morris accepted that his father loved all his children passionately, but, at the same time, he had seemed pathetic at supporting them. Jacob had been a successful businessman in Poland, so Morris couldn't understand why he had seemed to implode as soon as they had secretly left there for a better life in England, and ultimately in Ireland. When his beloved wife had then passed away, Jacob had appeared to descend so deeply into an abyss of despair that he could not be saved.

Another thing Morris recognised was that Jacob was an outstanding teacher, and had taught his family, in particular the boys, all about business, money, etiquette, and social skills. It had been thanks to his teachings that all the brothers in the family had become astute businessmen and readily accepted by their peers. Although Morris had given his brothers a hard time in Africa, he knew that they were smart and thought quickly in every regard.

Helena's light-hearted conversation snapped him back to the present. "When did you arrive? Are you here for good? Oh, you must tell me everything! Leave no details to the wind."

Morris raised his hands and chuckled, "Slow down," he smiled, "I have not made firm plans for the future yet, and yes, I have many years of news to tell you all." Then, casting a glance at the baby on her hip, he asked who that was, knowing that the answer would be Erin, as news of the second-born from this new marriage had long since reached him in Bulawayo.

"This," Helena propped the child higher on her hip, "is Paddy."

"Paddy?" Morris raised his eyebrows, not expecting to hear that.

"Well," Helena giggled coyly, "we wanted to name him Erin, but the midwife was illiterate, as most people are around here, and she recorded his name at the Births Registry as Aaron; the silly woman." Helena clucked her tongue in feigned disgust but smiled. "Anyhow, we don't like the name Aaron, so we have named him Patrick, or Paddy, a good Irish name."

"I see," Morris smiled without emotion as he became distracted by a commotion that began over her shoulder. A toddler came waddling into the room and turned directly towards the kitchen. "And whose child is that?" Morris questioned hesitantly.

"Ahh," Helena looked over her shoulder at the infant. "That's Ernest. He is two years old; my third child."

"Good grief!" Morris mumbled to himself, but it came out louder than he had expected, causing his father to cast a stern eye on him. "Well, I, umm ... my congratulations once again." Morris tried to cover up his rudeness but didn't manage too well.

At that moment, Rachel entered the room pushing a perambulator, and the moment Morris set eyes on the contraption, a piercing scream from a baby came tearing into the small room, causing Morris to screw up one eye as the wretched sound raked at a nerve in his ear.

"And that, my dear Morris," Helena smiled as she turned to address the disturbance, "is Tillie, your youngest sister."

Morris looked at Jacob, horrified at what he had just discovered. Jacob was not sure if it was a look of terror, disgust, or disapproval, and quickly moved to calm the situation down.

"Yes, Morris, our family has grown since you went away," he said with an air of authority, "some tea, perhaps?"

"Tea?" Morris looked perplexed and carefully sat down in his chair. "Indeed, thank you, tea would be very welcome. It is a little overwhelming to come home to find a new family, Father. I have returned to four half-siblings I didn't know I had."

"Five, actually." Jacob broke into a pleasing smile as he carefully poured the steaming beverage into a porcelain cup, "Helena is with child."

Only five minutes had passed since Morris had stepped under the roof of his father's home when an overwhelming need to escape invaded his very being. He had no time for screaming infants; the grubby, wayward hands of toddlers; or the excess fur from a moulting cat. He was uncomfortable with his father's marriage to his cousin, and the unexpected multitude of offspring they were producing. Had it not been for the very welcome arrival of his elder sister, Bloomy, Morris would have found an excuse to leave, his mind having been rushing about in search of both a plausible and an acceptable reason to depart.

When Bloomy arrived, however, Morris' spirits lifted immeasurably, and a certain degree of calmness was restored. Finally, a family member who had not changed in any way, and whom he adored, had walked back into his life as though she had never left.

Bloomy was looking radiant. Under her woollen overcoat, she wore a blue frock with matching summer shoes. Although she was apparently eating well enough, she had not gained any weight since Morris had last seen her eight years ago. Bloomy was still slender and tall and carried herself with a grace that reminded him of his mother. The joy of seeing his beloved sister vanished in a whisper when, immediately behind her, he noticed a strange man, pushing a further two infants in a perambulator.

When Bloomy saw Morris standing by the window in the lounge, hands clasped behind his back and smiling sweetly at her, she squealed in pure delight, rushing to him and flinging her arms around him in a tight squeeze, sobbing openly. Unlike his reaction to his father's hug, Morris willingly accepted her embrace, and, for a moment, nothing else in the world mattered to either of them. Brother and sister had been reunited in a close family bond.

Bloomy was the first to break the embrace and excitedly turned to the stranger. "Morris," she murmured, "this is my husband, Bernard Zeider."

"I didn't know you were married!" Morris shook Bernard's hand, although he was talking to Bloomy, staring at her disbelievingly. "Why didn't you tell me?"

Bloomy looked hurt. "I did write. Perhaps you never got the letter."

"I certainly did not," Morris stated indignantly, not quite sure what to make of this new and surprising development.

"And these are our two daughters, Esther and Jeanne," and, at the mention of their names, the two little ones set up a clamorous crying. Bernard took the cue to rapidly take them outside, leaving Morris to recover from a mild state of shock.

After a short while, the remaining adults thoughtfully left Bloomy and Morris to themselves while they attended to the children and prepared the evening meal. It was accepted that the two elder siblings had a special kinship, and it warmed Jacob's heart to see them engrossed in earnest conversation.

Suddenly, Morris sneezed three times in quick succession and fumbled for his handkerchief. "Excuse me," Morris apologised.

"I hope your journey has not made you ill," Bloomy soothed.

"No, I believe it is the cat. I find cats tend to irritate my nose and eyes. Perhaps we could go for a walk and get some fresh air before Father and Helena serve dinner?"

"What a wonderful idea." Bloomy winked at Morris and almost whispered with a coy smile. "I'd quite prefer to have you to myself if the truth be known!" Taking Morris' hand and pulling him to his feet, she called out to the others that the two of them would be going for a walk.

"Dinner will be ready in half an hour; don't be late," Jacob laughed, the joy of his son's return still overwhelming him.

Although Morris didn't need his fancy Derby hat, he took it with him as he exited the house, more because he didn't want to leave it unattended inside than for any other reason. As soon as they were on the pavement, Bloomy hooked her arm around the crook of Morris' elbow and continued chatting unabated, but this time her conversation was a little more unguarded and relaxed.

"Tell me about our brothers. How are they?"

"They are well, Bloomy." Morris smiled fondly as he remembered his siblings in the heart of the sub-continent. "David is an exceptional person. He works very hard; I have taxed him physically and mentally, mind you, but he does what I ask without objection, and always far better than I ask of him. You would be proud of David."

"I'm proud of you, Morris." Bloomy squeezed his arm affectionately as they continued to stroll past some terraced flats. "Who would have guessed you two would have been so successful in business over there. Father is beside himself with pride."

"Is Father working?" Morris cut in, feeling it essential to get some nagging concerns out of the way.

"No," Bloomy sighed. "I don't know what it is with him. He's been offered employment by some of the members of the congregation, but he always finds a reason why he cannot do it."

"Why? He is obligated to care for his family," Morris exclaimed.

"Morris," Bloomy said calmly, "some things with men cannot be explained. I have heard the other women at work discussing similar things that happen to some of the ladies in the community. It is as if," Bloomy paused and looked at the sky for a moment, "as if, on some days, there is a dark cloud that hangs over his shoulders, even though the sun is shining and the birds are in song. On days like these, Father won't leave the house, and sometimes this mood can go on for days. He won't eat and hardly talks. There is much sadness in the household."

"Is it an illness?" Morris looked her in the eye, confusion evident in his question.

"No, it is not an illness for he is well and in good health. Helena, Sally and I have learnt to let him alone. The cloud will lift, eventually, and he becomes his joyous self again. He eats well, and no, there is never a sign of illness. We daren't speak to him about it; there's no use. But Helena is perfect for him, and she is very faithful. It is good to see the support she gives him, even though she is much troubled about it."

"Well it makes no sense to me," Morris said bluntly. "I resent that he does not care for his family."

"Oh but he does, Morris, surely he does," Bloomy objected quickly. "As I said, there are many things we do not understand about people, and Father is one of them. I can assure you he loves each and every one of us. You are his shining light. Although Father would never openly say so, it is undeniable. You are a successful businessman, as he once was. You and David are supporting our family very adequately. Perhaps it might concern Father that you are a better man than him?"

"No," Morris said flatly. "No, my concern is that because I support the family, he feels he does not need to work."

"That's not it," Bloomy said gently as she pulled firmly at his arm and led him to the left at the next corner. "You may presently experience one of Father's unhappy dispositions. I must warn you that it is not pleasant, but you will soon learn that it is a kind of affliction, a serious affliction, that will render him impossible to deal with. And these afflictions come for no discernible rhyme or reason. You will see."

Morris thought about it for a moment, but it still made no sense to him at all. "Well, Sister, that brings me to another issue I must discuss with you, and you alone."

"Go ahead, brother of mine." Bloomy smiled sweetly at Morris, pleased that he would take her, of all people, into his confidence.

"I cannot stay in that house any longer than is strictly necessary."

Bloomy was openly shocked. "Why?"

"With the greatest of respect, Bloomy, I have changed. I'm not a child anymore, and I feel very uncomfortable with those children in the house. They are not my siblings."

Bloomy chuckled softly. "Oh Morris, you have been away too long, and you don't know them yet. You will come to love them as your own. You wait and see."

"I doubt that," Morris grumbled. "I've had this discussion with our brothers. Mother had seven children, and you and I belong to her family. These other children belong to Helena's family; they are not part of our family."

"Of course they are, Morris!"

"No, that's not how I see it, and that's final."

After a short pause, Bloomy sighed. "You have always been the stubborn one, Morris. Let us not discuss this any further, then. But you will stay with us for a while, won't you?"

This time it was Morris who sighed in resignation. "Alright, one night; but make sure that lazy cat doesn't come anywhere near me."

"Stay more than one night, Morris. Please," she implored, then quickly changing the subject before Morris could reply. "Tell me about your home in Africa."

"Hah!" Morris exclaimed, not realising she had just used the same tactic of diversion he often used in his business negotiations. "Our home in

Africa? We don't have a home like the one you have. In fact, we don't even have a home."

"How can that be, Brother?" Bloomy looked at him questioningly.

"We sleep on blankets on the floor in the back of our trading warehouse, between boxes, or wherever we find a spot."

"I don't believe you!" Bloomy said with a chuckle. "You are dressed to reside in a first-class establishment, and yet you choose to sleep on the floor?"

Morris laughed, "It is the truth. It is not uncomfortable, and something we are well used to, as you know. And it is much warmer than our cottage on the old farm; that I can say with certainty. Until now we haven't been able to afford to rent any accommodation, and it is most convenient to sleep at one's place of work. We all prefer staying there, as we are all together as a family. We left Louis in a coastal town near Port Elizabeth called East London for several months when he first arrived, and he did not like that one iota. We have been much happier together. David is the funny one, though, as he will always sleep with his back to a wall, as he did in our cottage in the farmlands. If all the boxes are stacked against every wall, he will spend ages moving the boxes just so that he can sleep alongside a wall. Harry will sleep anywhere, but Louis needs some extra space because he is so long."

Bloomy giggled at the memory of her younger brother's height and gait.

"We call him 'Giraffe'!" Morris suddenly laughed openly.

Bloomy attempted a laugh, but it wasn't convincing. "What does 'Giraffe' mean?"

"'Giraffe?'" Morris looked slightly shocked. "Heavens, Bloomy. It's a very tall animal with an extremely long neck and a head that reaches the top branches of the tallest trees. There are thousands of them in the African bush."

"Goodness me!" Bloomy was startled. "Are they dangerous?"

"No," Morris chuckled heartily. "They are quite beautiful creatures. They have a lovely brown pattern in their fur, and the oddest tongue: blue and extremely long. Giraffes walk and run very gracefully. For all their massive size, they are quite shy of us small humans."

"Oh, you must tell me all about the animals in Africa. I know only of the lion and the elephant."

"That is just the beginning. I'll tell you some funny stories about the animals and your brothers, but let's save those renditions for the dinner table." Morris promptly turned on his heel and allowed Bloomy to hook her arm in his left elbow once more. "We should not keep Father waiting any longer; I'm sure dinner is ready, and I'm famished. Tell me about Bernard."

"He is a lovely gentleman, and I am happy in my marriage. He is a shy and reclusive person, but his ambitions are very high, perhaps a little too high, and he has plans to make a fortune selling furniture."

"If he is quiet in nature, he might have a problem making a fortune as a salesman. Usually, those sorts of people are somewhat forthright. Where do you live now?"

"Bernard doesn't make a lot of money, so we are still living with Abba in the house you so kindly provided for us. He has plans to move into a home near here when we have saved enough."

"You and your family all live under father's roof, among all his other children? It must be overwhelming, but I will say no more, Bloomy," Morris replied, feeling justified in having made his earlier decision to find alternative accommodation.

"I have recently discovered that I am with child again," Bloomy beamed.

Morris stifled a sigh of exasperation. "Congratulations, Sister," was all he could manage in response.

Arm-in-arm in the cool of the evening, the two of them walked back to the apartment, enjoying their idle conversation and their renewed intimacy. Morris could not have been happier, though. He had an exceptional connection to his older sister, and even now – after eight years apart – Morris felt as though he had not left her side for one day. He knew she understood him and his ways, while her loyalty to himself and his brothers was absolute.

Dinner was an excellent affair. Helena and Ruben had prepared the most delicious meal, and after Ruben had given the traditional Hebrew blessing over the bread and wine, he gave thanks to their Lord for Morris' safe return and the knowledge that his sons in Africa were well and healthy. They consumed the meal with much hilarity and enjoyment with Morris taking centre stage and relaying many of the stories from their stay in Africa.

"What about lions?" Sarah asked excitedly. "Did you see any of those?"

"Oh yes," Morris smiled. Having just finished his meal, and having placed his knife and fork neatly together on the empty plate, he leant back comfortably in his chair. Bloomy noticed his polite etiquette and unconsciously twitched an approving smile that Jacob was quick to notice. "I was stalked and attacked by the creatures on several occasions."

"No!" Helena reacted sharply.

"Indeed I was," Morris frowned, "and a most unpleasant situation in which to find oneself. A lion can kill a man with one swipe of its paw, or a single bite."

Sarah stared at Morris in wide-eyed fascination. "Did you kill any lions?" she blurted out.

Bloomy promptly scolded her young sister. "Sarah," she exclaimed, but Morris merely smiled at her, ignoring Bloomy's reprimand.

"No, Sarah," he said. "On a couple of occasions, I would shoot at them to scare them away, but I'm not a hunter, and – as a matter of fact – I hate guns, so I avoid them at all costs; they truly scare me. Your brother David, on the other hand, is an excellent shot – a marksman, I would say."

"I cannot believe that," Jacob murmured. "My son David? He can use a gun?"

Morris immediately addressed him directly, "Father, David hunts animals but only for food. And he will only shoot what is necessary, as he loves the wild animals. In fact, David loves everything about the African bush: the animals, the plants, even the insects. His favourite possession is a telescope, and you should see him admiring the birds. I have never seen so many birds of such a variety in size and colour. There are thousands of birds, beautiful and ugly, minuscule and gigantic." Morris straightened himself in his seat, and the memories of Africa began flooding in. He needed to tell his family of their adventure in Africa, and a bit of embellishment would not go amiss.

"Do you know that the smallest bird I saw was no bigger than my thumb?" he continued, grasping his thumb and holding it out to make the point, which brought the desired effect, as everyone at the table stared intently at his stubby digit. "And the biggest bird I saw is called an 'ostrich'. It is larger and taller than you, Father. There are birds called vultures, and when they see a dead animal, they will swoop down in their dozens, summoning more and more, and devour the entire beast, apart from the skeleton, in barely half an hour."

Jacob's eyes were as round as saucers. Morris looked around the table, and everyone was staring at him in total silence as if he had recently kissed the Blarney Stone and was now spinning the biggest yarn of the country.

"I tell the honest truth," Morris defended himself, looking somewhat offended at their apparent incredulity. "David and I were stalking an ostrich one day, hoping to steal one of its eggs, which are as big as your dinner plate I might add, and we got into a spot of bother when it attacked us suddenly. It pushed me into a thorn bush that literally captured me and prevented me from moving, and then it turned on David and kicked him so hard it nearly killed him. His bruises were indeed something of a sight: quite black and blue all over."

The stories and memories continued almost until midnight when Jacob finally brought the evening to a close. He asked Bloomy to prepare a single room for Morris by apportioning all the youngest children among the remaining bedrooms. Sarah chose to sleep on the sofa.

Jacob took Morris by the shoulder and gave him a tight squeeze. "Good night, my son. My heart is very much warmed by your return and tomorrow evening we will go to the synagogue for the evening service and thank the Lord God Almighty for bringing you home to us. I have some friends there who would be interested in talking to you."

Morris smiled briefly, not wanting to spoil his father's joy by telling him that he would not be staying under his roof for long. He shook his father's hand firmly instead, bid him a good night, and retired to his temporary bedroom.

After taking a quick cup of tea and then walking Bloomy to her place of work, Morris was in no hurry to return to his father's home to endure the idle chat, the impossibly small children, and the ever-present cat. Straightening his hat, he strode off in the direction of town and immersed himself in the flow of the population. Morris called on a number of stores and places of business, always making mental notes of how companies operated in Ireland and comparing them to how business was managed in southern Africa.

Overall, it all looked quite similar, although he did pick up some curious nuances and styles of trading. Captivated by the aroma of a meal in an oven, Morris entered a somewhat expensive establishment called the Fitzwilliam Guest House and settled down for a full breakfast and a very welcome pot of coffee. Before leaving, he checked the room rates at the reception desk and enquired about their availability. Suitably pleased with his discovery, Morris slowly made his way back to Wood Quay, but not before enjoying some quiet time in a relatively large botanical garden that was open to the public.

Once home, Morris spent enough time talking to Jacob to be polite, before intimating that he was fatigued from his journey, and would be retiring to his room for a nap. Unexpectedly, he slept very heavily, and had to be woken by Jacob some ten minutes before they were due to leave for the Synagogue. Although he had not done much at all during the day, Morris still believed he had been very successful in avoiding the unpleasant and unnecessary social formalities he had expected to be forced to tolerate with his new family.

On arrival at the Synagogue, it couldn't have been more obvious that Jacob was an extremely proud father, heartily introducing Morris to just about every congregation member within his reach. They made their way with loud whispers to the far left of the place of worship, close to the Synagogue Ark where the scrolls of the Torah were kept. With a yarmulke on their heads and a prayer-book from a shelf, they approached their seats. Jacob hastily shuffled a confused gentleman one chair over and proudly placed his favourite son at his right-hand side, amid hushed apologies from an acutely embarrassed Morris.

The Rabbi conducted the entire service in Classical Hebrew, which Morris did not understand, for the most part, having not used the language since he was very young. All the men dressed in dark business suits and no women were visible at all. When the service was over, the gentlemen in the congregation made their way outside in subdued mumbles. As the evening was so agreeable, many of the men stood in groups, as was their tradition, to discuss their various affairs.

Because Jacob had often spoken about his boys in Africa, and as it was apparent that he was with one of those sons, almost all of those present paid their respects and introduced themselves to Morris. Many invited Morris to their homes for a meal, wanting him to relate his adventures from such a far-off, mysterious country. One big man with a very bushy, black beard shook Morris' hand during the melée of introductions, introducing himself as Yoni Goldberg. His handshake was unusually firm, and his pale-blue eyes caught Morris by surprise.

"Your father speaks highly of you. I understand that business in Africa is exceptional."

"Yes, sir," Morris smiled, "my brothers and I have been quite successful."

"And what of the Jewish community in Africa?"

"Oh, I wouldn't know about all of Africa, but in Rhodesia, there is a small community." Morris looked about at the throng of worshippers and continued. "There are probably more Jews in this Synagogue than there are in the entire town of Bulawayo. We have tried to form a branch of some organisation called the Zionist Movement, but until we know what it is all about, I renamed it the 'Friends of Zion'."

"You renamed it?" Goldberg smiled curiously.

"Yes, they asked me to be their Chairman for the inaugural meeting, and then appointed me as president."

"You are the president of the Zionist Movement in Rhodesia?" Goldberg's eyebrows arched in surprise.

"For the moment, yes. You've heard of the Zionist Movement, Mr Goldberg?" Morris seemed interested.

"Well yes, I have, actually," Yoni chuckled.

"I have not found it to be a very effective organisation, mainly because we don't know much about it," Morris shrugged. "I've resigned my presidency, it was too time-consuming and therefore interfered with my business, and – besides – I intend to live in Ireland now. They should be electing a new president next month."

"I would be most interested to hear all about the Jewish community there, and more particularly about your voyages to Africa and back. You must ask your father to arrange a meeting," Yoni insisted.

"Certainly, Mr Goldberg," Morris agreed. "I would be delighted." Of all the people he had made this promise to, this was the one invitation he intended to honour; there was something in the handshake that told him he should.

Jacob stepped into the conversation and shook the well-dressed gentleman's hand. "Mr Goldberg is from London," Jacob asserted. "Shabbat Shalom, Mr Goldberg."

"Shabbat Shalom, Mr Langbourne," Yoni smiled as he shook his hand.

"I was just introducing myself to your son. You should be well pleased with his return."

"Indeed, delighted," Jacob confessed, and even his eyes were smiling.

"I would very much like to hear what Master Langbourne has to say about his voyage to and from Africa. Perhaps we could meet on Sunday for afternoon tea at the place where I am residing."

"It would be an honour," Morris replied quickly before his father could say anything that might jeopardise the appointment.

"Splendid. I am staying at the Fitzwilliam Guest House in Upper Fitzwilliam Street, not far from here."

This was music to Morris' ears; it would be an easy way out of his father's hospitality. "I know where it is," Morris said with confidence.

"You do?" Jacob's eyebrows arched in surprise as he looked down at his son.

"Indeed," Morris casually glanced at his father. "In fact, I have booked a room there from tomorrow. My apologies for not mentioning this to you yet, Father, but there has been so much on my mind in the last few days it completely escaped me."

Jacob stammered briefly, but checked himself very smartly and smiled. "Very well, then. Sunday afternoon tea, Mr Goldberg?"

"Excellent," Goldberg beamed, "and please bring your lovely wife. I would be delighted to meet her. Good evening, Gentlemen." He shook their hands once more in farewell and melted into the gathered throng of black overcoats and yarmulkes.

During the walk home, Jacob questioned Morris as to why he had chosen to stay at a guesthouse when he was more than welcome, and in fact, expected, to reside under his father's roof and hospitality.

"Father, I well know I am welcome under your roof, and I am very grateful, but for the last eight years, I have been surrounded by people my age and older. I have also been living in my warehouse, which is large and peaceful, so I find it difficult to share a small house with infants."

"They are your family, Morris." Jacob sounded hurt.

"Yes, but..." Morris retorted bluntly, then changed the subject quickly. "I have changed, Father; I am not a child anymore, and I have a large business overseas to run."

"Fitzwilliam's is expensive! My home is free to you."

"I can afford it, Father."

Jacob let out an exasperated sigh. "You have not changed Morris. You are still the stubborn, determined, and independent young man I remember. It is just that I love you dearly and I would like to spend a lot more time with you."

"And we shall. I love you, too, Father, and always will, but I am restless. I have so much I need to do and the inordinate waste of time on that ship has made me very frustrated, and eager to get on."

Jacob reached over and squeezed his shoulder briefly. "I understand, Son. Will you at least stay with us until Sunday and celebrate the Sabbath in our home? It would mean a great deal to me."

"Certainly, Father," Morris reluctantly agreed with a nod and smiled at his father. It was only one more full day in his father's home, and he also knew that he wanted to spend a little more time with Bloomy.

"I still cannot believe what you have achieved in Africa," his father remarked. "You are richer than my wildest hopes." Jacob scratched at his chin through his manicured black beard, then chuckled jokingly, "I taught you well, Son."

Morris gave a hearty laugh, and this time he reached up and squeezed his father on his shoulder. "You taught all your sons well, Father. Tell me, who is Mr Goldberg?"

"A very influential man, and very well educated: Cambridge or Oxford, I believe. He lives in London but visits Dublin fairly regularly as he has an ageing mother here. Mr Goldberg sits on a Board of Executives for a large insurance company that specialises in marine insurance. I'm sure that's why he wants to talk to you about your journey to Africa."

"Marine insurance?"

"Yes, it's called Lloyds of London, if I recall. It would be to your benefit if you took note of his counsel – a very learned and respected man."

"In the brief time we had during our introductions I got the feeling he was quite important," Morris mumbled as he drifted into thought about the imposing man he had just met.

Morris checked into his room at the Fitzwilliam Guest House and unpacked the few belongings he had into the tall wooden cupboard, which was probably a little too big for the room. His lodgings were on the first floor of the building, and he was able to look down onto the street below. A door stood near the head of the bed, and for a long while, Morris pondered as to where it might lead. He was hesitant to try, in case it should open into the next bedroom. He knew he would not endure the embarrassment should he enter to find someone in there, particularly if that 'someone' were a lady.

After gazing out of the window for a few minutes, Morris realised that he could not quell the feeling that this mysterious door was evoking. Fearing someone might enter the room while he was asleep, he walked over to the door and knocked politely. Receiving no reply, Morris gently tested the doorknob and, finding that it opened freely, he cautiously pushed the door and poked his head through the opening. To his surprise, he found himself in a small room with a white-enamel freestanding bath and wash-basin, complete with hot and cold water taps, and a wooden commode.

"Hah…" Morris exclaimed aloud, "this is most convenient." Deciding to test the temperature of the promised hot water, he turned on the wash-basin tap and let the water flow freely past his fingers, all the while scanning the rest of the small room. It suddenly dawned on him that there was no other door to the water closet.

"Good Lord," he mumbled under his breath, then began to smile. "This is all for me! Well, I'll be…."

Morris had never seen, let alone stayed in, lodgings that had a private water closet attached to each room. He was mightily impressed, and when the water trickling past his fingers began to heat up to a most agreeable temperature, he began to grin uncontrollably. Morris had found the room rate affordable, and the unexpected amenities made it well worth every penny. He decided there and then that he had made the right decision moving from the family home, even though he was paying their rent, and concluded that Dublin was a most civilised town, and that he might very quickly become accustomed to its lifestyle.

Morris had another two hours to go before Jacob and Helena would arrive to meet with him and Mr Goldberg. Lying on the plush bed and taking a nap had crossed Morris' mind, but he was too full of energy to waste an afternoon in that way. So, donning his jacket, Morris took a walk around the streets and explored some of the side roads of the suburb. Just before 4 o'clock he returned to the guesthouse, made use of his private water closet, and then went down to the reception room to anxiously await the impending meeting.

* * *

Jacob arrived promptly with Helena on his arm. With her dress flowing down to her ankles and a cheerful scarf tied elegantly around her neck. Morris had to admit that she looked quite beautiful. Jacob wore his best suit, with his beard freshly groomed for the occasion. Indeed, they made a striking couple, despite the age difference between them. Notwithstanding his conflicting feelings towards their marriage, Morris was secretly pleased to see the couple so happy and in love.

'Perhaps I'm too judgemental,' Morris thought to himself, momentarily softening his stance, before becoming annoyed once again that Bloomy had not been invited.

As soon as Morris had greeted his father with a handshake and Helena with a kiss on both cheeks, Mr Goldberg entered the reception room from the internal stairway and greeted the family warmly.

"I hope you don't mind, but I have invited three other gentlemen and their wives to join us," Goldberg announced. "I believe they would be most interested in Master Langbourne's opinion of South Africa, as they had once considered leaving Ireland altogether."

Jacob was delighted at the prospect of additional company. "It will be an absolute pleasure," he beamed.

Morris, however, suddenly felt a little uncomfortable. "I'm more familiar with Rhodesia, Mr Goldberg, which is further north of the South African republics, but I will help wherever I can."

"Splendid!" Goldberg responded sincerely. "You need not concern yourself with that detail. First-hand news from that part of the world is scarce, so I am sure we will all enjoy hearing what you have to say. Now let's go in." He held his arm out to usher everyone into a side room, "I have booked this lounge and ordered high tea for the ten of us."

The group moved through to an opulent room where heavy curtains draped from ceiling to floor, and the thickly piled carpet swallowed every sound. Exchanging a great deal of pleasantries and polite light humour, they sat in one corner of the room, comfortably ensconced in luxurious chairs that had been set out in a reasonably large oval. While Mr Goldberg and Jacob carried on the conversation, Morris, in his usual manner, did not contribute, preferring to listen intently and to observe the social mannerisms of his father, Helena, and Mr Goldberg.

It didn't take Morris long to realise that, although fully accomplished in social etiquette and gentlemanly behaviour (thanks to his late mother's constant tuition before she died), the isolation and harsh environment of Rhodesia had placed these social norms lower down on the colony's priority list. Even though Bloomy had reinforced her family's social skills after their mother had passed away, to the point of being pedantic, Morris knew he had slackened a fair amount since he had left home.

Both Mr Goldberg and Jacob reclined easily in their seats, with their legs crossed at the knees. Helena sat bolt upright in a perfect posture, crossing her legs at her feet, her hands clasped gently in her lap, and smiling graciously. She appeared to take much interest in what the two older gentlemen were saying, though without uttering a word. Morris realised by comparison that he was slouching; his left elbow and leg rested casually against the armrest of his superb armchair; his left foot lay sideways on the floor, and his right foot stood on top of his left shoe. He very slowly corrected himself, straightening up as he stifled a fake cough, hoping that no one had noticed.

Within the next ten minutes, the other couples arrived, Mr Goldberg, Jacob and Morris standing to welcome them and making introductions all around. The first to present himself was a tall, thin man called Mr Albert Bondi, a pharmacist, who had an equally tall and slim wife. The next to arrive was an industrialist called Mr William Milner, and finally Mr Hyman Lobel, a baker by trade. He also had a small printing press that he operated from the rear of his bakery.

Morris noticed that his father knew all the men, but not the wives, and assumed they were all part of the same congregation at the Synagogue. In fact, Morris thought he recognised one of the men from the Friday-night service. A wave of apprehension overtook him when he suddenly realised that he was about to become the centre of attention.

Tea was served by two attentive ladies in the hotel uniform, their heads covered with matching scarves, accompanied by a man in formal attire. When they proudly set down their three tiers of cakes, pastries, and biscuits on a table in the middle of the room, Morris struggled to avert his eyes from the spectacular display. Once all the commotion was over, and the hotel staff seemed to melt away, Mr Goldberg drew everyone's attention to Morris.

"We would like to welcome you back to Ireland, Master Langbourne." Morris quickly acknowledged the salutation with a slight nod and polite smile before Goldberg continued. "We are very interested to know what it is like doing business in South Africa, and Rhodesia, as some of us here are considering setting up commercial operations over there. For the benefit of those that don't know Morris' story," he quickly glanced around the room, "he left Ireland, what, eight years ago?"

"That is correct," Morris agreed.

"And, correct me if I am wrong, you set up a tobacco business in Port Elizabeth in the South African Cape Colony which you recently sold and then began another business in Rhodesia as a general trader."

"Firstly," Morris pulled himself up and puffed out his chest slightly, "I would like to thank you, Mr Goldberg, for your introduction, your kind hospitality, and the tea you have so generously provided for us." Morris noticed a faint smile of approval from his father at the acknowledgement of Mr Goldberg's benefice. "In fact, my brother, David, and I set up a cigarette factory in Port Elizabeth as soon as we arrived there, which we sold after only one year."

"Only one year?" Mr Lobel interrupted, somewhat intrigued.

"Yes, sir," Morris nodded at the gentleman and continued. "We had begun trading and had employed twenty staff when an American competitor approached us and asked if we would sell our business to them. We were very fortunate, being in the right place at the right time and producing the right commodity. We could almost name our price.

"We had heard," Morris continued after a slight pause, "that Mr Cecil John Rhodes, the Prime Minister of the Cape Colony, was investing considerable resources and finances into a country to the north, called Matabeleland, ruled by a strong king by the name of Lobengula. We were hesitant to go, but having heard of great expectations there, we took the train from Port Elizabeth to a town called Mafeking in Bechuanaland, which is where the rail line ended. Nothing but bush, forest and jungle would be seen from there on. In Mafeking, we bought supplies from a Jewish wholesaler who . . ."

"Forgive me, I know a Jewish trader in Mafeking," Mr Lobel suddenly interrupted, raising his hand briefly. "That wouldn't be Julian Weil, would it?"

"Yes!" Morris exclaimed, totally amazed by the unexpected connection. "How do you know him?"

"Ahh, he is related on my sister-in-law's side. I've met him only once, many years ago. I believe he is doing quite well over there."

"Indeed," Morris replied, still intrigued, "he is doing exceptionally well. Mr Weil has been very instrumental in our success too. He gave us very generous credit terms when we were in danger of losing our entire business. We owe him a debt of gratitude."

"I would still regard him carefully, Master Langbourne. I hear he is not shy to make a profit off his friends . . . Or his family."

"Oh," Morris smiled wryly, "he has made some good money out of me, make no mistake. He puts a lot of gravy on his plate."

A soft giggle emanated from the ladies present, which pleased Morris and he relaxed a little more.

"So, go on," Mr Bondi prompted. "You set up a trading business in Mafeking?"

"No, we only purchased goods from Mr Weil to sell forward when we reached our final goal. Having placed our goods on six wagons drawn by oxen, we proceeded to travel northwards. We had intended to go to Fort Salisbury, but after walking for three months, we arrived in KoBulawayo (as Bulawayo was then named) and discovered that we were only two-thirds of the way to our intended destination. At that point, David and I decided that we had had enough of walking through the relentless bush, so we agreed to stop and set up our business in KoBulawayo."

"Three months? You walked through the African bush for three months?" Albert Bondi asked incredulously.

Before answering, Morris looked around the room and noticed that everyone was sitting motionless with their mouths agape - everyone except his father, who was smiling broadly.

"Err... Yes, three months," Morris replied in an almost matter-of-fact tone. "Unfortunately, soon after we arrived and began trading, a conflict broke out between the Matabele, and another tribe to the north called the Mashona. The Mashona people asked Mr Rhodes to use his private company, the BSAC, for protection. The BSAC stands for the British South Africa Company, which operated as an informal military unit in the area. Because the BSAC appeared to have intervened directly in the political affairs of the Matabele under their leader, Lobengula, the tribesmen rebelled against the BSAC, causing a brief, but very bloody war to erupt. The BSAC won the conflict through sheer firepower, and the administration took over the country by means of a Charter granted by the British Queen. That part of the country known as 'Matabeleland' was renamed Rhodesia, while the Ndebele place-name 'KoBulawayo', which means 'The Place of Slaughter' was renamed 'Bulawayo'. We almost lost our entire business because of that conflict; two of our wagon traders died.

"Then the Administrator, Dr Leander Starr Jameson, who on the first impression seemed a very kind and honourable gentleman, formed an army with all available soldiers in the country and attempted to overthrow the Afrikaner-Dutch government of the South African Republic, or 'Transvaal' to the south of Bulawayo. Why, I have no idea, but that folly failed dismally. In my opinion, his actions were completely irresponsible in that he left only 32 military men in Bulawayo to protect the citizens in the town."

"Did you meet this Dr Jameson?" Mr Milner interrupted, seeming very interested in the mention of the name.

"Indeed. I had a very cordial relationship with the gentlemen, but I mostly dealt with his assistant, Major David Seward, an interesting and helpful individual."

"I read about Mr Jameson in the newspaper in London recently. He has been repatriated to England after his capture to face trial, if I recall correctly." Milner stroked his beard thoughtfully with the palm of one hand. "It seems most odd that a learned and upstanding doctor of medicine would wish to attempt to overthrow a sitting government."

"I think he had political motives, and rumour has it that Mr Rhodes authorised this. I do try to make a point, however, of not involving myself in the shenanigans of politics, to the point where I have warned my brothers against even discussing politics; it's a dangerous game." Morris shot a quick glance at his father, who gave a barely discernible nod of approval.

'I couldn't agree with you more," nodded Mr Goldberg, reaching for his teacup and saucer. "Please, go on."

"David and I had only recently refinanced our business to start trading once again when, realising that we were all but defenceless, the Matabele rose up once more against the settlement."

"For heaven's sake, why?" Mr Bondi exclaimed.

Sensing that this was going to be a lengthy meeting, Morris sighed and leant back in his armchair, before replying.

"I believe they had many reasons," he said. "Firstly, you must understand that the culture of the African tribes is very different from ours. They don't have formal education, as we do, but rely on the folk law passed down to them for generations. They do not have formal religions, such as the Christian or Jewish faiths, but they do believe in the spirits of their ancestors, as well as a host of other complicated beliefs. We may call their religious practice 'witchcraft', but whatever it is, they believe in it very deeply and often live in fear of certain spirits. At the time when the European settlers first came to Matabeleland, the country, coincidentally, experienced severe drought, and the crops failed. Then a plague of locusts followed, which decimated anything that had barely survived the drought. Starvation became a real concern; everyone, including our family, was battling hunger."

Morris leaned forward in his chair and sighed once again as he carefully took his teacup off the saucer and stared at the ripples in the cloudy liquid. He wasn't sure how to best explain these things to the company present. If he didn't understand it completely himself, how would he explain it to these well-educated ladies and gentlemen of Dublin and London?

His memory of the Rinderpest plague flooded his mind; he would discuss that but decided he would not mention how it was the prime cause for the loss of the most substantial convoy of wagons the country had ever seen – his wagons along with all his stock, that almost caused his financial ruin. He did not want to delve into a discussion that might reveal that it was his volatile temperament that had sent Duluxolo, the only man who knew of the wagons' whereabouts, scampering into the bush, thus losing the location of the wagons for over a year. *'No, I won't mention that'*, Morris thought to himself sullenly, because he was secretly embarrassed by his actions that day. *'No, they certainly don't need to know about that'*, he thought again.

Suddenly, Morris noticed that it was uncomfortably quiet. He quickly looked up over the lip of his teacup, and everyone was staring at him intently. Realising he had been entirely lost in thought for an inordinately long period, he hastily returned to sip his tea to buy some time, as he had forgotten where he had left off.

"Excuse me," Morris apologised, placing his cup down on the table, "where was I?" Still unable to remember where he had ended, he cleared his throat and smiled at the concerned faces looking back at him.

"The drought? Your family's hunger?" Mr Bondi came to his rescue.

"Ahh, yes! Thank you. There was another development, something which most of humankind has not experienced, not that I am aware of, anyway. A ghastly and deadly disease swept through the land. Called 'the rinderpest', it affects only animals of the ungulate family: oxen, cattle, and buffalo, and spreads like wildfire. Once a beast contracts the rinderpest, the animal dies a horrendous death within hours. With most of the cattle dead, neither meat nor milk were readily available; and with the oxen dead, transport became impossible, so we could not receive any supplies of food or medicine and were quickly isolated. What the settlers failed to take into consideration, however, was that the Matabele believed that all these hardships – the lack of rain, the plagues, the hunger and the deaths – were all because of the white man's arrival in their land.

"Furthermore, before the white man's arrival, the Matabele lived off the land: the women farmed, the children raised cattle, and the men defended the villages, being skilled in warfare. Now the white man put the men to work with minimal wages, working in mines, clearing land, and doing menial tasks. Their pride was hurt.

"To top it off, in an attempt to prevent the spread of the rinderpest, the BSAC went around shooting any stray cattle in an effort to contain the outbreak. However, what they failed to understand was that the ownership of cattle is the Matabele's measure of wealth and status. Imagine what the tribesmen must have thought when some white men simply walked into their villages and shot the beasts without permission, leaving them to rot in the sun without even harvesting the meat for food. Of course they would rebel!" Morris briefly raised his hand to emphasise his point.

"The town of Bulawayo," he continued, "which had a population of about 4,000 citizens, and 32 soldiers, as I mentioned, was placed under siege by about 70,000 Matabele warriors. My two brothers, Louis and Harry, had just arrived from Ireland. It was a fearsome time, bearing witness to starvation, sickness, disease, and plagues."

Morris reached for his teacup and took a sip of the now lukewarm beverage. "We did have fresh water, though: someone had dug a well in the grounds of the Market Square and found a lot of clean water."

Once more Morris stared into his cup, deep in thought, as unwelcome, vivid memories came flooding back. "We were scared of being overrun by the Matabele because they have a very vicious way of killing their enemy. They have short, stabbing spears with very wide, extremely sharp blades. They come at their victim screaming their war cry, and when they plunge the blade into a person's stomach, they twist it so that the loss of blood is massive; entrails frequently escape the abdomen - there is no hope of survival and death comes quickly."

Morris was interrupted by what sounded like a soft squeal from one of the ladies sitting next to Helena. Everyone looked at her and noticed she had no colour in her face. Her head began to loll to the right, and the woman slipped into unconsciousness. Helena and the other ladies leapt to their feet and attended to her before she fell off her chair. Men quickly stood to offer assistance but needed to do nothing, since the deathly pale woman had been carefully laid down on the carpet. No sooner was she horizontal than she opened her eyes and attempted to sit up, which prompted the womenfolk to fuss over her, helping her to her feet, and quickly escorting her out the room.

"I hope your wife is alright," said Mr Goldberg to Mr Milner. "Perhaps you might like to accompany her to see a doctor."

"No, thank you, Mr Goldberg, she should recover well. It happens from time to time, and we know not what causes it," the hapless gent shrugged. "The ladies will attend to her better than I can, I'm afraid. Please, be seated; my apologies for the interruption, Master Langbourne."

"No apologies necessary," Morris said, feeling slightly embarrassed, as everyone took their seats once more.

"You were saying?" Mr Goldberg said as he reached for his teacup.

"Before you go on," Mr Milner politely interjected, "I must admit I am somewhat horrified to hear what you are telling us."

"I agree," Mr Lobel concurred. "In fact, I am surprised that you are even here to tell us these tales."

"Tales they are not, Gentlemen." Mr Goldberg placed his cup down with raised eyebrows. "News in Dublin is not so forthcoming, but let me assure you much of what Master Langbourne has related here has been reported widely already in the newspapers in London. The British take a deep interest in what is happening there."

Morris was somewhat surprised to hear of this. "I didn't know that," he murmured.

"Indeed. That gentleman you spoke of, Dr Leander Starr Jameson, who

45

led that failed attack on the Boer government has been hailed as a bit of a hero by the British papers."

"I regret I don't share that view, Mr Goldberg," Morris commented dryly. "Because of his stupidity, he left us virtually defenceless. After King Lobengula was ousted, his position was taken up by a demon-possessed medicine man whom they called the M'Limo. He rallied up the old armies and turned them against us.

"Thousands of people were slaughtered on both sides. The Matabele spear didn't stand a chance against the British Maxim machine gun, and when the traditional leader tells his people that he will turn the white man's bullets into water with his magical powers, what hope have they got? No," Morris sighed, "it was a massive military blunder by Jameson."

"Forgive me." Mr Lobel was scratching his head as he stared at a pattern in the carpet before looking Morris directly in the eye, "I can't understand something you said; 4,000 citizens with 32 military men for protection, and 70,000 of these spear-wielding warriors? The arithmetic doesn't add up."

The businessmen in the group softly mumbled their agreement as Morris' eyes darted around the room. He had to admit it didn't sound logical.

"I understand your assessment of the terms of battle, and I agree with you to a degree, but let me assure you I don't doubt the numbers. The figure of 70,000 may well seem to have been exaggerated, but I was within earshot of Major Seward when one of his captains confirmed a sighting of a 10,000-strong Matabele army on the east side of Bulawayo on just one particular day." Morris straightened up slightly and reached for his teacup; the remaining puddle of tea in the cup was cold.

Although fleeting, Morris' unintentional glance into the bottom of his teacup, with an accompanying flash of disappointment, was not missed by Mr Goldberg. He immediately looked over his shoulder towards the door and raised his hand slightly, summoning the attendant who had kept a respectful and watchful eye on his charges. Without a sound, the waiter immediately came forward, the silver teapot in one hand, silver milk jug in the other and a spotless white cloth draped over his right forearm.

"A refill, Gentlemen?" Goldberg politely called a pause in the conversation. Teacups were refilled during a brief lull as the men spoke quietly to each other. The ladies silently and gracefully returned into the room, with the gents standing to welcome them back. Mrs Milner apologised for her poor health, but assured the menfolk that she was well and in good spirits; some colour had evidently returned to her cheeks.

With teacups almost overflowing and a flurry of sweet delicacies transferred from plate to mouth, Morris took the floor once again.

"Getting back to the rebellion, Bulawayo was placed under siege by the Matabele armies. We were very fortunate in that the military personnel we had protecting us were extraordinarily astute and put the town into an effective laager, quickly devising ways of protecting the settlement against invasion. For almost three months, the population of Bulawayo was surrounded, and literally, a day or two before our protectors ran out of ammunition, we were relieved by forces coming from both the north and south. A great deal of bloodshed followed while the BSAC fought to overcome the Matabele, during which time we – my brothers and I, along with the rest of the civilian population – remained within the assigned limits. In the end, it was only because of the intervention of Mr Cecil Rhodes in negotiating a truce that the war in the south of the country effectively ended. That gave all of us a chance to rebuild and start trading once again.

"Since the town of Bulawayo is now very progressive and expanding at an incredible rate, I honestly believe that there is a lot of money to be made for any business that starts up in Rhodesia at this time. That is the reason I am here: I wish to open a purchasing office to supply our business in Bulawayo because many commodities are always in short supply over there."

"Well, I for one am not surprised!" Mr Lobel retorted. "If it takes three months to get your supplies there in a wagon, it's a wonder you are able to trade at all."

"Actually, thanks to Mr Rhodes' employing his personal finances, we have recently been connected to Mafeking by a railway line to Bulawayo," Morris retorted, "and freight can now be transported from Mafeking to Bulawayo in a mere two days. Not only that, but we also have a telegraph line that connects all the way through to Cape Town, which in turn connects to the entire world," Morris expounded excitedly. "Further to this, with the Union Castle steamships, I am now able to get goods shipped from Southampton to Cape Town in a short 17 days."

The assembled group sat in contemplative silence, frowning slightly as they exerted their minds to follow Morris' train of thought. The only person who did not have a frown was Jacob, who smiled as he admired his eldest son. *'I have taught my son well'*, he thought to himself.

Mr Milner broke the silence. "As much as I would like to expand my business into South Africa, I regret I am not brave enough to take my chances in an uncivilised and unstable country." His frail wife nodded her approval of his statement, not attempting to hide her sentiments.

"What line of business are you in?" Morris enquired politely.

"I'm a banker's technician," Milner said matter-of-factly.

"A banker's technician?" Morris cocked his head, slightly confused.

"Mr Milner is your everyday locksmith, not so, Hymie?" Mr Bondi joked, winking at Mr Lobel and letting out a chortle. Morris instantly realised all the men were friends.

Mr Milner glared at Albert Bondi for a brief moment, then allowed a smile to creep across his face. "If I simply manufactured locks and keys, Bertie, I agree, I would be a locksmith." He turned to face Morris again and continued, "I manufacture safes and strong-room doors for the banking sector. Indeed, locks and keys are a big part of my business, but I do more than just that. I also consult with bankers on their safety requirements."

"There is a tremendous opportunity in Africa for your services, Mr Milner." Morris beamed. "Why, only a couple of years ago, the first Standard Bank in Bulawayo consisted of a tent for an office and boasted a tin trunk as their strong-room."

"Goodness me!" Milner exclaimed, echoing the sentiments of everyone in the gathering. "Be that as it may, after what you have just described to me regarding these Matabele people, I will never set foot in Africa."

His wife looked visibly relieved.

"I respect that, sir," Morris smiled openly, "but my intention of opening a purchasing office here also includes the proposition of acting as an agent for commerce and industry. Perhaps you would allow my company to be your agent in Africa? I would effectively open your business and its products to the South African states, including Rhodesia and Bechuanaland, which covers an area about, oh… I'm not sure, but at least eight times bigger than England."

Another pause followed, the gentlemen looking somewhat perplexed at the business acumen emanating from such a young man. Even Jacob looked bemused.

"Are you saying you would represent my safe and strong-room doors in Africa on my behalf, and I would never need to visit that part of the world?"

"Absolutely, sir," Morris smiled confidently.

"So, through you, I would be expanding into an area eight times bigger than England, and I would not have to do any of the hard work?"

"Well, the population is only a fraction of that of England, but towns and settlements are springing up at an astonishing rate. We would need to agree on what products would sell in Africa, based on my first-hand experience obviously, and I will export and deliver your products to my distribution warehouse in Johannesburg. My warehouse is in very close proximity to the railway station, and from there I can distribute to a vast area. I will take a commission, obviously. My brother controls the Johannesburg warehouse, and once a product of yours is sold, I will pay your price," Morris nodded his affirmation. "But we could discuss the various terms later if you agree." Morris then quickly turned to distract Milner before the man realised that Morris had implied that he would not pay for the goods until sold. "What's your line of business, Mr Lobel?"

"I, er... I come from a family of bakers," Mr Lobel stammered, caught off-guard by Morris' rapid change in his focus of attention.

"Ahh..." Morris sighed. "Sadly, I cannot represent that line of business. You, sir, would have to go to Africa if you wanted to sell your confectionery there."

"I would assume that goes for me too," Mr Bondi mumbled, more to himself than to the party. "I'm a pharmacist."

"Correct," Morris agreed. "I cannot represent your profession either."

"Master Langbourne," Yoni Goldberg said slowly, drawing everyone's attention to himself, "I must admit I am fascinated with your perception of business, and certainly your determination to succeed. To be honest, I have never come across anyone as... as..." he struggled to find the word, "ambitious! Tell me, why is it that you choose to set up your purchasing office in Dublin?"

Morris shrugged. "My family live here. It's where I lived before I left for Africa. Why?"

"A man of your abilities and foresight does not belong here. London is where you need to be. It is the centre of industry and commerce in all of

Europe. That's where you need to operate from. You can achieve so much more there."

Suddenly a look of horror flashed across Goldberg's face, and he quickly looked Jacob in the eye. "Forgive me, Jacob, I did not wish to encourage your recently returned son to leave your home again."

Although Jacob was visibly upset, he put on a brave face. "No apologies necessary, Mr Goldberg. Morris is a very determined young man, and even a strong pack of mules could not stop him from doing what he wanted."

"I am a man of much influence in the business world of London," Goldberg hesitantly continued, "and I could make some very favourable introductions for young Morris to a number of important people. I am most impressed with your business acumen," he said, turning to address Morris directly.

Morris allowed a shy smile to escape his lips, and, ever so slightly, he nodded his gratitude.

London was going to suit him just perfectly, and he couldn't wait to get there.

Chapter Three

Bulawayo 1899

David finalised the sale for his customer and politely walked her to the door of their Fife Street store. He was the complete gentleman, offering to carry her purchases out to her buggy, and holding the door open to allow her onto the pavement.

"Thank you very much, Master Langbourne. You have been most helpful, and your store is an absolute delight," she sweetly praised.

"My pleasure, Mrs Rubinstein." David gave a very slight bow out of respect for both her compliment and her custom as she glided past him. "Do call again," he encouraged.

"Oh, I shall," she assured him. "I will bring my daughter, Hanna, next time. She would adore your shop. You've met my daughter, have you not?"

"Actually, no," David confessed. He wasn't really listening to her, his mind filled with other pressing business: being continuously polite and gentlemanly was testing him to the limit.

He had been frantically trying to code and stock the warehouse on Abercorn Street that morning when Harry, who ran the store, called him over to take stock of a wagon trader who had just returned from the countryside and needed to depart again at first light. Since he had been juggling three other customers in the store already by that time, Harry had not been able to deal with the trader's need. Just as David had started going through the wagon trader's consignment stock, however, the stationmaster had called in, demanding that David should attend to the local railway siding. A train had halted with several cartons of goods from Mafeking, and that the consignments needed to be offloaded immediately, because the train was shortly due to depart.

Just as David had thought that matters could not get any worse, Louis, in the Fife Street store, had sent a runner to ask him for assistance, because his shop was overflowing with customers, and he wasn't able to cope. It had been a very stressful morning, but almost every day was like that nowadays.

"Tomorrow?" Mrs Rubinstein asked more forcefully.

"I beg your pardon?" David suddenly realised he had been entirely lost in thought and hadn't heard a word she had been saying.

"I asked if you will be here tomorrow."

David apologised profusely. "Oh, please forgive me," he replied. "It is possible, but I cannot be certain. I tend to operate between our warehouse on Abercorn Street and the store here – wherever I am needed most. Why do you ask?"

Mrs Rubinstein gave a frustrated sigh. "I said I might bring Hanna here tomorrow to look at that silver tea-set you showed me."

"Of course!" David felt very embarrassed by his lapse of concentration. "By all means, do. If I am not here, please feel free to ask my brother, Louis, to assist you."

"Oh, but it is *you* I would specifically like to attend to Hanna."

"Me?" David arched his eyebrows in surprise.

"I believe only you would be able to convince her to let me buy that tea-set."

"Oh, I see ..." David sounded somewhat confused. He suddenly cleared his throat, "Well, by all means, then; do come in tomorrow, and – if I am not here – ask Louis to send a runner for me. I will only be two blocks away."

"Splendid," Mrs Rubinstein chirped happily and took her leave.

'I wonder what that was all about?' David thought to himself as he shook his head slightly, before turning around to get back to the next customer and almost walking slap-bang into Louis.

"David!" Louis hissed, "Please help me with that customer by the kitchenware, quickly. He's getting irritated." Although Louis was the younger brother, he towered over David, looking very flustered with a red glow erupting on his pale cheeks. Louis' ill-fitting suit didn't help his image much, and his tie looked as though it was about to throttle him.

"Of course," David said calmly as he side-stepped his brother, who immediately attended to yet a further customer. It was pandemonium that day.

Just before David reached the gentlemen in question, he caught sight of Thembela, the young Xhosa lady who replaced Nkosazana when she left their employ to marry Daluxolo. She was standing patiently against a wall staring at him, trying to snare his attention.

"My apologies for the delay, sir." David raised an open hand in a gesture of friendship, "Umm… one moment." He allowed his hand to form a fist, with his index finger quickly pointed up to accentuate the notion of literally "one moment".

"What is it, Thembela?"

"Boss Hurrie says come back. There are another two wagons that have returned."

David let out a huge sigh, and his shoulders slumped. "Fine, thanks, Thembela," and dismissed her with a forlorn look.

"A bad day, Master Langbourne?" the customer asked with an understanding smile.

"It's like this every day, I'm afraid. Thank you for your patience. How may I help you, sir?"

The customer picked up an off-white enamel tea-pot and turned it over in his hands carefully. "I need twelve of these in pink, with a pattern of yellow roses on the side."

"I beg your pardon?" David was stunned by the unusual request. Their supplies of enamelled porcelain came in only four colours: off-white, off-white with a blue handle, avocado green, and an insipid mustard-yellowish colour. Never had he heard of pink, and as far as he was concerned, such patterns or pictures had not been invented. David's face was a picture of confusion.

The customer laughed heartily. "I'm only teasing you, sir. It looks as though you could do with a laugh. I'd like six of these same tea-pots."

"You had me there," David chuckled. "Please bear with me: I have six of them in the storeroom. I'll be back in a moment."

"Forgive me for being so bold, sir," the customer caught David before he walked off, "but it would appear to me that you might require extra staff in a store as busy as this. Perhaps I might recommend a certain gentleman who would suit your requirements perfectly?"

"Possibly," David frowned. "I cannot deny we are swamped. I'll discuss it with my brothers and let you know. How do I locate you?"

"Brian Loxton, Food and Beverage Manager of the Charter Hotel."

"Pleased to make your acquaintance, Mr Loxton." David gave him a hearty handshake. "Excuse me while I get your teapots from the back."

David turned on his heel and almost jogged over to the storeroom, grabbing the door handle and stepping through in one fluid motion. Unfortunately, at that exact moment, Louis was on the other side of the door and reaching for the handle. The collision was quite spectacular. Since Louis was in half-stride, his arms laden with boxes and bracing to open the door, he was no match for David's weight and momentum. He went hurtling backwards, arms flailing, and boxes flying in every direction.

"Oh, my word!" David exclaimed, "Are you alright?" He stared at his brother who lay on the floor rubbing his forehead.

"Hell, David," Louis slowly started to sit up, "this is ridiculous."

David closed the door and squatted alongside his brother. "How's your head?"

"I'm alright. Just a little bump. We need help, David; this is crazy. Since Morris left, we have struggled to do all the work and keep the admin up to his standards. And it's getting busier by the day," he added.

"You're right," David had to agree. He rocked back and sat heavily on the floor, letting out a deep sigh. "It's a good problem to have, but I'm tired now."

The two brothers locked eyes, desperation evident in their scowls. Louis started to smile and shook his head gently in disbelief. David returned the smile and then began to chuckle. Within moments both boys were laughing freely as they sat on the floor in the dingy storeroom.

"Come on." David composed himself as he struggled to stand up, and, grabbing Louis by the hand, helped him to his feet. "We've got customers waiting outside and a business to run. We'll have a family meeting tonight with Badger about getting some help."

Using their assigned code names had become second nature to the brothers, but they only used these codes amongst themselves. Strangely, it bolstered the bond the boys had with each other, almost making them feel they were part of a secret and elite group that only they could belong to. They had other variations of their names too: the Matabele people struggled to pronounce certain letters in the English alphabet, and so Louis was referred to as Rooie, David, Deved, and Harry was Hurrie.

"Sounds like a very sound idea. Do you think everyone heard us out there?" Louis tucked his shirt in and began picking up his spilt cargo.

"More than likely, but I hope not," David grinned as he helped retrieve the scattered boxes. "I have to get back to Abercorn Street; two more wagon traders have returned."

"You are not leaving here until I say you can. This is my shop don't forget," Louis chuckled.

David laughed. "I'll deal with that customer of mine, and then I'm out of here. Good luck!"

"We'll see about that," Louis scoffed. "Right-o, time to face the crowd," Louis mumbled as he walked through the storeroom door and onto the shop floor.

David walked over to the back of the Abercorn Street warehouse where he carefully covered a substantial pile of merchandise on the floor with a very heavy, grey blanket. Although the blanket was not large enough, and some of the stock protruded from underneath, he didn't care. He then went to fetch another blanket to cover a second pile that was being attended to by Louis. These small mountains of stock were for two wagon traders who would load up in the morning for yet another excursion into the bush.

"Have you finished the paperwork yet?" David asked Louis.

"Yes, this is the last lot," Louis replied, as he placed a packet of a dozen gentlemen's shaving mirrors onto the pile, each no bigger than the palm of his hand.

"Who has the time?" David called out.

Harry angled his pocketwatch towards the flame of the candle. "I make it half-past nine."

"Are you finished with your order?" David asked Harry.

"Yes, I have just finalised the last entry. We had some good trading today," Harry grinned.

David carefully laid the second grey blanket over the last pile of stock and stepped back to look at the evening's work. "Let's call it a day. I think we are ready for the traders first thing in the morning. Anybody hungry? Because I am starving!"

"I have not had anything to eat since breakfast," Louis complained.

"I suggest we go down to the Charter Hotel and get something to eat," David proposed, wiping his dusty hands on his trousers.

Harry glanced at his watch again and frowned. "I'm afraid the kitchens at the Charter closed half an hour ago. We will have to see if we have any food in Thembela's cupboard."

David's shoulders slumped, because he knew there was no food in the warehouse, and he was extremely hungry. "I don't think we have anything here, fellows. I think we will have to settle for some coffee."

"That means we will have to light the fire again," Louis grumbled, "and I can't be bothered to do that just for a coffee."

David sighed again, he was exhausted, and his feet hurt. He wondered how it was possible that they were making such good money and still remain starving.

"I tell you what," David tried to smile, "let's get an early night and tomorrow morning we will go down to the Charter and have a big breakfast before the morning gets underway."

The boys mumbled their agreement because, in truth, there was no other option available. The three walked out the back door and washed their hands and faces in the old sink, using a piece of pungent green soap that had fallen into the dirt, and so needed itself to be wiped clean before it could be used. Afterwards, they went back inside, locked the warehouse door, and retrieved the bedding that had been rolled up and stashed away on various shelves. David, as was his custom, placed his blankets against a wall and slowly went down on his haunches with a short grunt, then rolled over onto his back, untying his shoelaces as he lay there. He was drained. The other two boys just settled down where their bedding fell.

"Fellows," David spoke to the roof above him, "I think the time has come to get some help. I don't think we can continue in this way for much longer."

"I was wondering when you were going to bring that up," Louis murmured.

"I agree," Harry piped up. "We will start losing customers if we can't service them, and that will affect our reputation. Remember what Morris always said: 'Reputation is paramount.' "

"I spoke to a customer today, a Mr Loxton, who suggested that we should employ extra staff. I was rather embarrassed because he had been waiting for some time and that was not a good thing."

"Neither is it a good thing for a customer to have to advise us that we need more staff," Harry grumbled irritably.

David ran his fingers through his hair. "He suggested a person he knew who might make an excellent employee, so I took the liberty of asking him to send this person to me."

"Thank you, David." Louis sounded very relieved, "I could certainly use the help at Fife."

"Wait a minute!" Harry exclaimed, "I need help at Abercorn."

"Don't worry, Brothers; we will probably end up getting a good three or four people to help us. Heaven knows we could certainly use them."

It was Harry who pointed out the obvious. "I don't know what Morris will think. It is an expense to the business, and I know he will oppose this decision vehemently."

"Well, he is not working here and can't see what's happening, so I'll make that decision. I realise that we have reached a stage in our business when we will go backwards if we cannot look after our customers. I will deal with Morris," David said softly. He knew this would have been a robust conversation with Morris if he had been in Bulawayo, but as conversations with him in Ireland would have to be via telegram, he wouldn't be able to argue much at all.

"Personally," Harry offered, "I believe we need two people in each store and one person to look after the wagon traders."

"What will you do, I wonder, once everyone takes over your responsibilities?" Louis mocked his older brother.

David, however, was not listening. "Morris insisted we had to initiate the Johannesburg office once he signals that from Ireland," he mused aloud. "I'm petrified that that will happen sooner rather than later because we are not prepared." David lapsed into thought again, and a brief silence encompassed the room before he spoke aloud once more. "I'll have to take you to Johannesburg, Louis, to get that side started with Danie Coetsee, and then I'll have to go to Cape Town to organise the docks and rail transfers, which would leave Harry here all on his own. Therein, Gentlemen, lies the next problem."

Harry was curious. "So what is your plan?" he asked.

David sat up gingerly and looked across at his two brothers, who were lying flat on their backs. "I say we ensure that both Fife and Abercorn are staffed with fully trained personnel within two weeks," he replied. "I'll need your help, boys. You need to train these recruits as fast as possible. Can I depend on you?"

"Of course," Louis agreed without moving.

Harry expressed his concern. "So, I'll be the only brother left to run every operation here?"

"Yes, and you will do it admirably," David smiled. He stood up, walked over to the candle and blew it out, plunging the warehouse into blackness, before fumbling his way back to his bedding, and gently lying down again. He knew the next few days were going to be very difficult.

Louis spoke into the dark, "David, we are making a lot of money now. Any chance of declaring another dividend?"

"In good time. Why, what do you need? You can use some of the petty cash if you need to buy something."

"No," Louis said drowsy, "they are selling very affordable plots of land in that suburb, ironically called Suburbs, and I wouldn't mind buying a plot on which to build a house. I'm tired of living in a warehouse and sleeping on a blanket."

"The Administration was hard-pressed for imagination the day they named that suburb," Harry mumbled sarcastically.

David was about to say something silly to put an end to the conversation but suddenly remembered his earlier thoughts. They were very prosperous, making a lot of money, and yet they were hungry. Indeed, the extreme workload had something to do with it, being more of an issue of time constraints than finances, but here they were: pretty well off with cash in the bank and sleeping in a warehouse on the floor.

"A house?" David mulled aloud.

"With a bed and a pillow," Harry added thoughtfully through a yawn.

"I'll bet Morris won't be sleeping in a warehouse when he gets to Ireland," Louis grumbled.

David couldn't contain the laugh that burst from his lips.

"Good night, Gentlemen," David chuckled.

The boys bid each other a pleasant night, and very shortly the warehouse fell silent.

Chapter Four

Ireland 1899

Helena came through from the kitchen holding a steaming casserole dish between two towels, before placing it on the dining table. She was followed immediately by Bloomy, who held a similar casserole dish overflowing with boiled vegetables. It, too, was steaming profusely.

"Dinner is ready," Bloomy sang out.

The table was decked most elegantly, with the best cutlery and crockery laid out in a splendid display of opulence. The affluent look of the dining table clashed starkly with the sparse aspect of the rest of the dwelling.

"A dinner fit for a queen," Jacob gushed.

"Bloomy deserves all the credit, my adoring husband," Helena beamed. "She did all this while we were out for tea with Mr Goldberg."

Jacob motioned everyone to sit. The infants had been put down, but Sarah and Rachel politely and silently took their seats at the table with the adults. Morris noticed that they were very well behaved and silently wondered how long their quiet demeanour would last.

"I was very proud of your brother today," Jacob said to Bloomy.

"Yes," she replied with a broad smile, "Helena was telling me about your meeting." She turned to address Morris, "I hear that you held yourself well among those important businessmen."

"Exceptionally well!" Jacob boasted. "Morris was the star of the show. It seems I have taught you well."

Morris was a little uncomfortable with this statement but didn't show it. He believed that his true mentor had been Jack Shiel, the manager of the Standard Bank in Port Elizabeth. It was their lengthy discussions over dinners at the Grand Hotel that had put Morris on the path to becoming a very astute businessman. Furthermore, he had not found it challenging to learn all that he had been taught, which had taken place mostly in Port Elizabeth, since he thoroughly enjoyed all aspects of business, trading and money.

Nevertheless, he rather chose to indulge his father out of respect. "Yes, Father," he replied, "you have taught me well; and Bloomy, I must give you a great deal of credit for bringing me up the way you did after Mother died. If it had not been for you, I would not have presented myself in such a way that senior society would have accepted me. That goes for David, too."

"Your table manners have slipped a little, I have noticed," Bloomy grinned. "It looks as though I might have to remind you of a thing or two."

Morris laughed, "It is rather wild and uncivilised in Africa, my sister. I think you are fortunate in that I have retained any manners at all."

Everyone laughed at the remark before Jacob brought them all into prayer, to thank the Lord for the food, and for his wonderful family. A special bottle of red wine was opened, and the offering was blessed by Morris, who still remembered the Classical Hebrew blessing for wine.

As the meal came to a close, Jacob returned the conversation to the meeting they had attended at the Fitzwilliam Guest House.

"I was saddened to hear that Mr Goldberg believes you should go to London," Jacob reflected mournfully.

"It is vitally important that he be able to introduce me to many influential people. It is not something the average man who starts a business has in his arsenal. It is a head start in a business that cannot be measured in monetary value."

Bloomy looked hurt. "You are not thinking of going to London, are you?"

"I would have to live there if I was going to run my business from there. And Mr Goldberg is right: London is the centre of business in all of Europe. My prospects in Dublin are rather limited."

Sarah looked as if she were about to cry. "I'll miss you," she protested and turned to Helena for support. "My brother has only just come home, and now he's going again."

Morris quickly put his hand on her shoulder to comfort her, privately touched that she felt this way about him. "It will be fine," he soothed, "You can come and visit me in London."

The entire family looked at Morris blankly. Instantly he realised that they could never afford to travel to London. As it was, he was supporting them through Langbourne Brothers in Bulawayo.

"Once my business in London is up and running and making a profit, I will purchase passage for all of you to come and visit me. You will love London," he added smiling broadly. "There are the most exceptional clothing stores for women, boutiques, haberdashery departments, beautiful parks, and lovely buildings. I've seen it; David and I went to London before we left for Africa."

A sombre atmosphere hung over the room. Morris' attempt to liven up the sentiment of his impending departure had failed dismally.

"It will be sad to see you go so soon," Bloomy was almost tearful.

What had started as a very lively and happy family dinner was rapidly going downhill, and Morris knew that he was the cause of it all. He had to leave the table because he could not cope very well with emotional gatherings.

When Helena told the young girls they had to prepare for bed, Morris seised the opportunity and excused himself as well. Bidding his family a restful night, and retrieving his Derby hat from the nail by the front door, he took his leave and walked towards the Fitzwilliam Guest House – very relieved to have somewhere else to go.

Morris woke to a beautiful day: the sun was shining with hardly a cloud in the sky. He drew himself a deep, hot bath in his private water closet and relaxed in the calming water for a while before shaving and making himself presentable. Morris stood afterwards at the window of his room, watching the morning's activity beginning to unfold on the street below, before preparing to go down for breakfast. He had noticed, just up on the corner, a restaurant with some tables spilling out onto the pavement. One or two patrons were already reading the complimentary newspapers that had been placed on alternate tables.

Morris changed his mind and decided that he would breakfast at that restaurant this morning, and not at the accommodation's dining room. Although a slight chill was present in the air when he reached the street below, he felt invigorated, his skin still tingling from the hot bathwater.

Selecting an empty table with a newspaper upon it, he picked up the menu and studied it momentarily, quickly deciding on a traditional breakfast, but without the offered bacon. Then, picking up the paper, he began to read the headlines. He had not gone far when a waitress approached and asked for his order. She had a thick Irish accent.

"Top of the morning to you, sir. And what may I be gettin' you for breakfast today?" she enquired briskly.

Reaching for the menu again, Morris pointed to the line that described the breakfast he wanted. "I'll have your traditional breakfast please, without the bacon, and a cup of black coffee, thank you." Looking up at the waitress to see if she understood, he found himself suddenly shocked.

"Good grief!" exclaimed the waitress.

"Elaine!" Morris was startled. Apart from his family, she was the last person he had seen in Dublin before he left for Africa eight years previously. "What are you doing here?" He stood up, awkwardly trying to decide whether he should shake her hand or hug her.

"Look at you, Morris; I can't believe it. All dressed up and important lookin'. Just look at you!" She took a step back and eyed him up and down. "Where have you been?"

"I've just returned from Africa,' Morris replied, "I have been there for all this time since we last saw each other. I was only thinking about you yesterday and wondering how things worked out on the farm. In fact, I was going to hire a buggy to visit the farm and see if you were there. Obviously, it didn't work out, since you have employment here. What happened?"

"It's a long story, Morris." A look of sadness clouded her face.

"What time do you finish?" Morris asked Elaine. "Perhaps we can meet at the end of your shift."

"I would very much like that," her eyes lit up. "I only finish at 2 o'clock, though."

"Excellent," Morris beamed, "I will be here at 2 o'clock sharp."

"Wonderful! Allow me to get your breakfast now. I shan't be long Morris. So good to see you," Elaine called as she walked back into the restaurant, a slight spring in her step.

Morris sat down and pushed his chair back slightly, reclining easily and crossing his legs as he picked up the newspaper. He shook his head slightly in disbelief at having stumbled across Elaine, especially as he had intended visiting the farming area to see her. He was also curious to go past the old cottage, for old times' sake, to remind him of where he had once lived.

The news in the paper was rather uninteresting, but he did see a small article at the bottom of the second page, referring to South Africa. Concentrating on the report, he read that the tension between the Government of the South African Republic (or Transvaal) and the British Government had reached boiling point.

It was old news as far as Morris was concerned. The peace between the Boer Republicans and the British had been tested ever since Dr Jameson's failed attempted coup about two years earlier. Morris quickly scanned the next few pages, but that was the sum total of the news on Africa.

"There we go, Morris," Elaine interrupted his thoughts by placing a steaming cup of coffee beside him. "Your breakfast will follow very shortly. Africa has obviously been good to you. Just look at you! I can't believe your transformation from farm labourer to this!" She smiled broadly from ear to ear.

"Yes, a lot has happened in my life," he replied, sheepishly.

"Africa!" Elaine exclaimed. "Whatever made you go there? Goodness me. And your brother David? How is he?"

"Very well, thanks. I left David in Africa."

"Oh, such a pity, I liked him. What is he doing there?" Elaine's questions were incessant.

"It's a long story. We will exchange all our news this afternoon."

"I can't wait. How long has it been? Five or six years?"

"Eight, actually. A lot has happened."

"Oh, I don't think I can wait for 2 o'clock. Enjoy your coffee, Morris; I'll be back." Elaine walked backwards a couple of steps while keeping her eyes locked on him and clumsily bumped into a chair, before turning around and scuttling busily into the restaurant.

Morris watched her disappear indoors. Elaine had changed a great deal. She had filled out beautifully and had some shape to her body now. When he last saw her at O'Connor's farm, eight years previously, Elaine had been as skinny and shapeless as a flagpole, and her complexion had been pale and insipid. Now she had some curves to her hips, and her waitress blouse was tight across her chest. Her cheeks flushed slightly, and her smile was contagious. She was, Morris thought, a rather attractive woman, and a far cry from what she had looked like when last they had met.

Since he had nothing to do until after lunch, Morris proceeded to drag out his breakfast, while watching Elaine from the corner of his eye, flitting in and out of the restaurant, serving customers, checking on him, and topping up his coffee. Eventually, nature called, and he excused himself, paid his bill, and reconfirmed his meeting with Elaine before sauntering back to the Fitzwilliam, looking forward to hearing her story.

As he entered the guest house, he bumped into Mr Goldberg, who appeared to be settling his account at the reception desk.

"Good morning, Master Langbourne," Goldberg enthused, "I trust you slept soundly."

"Indeed, thank you. I hope you did likewise."

"Always," he chortled. "Morris, please join me for a coffee in the lobby. I am about to depart but would like to have a quick discussion with you about some matters I have been pondering during the night."

Morris readily agreed but excused himself briefly while he went to his room to collect a notepad and pen – really an excuse to get to his bathroom because the three cups of coffee that Elaine had served him were rapidly filtering through his system. By the time he re-joined Goldberg in the lobby, he found the gentleman seated in a corner containing two plush chairs, while a waiter was already serving a round of coffee. Morris took the proffered seat and placed the notepad and pen on the coffee table. He had no real intention of using them, as he never wrote things down, relying solely on his memory.

Mr Goldberg had two main topics to discuss: firstly, as to whom Mr Goldberg intended making introductions for Morris in London; and secondly, to discover when Morris planned to leave. Morris became quite excited at the prospect of meeting all these influential business leaders, whose future support might bode well for his company and the activities he wished to conduct. Goldberg also had contacts in the Far East - Hong Kong and Japan, to be precise - and suggested that once Morris' business was sufficiently profitable and in need of expansion, he might like to gain introductions with those contacts. The prospect of having to conduct business with such people in so distant a country was of some concern to

Morris, but after discussing the matter in more depth, he began to realise that it would undoubtedly improve his range of stock, and more importantly, his profitability.

Although Morris had intended staying in Dublin for one week, the excitement of starting his business became too much for him, and he decided he would leave for London within a few days. This decision prompted Mr Goldberg to ask Morris about his accommodation plans. It caught Morris off guard because he had not given it any consideration.

"When I get to London I will make arrangements for a warehouse and living accommodation," Morris declared.

"May I suggest that you stay in my home for the first few days until you find your feet?" Goldberg urged. "My wife would be delighted to have you stay with us, and it would give you a chance to find what you are looking for without undue pressure."

"That is very kind of you, thank you, sir."

"We live in a flat in Berkeley Square, near Hyde Park. We are located fairly centrally, which will allow you to make many enquiries without too much bother."

"That would be perfect, and I believe I will only need about three days to establish myself." Morris did not want to presume on his host's hospitality any longer than was necessary.

"Splendid!" Goldberg reached over and took Morris' pen and notepad. "Do you mind?" he asked, as he began to scribble something on it.

"Go ahead," Morris agreed quickly, with a smile.

"This is my address. When you get to London, just ask anyone where Berkeley Square is, and they will point you in the right direction." He handed Morris the pad. "I can expect you before the end of the week then?"

"Yes, indeed," Morris agreed happily. "Thank you for your kind offer of hospitality, and I am most grateful for all that you plan to do for me when I get there."

"Absolute pleasure, Master Langbourne," Goldberg said as he heaved himself up. "Right-o, I must be on my way. My regards to your father."

With that, they shook hands, and Goldberg took his leave. Morris made his way back up to his room and lay on the bed for a while, deep in thought as to how his future might unfold. He made some mental notes of things that needed attention, how he would accomplish them, and in what sequence he would have to manage it all to get everything in place. Finding a warehouse, although at first appearing to be a priority, suddenly became the least important issue.

"No, I need an office," Morris spoke to the ceiling.

He realised that the foremost priority was to coordinate all the agencies he wished to represent, such as Mr Milner and his strong-room doors, and this would likely involve a fair amount of travelling, both around the countryside and into the industrial towns. It would be a waste of time and money to rent a warehouse immediately as it might take some months before his purchases began to arrive. If he planned it correctly, Morris thought, he could arrange that all his various purchases arrived at the warehouse at about the same time, and therefore he would only need to begin his lease agreement around then, thereby saving him two months' rent or more.

"An office is what I need first and foremost," Morris said aloud to himself as he stared at the ceiling. "Maybe a suite with a second office that I can use as a bedroom? Yes!" Morris exclaimed and leapt off his bed. The excitement was getting too much for him; he needed to go for a walk.

At precisely 2 o'clock, Morris arrived at Elaine's place of work and stood a respectable distance from the seating arrangements, so as not to look too expectant. At two minutes after the hour, Elaine duly appeared, minus her apron and smiling gleefully, before taking Morris by the arm and leading him down the street.

"I thought the end of my shift would never come. How wonderful it is to see you again, Morris!"

"Indeed, I am so pleased to see you, too," Morris beamed. "So tell me, what happened after I left the farm?" Morris, as usual, went straight to the point.

"Oh, I don't think my story is as fascinating as yours," Elaine smiled coyly. "Just look at you, dressed like a governor and all. You first, Morris, I can't wait to hear your story. And David, tell me all about him."

Morris sighed, knowing he would have to lead the conversation, but when he realised they had all day, he reigned in his impatience. For the next half hour or so, Morris related many of the adventures he and his brothers had experienced since 1891. The more he remembered all the excitement and dangers they had been exposed to, the more animated he became. Drawing to a close, Morris came to realise that he and his brothers had been extremely fortunate in very many ways. They had survived a long journey by sea; somehow managed to escape being killed by numerous – many unseen – wild animals, insects, and diseases; and had narrowly escaped death during two Matabele wars. And yet, through all of this, they had come out victorious in the commercial world, building a business that was the envy of many other, well-established businessmen.

"My-my, Morris," Elaine shook her head in disbelief, "that is some story if ever I heard one. I can safely say that my story is nothing like yours; in fact, quite the opposite."

"I'm sorry to hear that, Elaine. Pray tell me all," Morris encouraged her. They had arrived at the entrance to a beautiful green park with a bench just inside the gate. "Let's sit for a moment," he suggested,

Morris dusted off a few leaves that had landed on the bench and motioned for Elaine to take a seat. He then sat beside her, turning slightly to face Elaine in anticipation of hearing her tale.

"Well, two days after you left the farm, that dreadful policeman arrived with a man from the government."

"Sergeant Garnet, if I recall his name correctly," Morris stated.

"Yes, that's him. And an awful man he is, to be sure." Elaine shook her head in despair.

"I must say I had a horrible feeling about him. What happened?" Morris frowned.

"Well, he came around with that government man, as I was saying, parading his authority and acting superior and suchlike, and even intimidating that government fellow. He wasn't very nice to me either, insinuating all kinds of unmentionable stuff about me, trying to be funny, I suppose. So when I thought the time was right, I produced that letter you and David wrote for me."

"Yes, I remember. I was going to ask you about that," Morris said gravely.

Having listened to something Sergeant Garnet had said, Morris had believed that the late O'Connor had no family and that he had no real friends either, and had therefore forged a Last Will and Testament in favour of Elaine. It was a long shot, but he had believed there was a good chance of her getting away with it, and he would have far preferred that she received the proceeds of the farm before some corrupt government official, who more than likely had not needed it anyway.

"Well, it worked a treat, caught Garnet right off guard, it did," Elaine sighed, "but reflecting on it afterwards, it probably wasn't the right time to present it. I should have presented it to a government official, and not in his presence."

"Did he take it off you?" Morris asked with concern.

"Yes, he said he needed to verify the signatures of the witnesses. He was very sly; he took it out of my hands, read it carefully, then with much pretence of authority, folded it and placed it in his pocket. It was out of my hands, literally."

"What about that government official?"

"He was pathetic. Garnet told him he would have to verify the witness' signatures and apologised for wasting the man's time. He seemed very pleased to be dismissed by Garnet, and looked like he couldn't wait to leave the farm and to wipe his hands of Garnet, too!"

"But how could he have even verified the signatures of the witnesses? As you know, there weren't any witnesses."

"Well, there you go!" Elaine exclaimed, slapping a hand on her knee to stress a point. "The dirty rascal said he recognised the signatures and would be verifying them with the respective signatories."

"What an evil man!" Morris shook his head and looked into the distance, contemplating the outcome. "He had no idea whose signatures were on that paper."

"So, it did work, Morris, your idea worked a treat. Sadly, however, it was I who was the foolish one, letting Garnet take the letter from me and all."

"It's not your fault, Elaine. That man is a nasty person."

"Nevertheless," Elaine smiled contentedly, "what we did was illegal, so I am comfortable in my heart, knowing I didn't get anything through nefarious means."

"Do you know who got the farm in the end?" Morris asked, his voice steeped in suspicion.

"Yes. I'm sure you already have a good idea." She smiled coyly.

"Garnet?" Morris offered.

"As I said, he is a dirty rascal. Two days later, he returned to the farm and gave me two hours' notice to leave."

"I'm sorry." Morris looked hurt.

"Oh, don't be," Elaine continued to smile, "I was packed and through the farm gates in thirty minutes, and he stood there with his arms folded, all so pompous-like, and so full of himself, while he watched me walk away. I have never been back, but I've had a few jobs since then, and the pay is much better than what O'Connor paid me, after all."

"When he paid," Morris said sarcastically.

"Yes, when he paid," Elaine laughed. "It's not an easy life I have, but I get by and I'm not worried about Garnet either. It seems he left the police, taking his pension, and stocked the farm with livestock: sheep I believe. Apparently, he fell down a dry well about three months after he occupied the farm and broke both legs."

"Serves him right," Morris grumbled.

"Oh, it gets better," Elaine chuckled, "it took them two days to find him, and because of the delay, he is disabled now; his legs never set properly, and while he was in hospital his livestock got stolen, or simply wandered away. Because he is disabled, he can't farm anymore, and the police force won't have him back. Last I heard, he was trying to sell the farm, but because of the stigma of his accident, and O'Connor's fatal fall, nobody wants to touch it for fear that the bad luck of the farm will befall them."

"Huh!" Morris took off his Derby hat and scratched his head in thought. "I almost feel sorry for the man."

"Oh, don't waste your feelings," Elaine said, "I haven't told you the half of what that man is capable of."

Morris looked at her curiously but felt it best to leave matters alone for the moment. Although there was some venom behind her eyes, she seemed at peace with herself.

"Let's keep walking," Morris suggested, standing up and offering Elaine his elbow.

The afternoon flew by, with Morris doing most of the talking, relating stories about Africa, her people, wildlife, and her enchanting scenery and seasons. The evening was upon them before they knew it. Elaine's accommodation was not too far away, so Morris happily walked her home, somewhat sad that the day had come to an end.

"Will I see you again?" Elaine asked anxiously.

"Of course," Morris replied with a grin. "I have some business to attend to before I go to London. I do believe breakfast at the Tavern is on my agenda first thing in the morning."

"Wonderful!" Elaine squealed, "I will ensure you are attended to by the best waitress in town."

Morris laughed; it had been a perfect afternoon in Elaine's company, and he had definitely struck a chord with her. He was sure she had also enjoyed their time together. They bid each other a pleasant evening and then parted company.

As Morris strode down the street, his thoughts were churning over something Elaine had said during their conversations. He reached a crossing, and – instead of turning left towards the Fitzwilliam Guest House – he turned right, towards his father's home.

Arriving there some twenty minutes later, he knocked impatiently on the front door, before Bloomy appeared a moment later.

"Morris Marks!" she exclaimed excitedly, "How wonderful to see you, Brother! Come in, come in."

'Marks' was Morris' middle name. His late mother was the only person in the world who had addressed him by this second name, and then only when he was in some form of boyhood trouble. It was a sign that Morris was about to be severely reprimanded by her. To hear his sister use this as a form of endearment made him laugh; he had not heard his second name mentioned in many years, and in fact, had virtually forgotten he even had a middle name.

Morris gave his sister a peck on the cheek. "I won't be staying long," he said.

"But you will stay for dinner, surely?" Bloomy asked, making the question more an order which Morris knew he could not refuse. "And I don't like that look on your face. The last time I saw that look in your eyes, you and David left for Africa."

Morris became serious again. "I need to speak to Father if he is in."

"Yes, of course, the whole family is here," she said sarcastically, implying that he was the only one who was not. "Dinner?" she asked again, but with an authority that turned the request into a statement.

Being quite hungry by this time, he accepted the invitation without complaint. "Splendid, thank you, providing I am not putting anyone out."

"Never," Bloomy responded with a smile, pulling him inside by the waist and closing the door. "You are family, Morris. Now come on in."

Since the entire family was either seated in the lounge or preparing the evening meal in the kitchen, Morris was welcomed warmly by everyone.

Although he needed his independence, part of him enjoyed the love of a family, so he was quite happy to soak up the attention and proceeded to immerse himself in the pleasure of the moment.

While Bloomy and Helena were fully occupied in the kitchen, Morris took Jacob gently by the elbow and casually turned him so that their backs were to the ladies.

"Father, do you have a friend who is an attorney?" He lowered his voice so that only Jacob could hear.

Jacob raised his eyebrows in concern and lowered his deep voice. "I do, why? Are you in trouble, my son?"

"No, not at all. I am sorry to have given the wrong impression. Fear not." Morris looked over his shoulder nervously to make sure no one was in earshot. "I need a commercial attorney to draw up some urgent paperwork for me."

Jacob visibly relaxed. "Oh, I see. Yes, Mr Pichanick. An excellent Jewish lawyer, specialises in commercial law. He goes to the same synagogue as me. In fact, you met him at the synagogue on the evening we attended together."

"I met a lot of people, Father," Morris reminded him. "This is most helpful. If you were to be so kind as to give me his details before I leave tonight, I would be most grateful. I will see him tomorrow at ten o'clock."

Jacob chortled and turned to lead them back to the kitchen activity. "Usually a lawyer will tell you when you can see him, not the other way around, my son."

"He will see me," Morris said with a smug smile, "and I will pass your regards onto him in the process."

Jacob laughed aloud. "You are quite a forthright young man."

Morris shrugged. "I may well be," he admitted to himself.

Later that night as Morris slid into his bedding at the Fitzwilliam, he lay on his back and closed his eyes, waiting for sleep to overcome him gently.

A very slight smile crept into the corner of his lips as he started to breathe deeply. He was going to enjoy the next day – immensely.

When Morris walked out of Mr Pichanick's office, he was smiling from ear to ear. His day was progressing exceptionally well. Breakfast at the Clover Leaf Tavern and catching quick quips with Elaine had been refreshing, and he had not needed to wait for a meeting with the lawyer, as predicted.

Mr Pichanick had been delighted to see him, and the meeting had lasted barely ten minutes. As far as Morris was concerned, Mr Pichanick would serve him exceptionally well.

After a short walk back to the Fitzpatrick, he boarded a rented buggy, pulled by two horses, the convenient form of transport had been arranged courteously by the Guest House Concierge.

"Where to, sir?" the buggy driver called over his shoulder, as Morris settled into the back seat, feeling very smug. The driver was an older man with a sparse and scraggly beard. He wore a grey business suit which had seen better days, while his white shirt was frayed at the collar and starting to show signs of yellowing.

"I don't know the address, but I can guide you there. If you would be so kind as to head out of town in a south-westerly direction, towards Rathcoole, that would be just fine."

"Certainly, sir," the driver nodded and flicked at the reins, causing the two large stallions to break into a gentle trot, their hooves sounding hollow, but soothing clopping sounds echoing off the surrounding walls.

"I'm heading into the farmlands, about an hour from here, well before Rathcoole," Morris called to the driver as they picked up some speed.

"Certainly, sir, I know the area quite well. Which farm, might I ask?"

Morris cocked his head and looked at his driver's back. He wondered how well he knew the area. A gust of wind almost blew Morris' Derby hat off, and he grabbed at it.

"I don't know the name, come to think of it," Morris replied. "A friend of mine used to work there, but I believe an ex-policeman now owns the farm."

"Ahh…" the driver nodded slowly. "I have heard that a copper acquired a farm in the area after the murder of the previous owner."

"Murder?" Morris queried.

"Yes, gruesome murder it was, too." The driver sounded as if he was going to enjoy sharing this story, and waited for a response from his passenger.

Morris didn't disappoint him. "Gruesome? What happened?" he asked, confident now that this would be the farm Garnet had purloined.

"Well, the story has it that, in the middle of the night, some ruffians entered the farm with the intention of relieving the farmer of some livestock. The farmer accosted them but was overpowered by the miscreants, and they tied him and his wife to a pole in one of the barns and beat them both to death with iron bars. It took two weeks to discover the murder."

Morris studied the back of the driver's head. It was possible that he was talking about another farm, but Morris' brain kicked into high gear, and he smiled. What if the driver was passing on a rumour?

"I heard the farmer was murdered with his wife and six children?" he tested.

"No," the driver replied pensively, "I don't think he had any children."

"I heard it was four boys and two girls."

The driver jerked his head up slightly and momentarily pointed his finger at the sky. "Actually, I think I might have heard that, now that you mention it."

'This is going to be good', Morris thought to himself, before carrying on aloud. "Yes, four boys and two girls, and they think the eldest son was friends of the robbers, but – because the robbers thought the boy might turn them in – they killed him also."

"Now that you mention it, I believe that is exactly what happened," the driver agreed.

"Yes, they beat the family to death with iron poles and drowned the eldest son in a bucket of water. Terrible that was." Morris was now embellishing the rumour gleefully.

"Well, I didn't know that, sir," the driver confessed. "They do say that nobody wants to live on that farm because of that gruesome murder. That I truly heard, I did."

"Yes, I do believe that farm is jinxed," Morris said nonchalantly, pressing his agenda. "In fact, I believe the man who owned the farm before him was also brutally killed on that very same farm."

"Is that a fact?" the driver exclaimed with a noticeable shiver.

Morris let his imagination run briefly amok. "Yes, to be sure. While he was sleeping in his bed, a rafter came loose in the bedroom and impaled the farmer right through the chest. Did you not hear about that ghastly incident before?"

"No, sir, I didn't, but I did hear that funny things were likely to happen on that farm, and so nobody wants to go there."

The houses of Dublin had begun to thin out, and the scenery gave way to a series of rolling, green hills. The driver was now nervously looking about, which suited Morris' intention very well. After seeming to look casually over the landscape, Morris suddenly sat bolt upright, a movement guaranteed to be felt by the driver, and leant towards him. "I also hear that even animals won't stay on the farm," he whispered hoarsely. "When we get there, let's see if we can spot any livestock on the farm. I'll bet my new shoes we don't even see so much as a goat."

"Why are you going there?" the driver asked, fear creeping into his voice.

"Oh," Morris carefully leant back in his seat, "I have a message I need to give the owner. I shan't take long at all."

"I might wait for you on the road if you don't mind, sir," he said nervously. "Don't want to spook these here horses, you understand?"

"That will be fine," Morris agreed. "I doubt your horses will want to enter the property in any case." Morris looked out at the verdant hills and quaint farmhouses that dotted the panorama. The whole journey was proceeding entirely to plan.

"Just a little further up on the left, please, driver," Morris directed the buggy driver to the gate of the farm. He had been only about fifteen years old when he had been employed there and had been treated very poorly by Farmer O'Connor. That was before the farmer had died tragically in a freak accident.

As the farm came into view, a cold chill ran down Morris' back. He was not at all superstitious, but he had memories of the farm that he did not care for. Together with all the other staff on the farm, Morris had been ill-treated: the cold and wet days, punctuated with hunger and scarce pay, had marked a notably low point in his life. He remembered vividly the sight of Mr O'Connor, lying dead at the entrance to his big barn, his skull punctured by the locking mechanism of the attic storage area above. Worst of all, Morris had been accused falsely and had thus been arrested, albeit briefly, for the suspected murder of his employer.

Morris asked the driver to stop a few yards before the ramshackle gate that had now fallen off its hinges. Not too far away, the farmhouse looked foreboding: its wooden walls had turned grey from the harsh weather and the roof sagging dangerously. The sinister barn, with its ominous attic door, stood looming over the dwelling, as if brooding over the fate of the farmer's utter neglect of his farm. A thin trail of wispy smoke climbed skyward from the chimney of the farmhouse.

Wrapping the key to his room at the Fitzwilliam in his clenched hand, so that the point protruded out from the back of his fist, Morris carefully alighted from the buggy, deliberately leaving his Derby hat on the seat.

"I'll be back in about two or three minutes," Morris said politely. "I won't be long at all."

"I'm happy to wait here for you, sir," the driver murmured, tipping his hat in agreement.

Morris smiled back at the old gentlemen and began as if to walk off. Then he stopped momentarily, turning to face the driver again, but standing right next to one of the horse's flanks.

"I must apologise," he said to the driver. "Did I leave my hat on the back seat?"

The driver swivelled to look over his shoulder, and, seeing the hat, reached over to collect it for Morris. At that precise moment, however, Morris jabbed the horse he was standing beside with the key in his fist. Surprised by the sudden prod, the horse immediately lurched forward and neighed in objection to receiving such cavalier treatment, causing the driver to almost topple into the rear passenger compartment of his buggy. The effect was far more dramatic than Morris had hoped for, and he had to stifle a laugh. He quickly grabbed the horse, while the driver struggled to regain his composure before apologising profusely.

"I don't know what got into the horses," he said, once the situation had been calmed down at last.

Morris pretended to look at the farm in some anxiety. "Do you think they are nervous about this place? And look: not a sheep or goat on the farm."

"This place is creepy; I'll give you that, sir," the driver almost shivered. "You can feel it, can't you? Even the horses are spooked!"

"Indeed," Morris acted as if very concerned. "Keep a watch on your horses while I get my hat, and I will be as quick as I can. I don't want to stay here a minute longer than necessary."

Morris pocketed his key, quickly retrieved his hat, and took off down the path towards the homestead. As soon as he walked through the broken gate, he noticed an eerie feel about the whole place. Everywhere he looked, the grass appeared overgrown; the trees seemed to have fewer leaves on them when compared to the surrounding properties, and the ground looked sodden. The whole place had an air altogether of cold and damp and was most uninviting. Morris looked around, the thought of the familiar cold and isolation from his childhood causing him to button up his suit jacket and plunge his hands deeper into his coat pockets. With a sigh, he checked over his shoulder to make sure the buggy was still there and saw the driver watching him intently, a look of concern on his face.

Morris turned and walked towards the homestead, allowing himself a brief, smug smile. It was time to move on to the next phase of his plan.

As he neared the dilapidated building, the front door opened slowly, and a decrepit old man appeared. It was Sergeant Garnet, Morris realised. He had changed so much in the last eight years that Morris would have walked right past him in the street had they encountered each other anywhere else.

Garnet leaned heavily on a walking stick, his hair unruly and unkempt and now a pale shade of grey. Morris instantly noticed that he had lost a great deal of weight and was in need of a shave. He had transformed radically from the days of the proud, somewhat insolent, policeman, and Morris felt almost sorry for the man the moment he laid eyes on him.

"What do you want?" Garnet snarled at Morris.

Although Morris wanted to return an equally rude retort, he knew that it would ill serve his purpose.

"Good morning, sir," he graciously replied, "I regret the intrusion, but I urgently seek the landlord of this property."

"And who might you be?" Garnet shot back, holding the door frame with his free hand for support. Morris wanted to smile: Garnet did not recognise him.

"My name is Marks," he prevaricated. "I represent my Principal, a Mr Danie Coetsee in London. He is looking for a farm to purchase in this area, and I wondered if you might know of a property that is for sale?"

Garnet cocked his head slightly, "Have I met you before? You look familiar."

"I doubt that," Morris chuckled, "I'm from London. Never been to Ireland before," said Morris, continuing the masquerade.

"Well," Garnet shifted his weight uncomfortably, "this farm is indeed for sale. Very fertile. It has produced some fine potatoes in the past."

"Is that a fact?" Morris seemed pleased and cast an inquisitive eye over the fallow land all about them. "I see no crops."

"I took a bad fall a while back and have not been able to recover sufficiently to farm the land actively. That is why I am interested in selling."

"How very unfortunate for you. I am sorry to hear that." Morris sounded genuinely concerned. "My driver mentioned that the owner of this farm had had a nasty accident. He also told me that the previous owner died on this farm: a multiple murder, his entire family."

"What rubbish!" Garnet exclaimed.

"And a suicide before that," Morris said, pressing on with the rumours.

"Codswallop! I was a policeman before I bought this farm and I can assure you, sir, that that tale is completely false."

"He believes it." Morris pointed his thumb over his shoulder. "He would not even enter the gate to bring me to this doorstep. I had to walk down your driveway. He claims the entire district talks about the murders on this farm."

"Absolute rubbish. I'll have a word with the old codger and put him right," Garnet protested.

"By all means, call him down here if you like," Morris shrugged, looking unconcerned.

Garnet let go the door frame and took a step forward. He bellowed to the driver to come to him and gesticulated wildly with his free arm. The man refused point blank and made his objections very clear with gesticulations of his own.

"You see?" Morris grinned.

"Imbecile!" Garnet muttered and stepped back to the door for needed support.

Morris then turned deadly serious, which caught the sergeant entirely off guard. "What's your price?"

"Well, it is worth at least £6,000, which is what I paid for it," he replied, looking Morris in the eye.

"You paid £6,000 for this farm?" Morris shot back in feigned shock.

"Yes," Garnet continued, totally assured. "That was about eight years ago and today…"

"I tell you what," Morris rudely cut him off, "With the unsavoury history of this place, and considering the state it is in, I will make you an offer."

"You will?" Garnet looked at Morris with some suspicion.

"Yes," Morris replied sternly. "We will offer you £100 and…"

"You must be…" Garnet interrupted him.

"I'm not finished," Morris almost growled and shot his hand in the air, cutting him off abruptly, which caught the ex-policeman by surprise, "Mr Coetsee will offer you £100 under the following conditions; firstly, the offer is open until 4 o'clock tomorrow afternoon. At one minute past 4 o'clock, the offer will cease. Secondly, I am visiting several other farms in the area for the remainder of the day, making various offers. The first person who accepts an offer made before 4 o'clock tomorrow afternoon also wins a bonus prize of six bottles of fine whiskey. Anyone accepting this offer will need to attend the offices of Mr Pichanick, an attorney-at-law, on Fitzwilliam Street in Dublin, opposite the Fitzwilliam Guest House. They will be required to bring with them the deeds of the property for immediate transfer of title."

"That is a ridiculous offer," Garnet snarled. "You can tell your Mr Coetsee, or whatever his name is, he is wasting his time with me."

"Fair enough," Morris smiled sarcastically. "Now, if you will excuse me, I have urgent business to attend to, and I must be honest, I feel very uncomfortable standing on your property. It feels jinxed." Morris looked about him with fear etched on his face.

With that he quickly turned on his heel and walked off the property as fast as he could, deliberately pretending to be scared, casting suspicious glares left and right as he went. The moment he got to the buggy he clambered in, ordering the driver to get going, a request the man did not hesitate to comply with, flicking the reins and barking at his docile horses.

As the buggy took off noisily down the dirt road, the driver spoke to Morris over his shoulder, "You are brave, sir. I had a bad feeling about that place."

Morris leaned back in his seat and sighed contentedly, taking in the lush scenery once again. "Oh, there is nothing wrong with that farm. Apparently, it is the farm next door that has had all the deaths and murders. The farmer was absolutely delightful and offered to take my message across on my behalf. We can go home now."

While sitting at the desk in his room later that afternoon, trying to compose a letter to David, Morris looked at his pocket watch. Much to his annoyance, he had forgotten once again to wind it up that morning, and it had now stopped. He tossed the pen down and stood by the window with a frustrated sigh. Morris estimated it was approximately 2 o'clock, about the time Elaine would finish work in the tavern. He decided he would walk downstairs and try to catch her if she were not busy because he wanted to spend a few hours in her company. But just as he reached for his jacket, hanging smartly in the only cupboard in the room, there was a knock at the door.

"Coming…" Morris called, shuffling into his jacket, and opened the door to reveal a bellboy, not much older than 14, standing to attention in the hallway.

"A gentlemen to see you in the lobby, sir," he announced proudly in his crisp uniform.

"Thank you," Morris nodded his appreciation, and stepped out of the room, closing the door behind him.

The bellboy allowed Morris to walk ahead of him along the thickly carpeted corridor and down the single flight of stairs. Lining the passageways were watercolour scenes of the countryside similar to that which Morris had passed through earlier in the day. Standing stiffly in the Lobby was a cleanly shaven, and quite dapper Mr Pichanick, who – although softly spoken – was yet an imposing man: well over six foot and slender.

"Good afternoon, Mr Pichanick," Morris greeted the gentleman with a welcoming smile. "Is there a problem?"

"On the contrary, Esquire," the lawyer replied with an uncharacteristic grin.

Morris looked at him blankly for a moment, then began to chuckle. "Esquire?"

"Indeed," Pichanick nodded, his grin turning into a broad smile.

"Garnet has been to see you already?" Morris asked, checking his pocket watch in surprise, but not actually looking at the time.

"I don't know how you did it. I expected the man tomorrow, as you intimated, but it seems that he could not wait to get into my office and sign his title deed over." Mr Pichanick reached into his breast pocket and extracted an envelope containing some documents which he handed to Morris. "For you, Esquire."

"'Esquire…'" Morris repeated, taking the envelope. "Is that a title normally given to a landowner?" Morris pretended to ask, although he was stating a fact. "Did you give him the money I gave you and those bottles of whiskey?"

"As you instructed," Pichanick nodded.

"Well, I never! I certainly didn't expect Garnet to arrive today. Tomorrow perhaps; but not today. He must have been desperate."

"I just need you to sign those documents, and I will register the transfer tomorrow."

Morris motioned for Mr Pichanick to take a seat at a small table by the window. They both sat in silence while Morris cast his eye over the paperwork.

"Ahh..." Morris looked up at his lawyer, then back at the documents. "I see a small error here; I wonder if you would kindly amend this for me? You have the purchaser as 'Coetsee'."

Pichanick looked concerned. "That's how I was instructed, Mr Langbourne."

"My apologies, Mr Pichanick, I meant 'Langbourne Coetsee'; it's the name of my company."

"I do apologise." The lawyer seemed calm, but Morris could see he was a bit flustered. "I obviously misunderstood you. It's easy enough to rectify, though."

"No problem at all, Mr Pichanick," Morris beamed and handed the papers back to him.

Of course, Morris had deliberately withheld the name 'Langbourne' because if the corrupt former policeman had seen the name, he would have put two-and-two together very quickly. He had already mentioned that he recognised Morris from somewhere, but Morris was sure the contrast between a poor, 15-year-old farm labourer and a successful 23-year-old businessman would have played havoc with the man's recollection, especially after an eight-year gap. Yet, any chance of linking the name to the face would probably have posed a problem, and that would have made his ridiculous offer precisely that: ridiculous.

"I'll have the deed formalised by ten o'clock in the morning. If you would care to call into my offices any time after that, I will give you the completed documents to prove your entitlement."

"Thank you, Mr Pichanick." Morris stood and shook the gentlemen's hand, "I will settle your fee in the morning, then. It has been a pleasure working with you."

"Likewise, Mr Langbourne." The lawyer shook Morris' hand vigorously and then departed.

Morris watched him exit the building before donning his felt hat, stepping outside, and standing on the steps of the guest house, surveying the street in front of him. The sun was shining, and the air was crisp. Having crossed the road, Pichanick traversed the three steps to his building in one bound and disappeared through the heavy wooden doors. Men in long, woollen overcoats and women in dark dresses with billowing skirts walked the pavements without haste or concern, while the occasional buggy or coach passed by.

It was a good day, Morris thought, although it felt rather strange that he was now the owner of a farm, a piece of Irish land, even though the property was in a sad state of disrepair. It was an extraordinary feeling, knowing that he had bought the land for almost nothing, purely because he knew, thanks to his conversation with Elaine, that Garnet couldn't sell the property and it was making him destitute. It was the second time in his life that he could practically name his price on the basis of some little tidbit of information he had accidentally come across, the sale of his tobacco business having been the other time. Information, Morris had come to realise, was vital when negotiating a deal of any sort.

Straightening his hat and doing up a button on his jacket, Morris joined the flow of pedestrians with a distinct spring in his step, heading to the corner tavern to see if he could catch up with Elaine. Just as he was about to enter the establishment, Elaine walked out, and her face immediately lit up.

"Morris, how lovely to see you!" she exclaimed. "I was hoping I would see you again."

"Yes, likewise," Morris beamed back. "Have you a moment? I'd like to talk to you about something."

Elaine laughed. "Now what possibly could I have planned for my busy day? No, I have absolutely nothing planned."

"Good!" Morris held out his arm, and Elaine looped her arm in the crook of his elbow as they walked down the pavement.

"I bought O'Connor's farm today for my brothers and me."

"You did what?" Elaine exclaimed and stopped mid-stride.

"Come, let me explain why," Morris said calmly and resumed walking.

As they strolled along, Morris related what he had done, and the deception he had played on his buggy driver to enhance his negotiations with Garnet. He told her that he had baited Garnet with whiskey, convinced him the farm was jinxed and offered him virtually nothing for the farm. Elaine was nevertheless concerned that Morris had paid any money whatsoever for the land, since she knew it to be useless, derelict, and unproductive.

"I had to offer Garnet something. Some money had to change hands for him to begin to consider the deal, so what I offered him was just a token. The whiskey was a sweetener because I remember he used to drink heavily when O'Connor was alive. You might recall he mentioned that to us when we were… arrested."

"Yes, I remember."

"Anyhow, the farm is fertile. I know it grows good potatoes," Morris chuckled. "Heaven knows I harvested many sacks of them. In any case, it is a good investment as the land is certainly worth more than £100."

"Did he remember you?"

"No, although he thought we had perhaps met. I even gave him a false name. If he had known it was me he probably wouldn't have taken the bait, and besides, who knows what he might have done? Arrested me a second time for trying to swindle him," Morris chuckled.

"That's not funny, Morris," Elaine scolded him. "You have no idea what that man is capable of."

Morris looked at her keenly. He hadn't expected that reaction from her and wondered what Garnet had put her through. He decided to change the subject.

"I was wondering," Morris continued, "if you would like to move back to the farm, to live there and manage it for my brothers and me? You won't pay any rent, and in fact, we will pay you to stay there."

"Why me? I don't know anything about farming. What about you?"

"I have business to do in London. In any case, David and I wanted you to have the farm before we left Ireland. It just seems fitting that we can now fulfil that wish, and – more importantly – we have done it legally and removed Garnet from the property."

"Talking of whom," Elaine jutted her chin out in a direction across the road, "look who's there."

Struggling to climb aboard a buggy, with the driver assisting by pushing him up in a most undignified manner, Garnet collapsed onto the rear seat and gathered his crutches to himself.

"Let's go talk to him," Morris winked at Elaine, "I have something to tell him as his new landlord."

Elaine tried to object, and even tried to pull Morris back as he strode off in the direction of the coach, but she was given no choice but to follow.

"Mr Garnet?" Morris said, as pompously as he could manage.

"Ahh… Mr Marks," Garnet looked at Morris, embarrassment overtaking him.

"I see you accepted my offer sooner than I expected."

"Indeed. I'm rather crippled now, so farming is not suited to me anymore," he opined, "so your offer, although offensive, appeared to be a sound option for me at this time of my life."

"A wise decision, Mr Garnet," Morris grinned openly.

Garnet shot a glance at Elaine, then back at Morris. "We have met before, haven't we?"

"Yes," Morris smiled. "Oh, forgive me, you remember Miss Witton?"

Garnet looked at Elaine again, a frown creasing his forehead, and then glared at Morris. "Your name is not Marks! It's Lambert or Lantern."

"Langbourne," Morris couldn't wipe a smug smile off his face.

"That's right, I remember you now. You tricked me!"

Morris puffed out his chest "We all know what you did, Mr Garnet, and now I have bought that property, and everything on it, fair and square, perfectly legally. I am now the landlord of that property, and this, sir," Morris gestured to Elaine, "is my new manager."

"Well," Garnet looked about him to see who was listening, and searched for a retort, but he was at a loss for words.

"Therefore I need to insist that you leave my farm forthwith and never set foot on it again."

Garnet glared at Morris venomously. "You are welcome to that farm, Langbourne. It will be your comeuppance. You will see no trace of me or my possessions within the fortnight, I can assure you of that."

"Actually," Elaine suddenly cut in, causing the men, including the buggy driver, to look at her in surprise, "you will recall you gave me two hours to vacate that property. Therefore I will be equally generous and give you two hours yourself, starting now."

"How dare you, young woman!" Garnet burst out, his anger now overtaking him, but Morris raised his hand abruptly.

"No, sir," Morris scowled, "I think Miss Witton has a fair point."

"Driver," Elaine turned to face the man who was completely engrossed in the conversation, his eyes darting from speaker to speaker, "kindly take Mr Garnet to the farm forthwith. It takes about an hour to get there, so he doesn't have much time, and the clock is ticking."

The driver nodded with a strained smile and smartly clambered aboard his buggy, flicking the reins and calling to his horses to move along. As the horses lurched forward, Garnet was dumbstruck as he jerked violently into the back of his seat. Morris and Elaine stood just as silently in the street, watching the buggy disappear down the road and out of view.

"I'm your manager, now am I, Morris?" Elaine scowled, but there was a smile lurking in her expression.

"Should you be agreeable, you are to be the manager of the Langbourne Coetsee farm, which I and my three brothers, David, Louis and Harry own. We require you to live on the farm in order to return the land and its dwellings to an acceptable standard and to make it profitable in whatever way you see fit. You will draw a wage, of course, and share in the annual profits equally between the five of us: four Langbourne brothers and yourself. If we ever sell the farm, you will share in one-fifth of the proceeds, less £100, being the purchase price, which, of course, belongs to me."

"And what money will I have to bring the homestead up to standard, and purchase livestock and seed?"

"We will agree on a budget that my brothers and I will fund, but we can do that tomorrow. Are you hungry?"

Elaine looked at Morris askance, "Possibly..."

"Good. Let's go," he said, smiling as he offered her his elbow again. "I want you to meet my family, especially my sister Bloomy. She is the best cook in Ireland, after you, that is."

Chapter Five

Rhodesia 1899

The morning was crisp and clear in Bulawayo, and the distinct smell of early morning culinary delights drifted down the streets from the various establishments, which keyed the boys' appetites to ravenous. It was half-past six in the morning, and the three Langbourne brothers were the only people out on the street, sharing the fresh, early-morning air with just a few cats and dogs. As they strode towards the Charter Hotel, their minds were fixed on only one thing: food!

They were the first customers of the day to be served by a charming Ndebele waiter in a fresh, white uniform. A welcome cup of hot coffee temporarily staved their minds off their stomachs, before they ploughed through a hearty breakfast of eggs, sausage, steak, potatoes, sautéed onions, followed by several slices of buttered toast. The brothers thus were left in good spirits, almost ready to face another gruelling day at their various tasks.

In the meantime, they engaged in light conversation about numerous current aspects of the business, with Harry continually checking his pocket watch and almost counting down the minutes before they needed to leave and open their commercial concerns to the general public. He was known to be exceedingly punctual, annoyingly so at times, but his siblings secretly enjoyed this little quirk of his that kept them on the straight and narrow.

Just as David signalled to the waiter to bring the bill, Brian Loxton entered the dining area and – seeing the Langbourne boys – came over to greet them cheerfully.

"Good morning, Gentlemen!"

Mr Loxton was a tall, athletic man with sharp facial features. With the aid of a popular hair-cream, he combed his jet-black hair tightly against his scalp, a style which highlighted his ears and forehead. His smile was contagious, and he always appeared to be happy to speak to anyone who was in his vicinity.

David stood up and extended his hand. "Good morning, Mr Loxton. These are my brothers, Louis and Harry," indicating his siblings, who had also risen to their feet out of courtesy.

"Pleased to meet you," said Loxton, shaking hands all round with a very firm and confident handshake. "I trust your breakfast was acceptable."

"Delightful," Louis beamed, while Harry mumbled a similar compliment.

"We were discussing the employment of extra staff to help us operate our business," David began, as he gestured to Brian to take a seat at a convenient fourth chair at their table. "I told my brothers that you knew of a person who might be suitable, and we would like to meet with him."

The assistant manager smiled. "I will arrange that at once. His name is Michael Johnson, a good friend of mine, and I can recommend him to you with confidence."

"Excellent! Thank you, Mr Loxton. We are looking for more than one employee – four to be exact, so if you were to have any other suggestions, they would be most welcome, I am sure."

"Well," Brian puffed his chest out, "I might also be on the market, as it were."

"Are you looking for a change in your career?" Louis asked out of curiosity.

"Yes, I need a change. The hospitality industry is not exactly what I had in mind as a profession, but it was all that was available when I arrived in Rhodesia, so I gave it my best shot."

David glanced at his brothers, and the smiles on their faces spoke volumes, but it was Louis who was the first to claim his man.

"I think you would be perfect at Fife Street," he said.

David beamed, flashing a wink at Louis. "When could you start?" he interjected.

"I am required to give two weeks' notice," Brian noted with some small concern.

"Good! Then perhaps you may wish to visit our warehouse on Abercorn this evening, at which point we might discuss such matters as a mutually agreeable salary, the hours of work, and so on."

"Thank you, sirs." Loxton stood to leave and shook hands with the brothers. "I will see you then. Perhaps I might take the liberty of asking Mr Johnson to join us so that you will be able to interview him after our discussion."

A moment after he left, the boys huddled together to discuss the exciting prospect of having their own employees so suddenly. Harry was a bit put out that Louis had captured Loxton for his own, but was comforted by the knowledge that a further opportunity lay with Mr Johnson.

David leaned back in his chair. "It may turn out, fellows," he said, "that Johnson might be more suitable to Fife than Loxton. Let's wait and see what happens at the interview tonight."

Harry glanced at his pocket watch. "Where's that bill? It's getting late, and we need to open the stores. You," he nodded at David, "have two anxious wagon traders who are probably waiting at the back right now and are in a mad hurry to load up and go."

David smiled to himself. He was confident that Harry was the right choice to leave behind in charge of the Bulawayo operations.

Business for all three brothers was as frantic that day as had become the norm. Their spirits were buoyed, however, by the excitement of becoming employers, with the added prospect of having their workloads considerably relieved. The morning had thus passed into the afternoon so quickly that none of the boys had noticed the passage of time.

David was at the warehouse, moving goods from the storeroom to the sales floor when he saw an Ndebele man, dressed in a khaki uniform, consisting of a smart, short-sleeved tunic and a pair of pants reaching as far as the knees. Standing at the front door, he looked rather out of place. It was becoming more common to see Matabele men wearing European clothing, especially in those uniforms representing particular industries or types of business. David put his load down and walked over to the man.

"I see you," he said in his best siNdebele. "How may I help you?" He noticed that the man wore a shiny leather belt around his waist with a polished brass buckle - something that a government department might issue to its staff.

"I see you, sir," he broke into a broad and friendly smile. "I am from the Post Office. I have a telegram."

"Excellent!" David exclaimed. It could only be from Morris, and David quickly assumed Morris had arrived in Ireland quite safely. "Thank you."

The Post Office man handed David a brown envelope and opened a small notebook. "You must write your name here, if you please, sir," he suggested.

David took a pencil out of his pocket and scribbled his name where he saw a small "x" next to the name "Langbourne Brothers" and returned the notebook to the young man. They exchanged a few more, brief pleasantries before the Post Office man departed, but the moment he walked out, Thembela slipped into the warehouse, looking somewhat concerned,

"Boss David," she panted, "Boss Rooie says you must come now. Someone is waiting to see you."

David sighed. "Alright, thank you, Thembela," he nodded, looking over his shoulder to meet Harry's eyes. David signalled with a simple gesture of one hand and a nod in the direction of the door that he would be running down to Fife. In the middle of serving a customer, Harry acknowledged the signal with one of his own, a signal so slight that the customer never noticed, but David caught it and understood.

Signals and codes were almost a secret language between the boys. Without realising it, they could communicate a host of messages between themselves over large and busy areas just by looking at each other. A simple twitch of an eyebrow, a bent finger tapping the nose, a very slight nod or shake of the head, all were signs and signals that had a meaning in a specific situation. They were not deliberate or learned codes or signs, just something that they had developed among themselves, and which they all understood. For Harry, it was a precise click, for David a short soft whistle, and Louis would run his fingers through his hair to catch a brother's attention. Each brother had his own way of communicating with a particular sibling.

Now confident that Harry knew he would be running to Abercorn, David turned on his heel and trotted down the road. It only took a minute to get there, so he was hardly out of breath when he entered the shop by the rear door. The moment he walked in, he saw his lanky brother talking to a relatively large and rotund gentleman. When Louis saw his brother enter, he almost invisibly nodded towards the right side of the store where a woman in an elegant dress stood with her back to him. Without breaking his stride, David approached her.

"Good morning, Madam," David apologised politely. "I'm sorry to have kept you waiting."

The lady turned around, and he recognised that it was Mrs Rubinstein. "Good afternoon, Master Langbourne," she greeted him with a mischievous smile.

David quickly glanced at his pocket watch in surprise. "Good grief! Is it afternoon already? How are you, Mrs Rubinstein?"

"I am exceptionally well, thank you. I have brought my daughter along to look at your silver tea-set." She glanced over David's shoulder and nodded in that direction, momentarily dropping her voice to that of a whisper. "Do try and convince her that we need it. Hann-aah!" she called.

When David turned to meet Hanna, his entire world appeared quite suddenly to fall apart. Before him stood the most beautiful girl he had ever seen: someone of perfection in every aspect. With glossy, black hair cascading down to frame a delicate porcelain face, she had the most liquid-blue eyes and a smile that radiated pure joy. She wore a tight-fitting, white blouse with delicate frills down the front, reinforcing her femininity, and a floral skirt that accentuated her wasp-like waist.

"Hello," she said, smiling sweetly.

Having never been at a loss for words before, David stood completely dumbstruck; even the simplest of responses eluded him. His stomach was in a knot, and he was sure his heart had stopped beating; indeed, even his breathing had stopped.

"My name is Hanna," she continued, after noticing that David seemed dumbfounded for some peculiar reason.

Fortunately for them both, however, a sense of reality came flooding back when David realised he was appearing like a fool and that he needed to pull himself together.

"Uhh… Umm… Hello." He finally managed to get some sort of a word out of his mouth, but it came out an octave higher than even he had expected. Immediately, he made some pretence of clearing his throat. "Ahem... I'm David. Very pleased to meet you." Finally, he had recovered enough of his senses to string an acceptable greeting together.

Even more mercifully, Mrs Rubinstein came to his rescue. "David," she purred, "would you mind showing Hanna that silver tea-set you showed me yesterday?"

David wrenched his attention away from Hanna before noticing that Mrs Rubinstein had the kind of cunning little smile on her face that was a little off-putting. He glanced around the shop in confusion, trying desperately to remember where the tea-service might have been located. He noticed Louis looking at him with a curious expression on his face, as if to ask what the matter was.

"Uhh... come with me, please." David walked off to the far side of the store, relieved at having to turn his back on the ladies momentarily, in order to reclaim his equilibrium.

Although Mrs Rubinstein never bought the silver tea-service in the end, David relaxed a little more as time went on, but still struggled desperately not to look directly at Hanna, because, each time he failed to restrain himself, her smiles were enough to melt his heart to butter again. As he walked the two ladies to the door, he thanked them for coming in and politely confirmed that he had been delighted to meet Hanna in person.

"Please do join us for dinner tonight," Mrs Rubinstein suggested, "I'd like you to meet my husband."

David was caught unawares, but the thought of seeing Hanna again appealed to him so mightily, and he was about to accept the invitation with enthusiasm when he suddenly remembered that he couldn't.

"I would very much like to," David beamed, "but unfortunately I am conducting some interviews at the warehouse this evening, and I'm not sure how long that will take."

"Tomorrow then?" Hanna smiled, excitement in her voice.

"Yes," David said immediately, then embarrassingly realised his response was probably a little too enthusiastic, "tomorrow would be wonderful. Thank you."

David watched as the ladies gently departed to stroll sedately along the pavement and, just before they rounded the corner, Hanna looked back over her shoulder. When she saw David standing, still holding the door open, she smiled at him once again. Suffering once more from an irregular heartbeat, David wanted very badly to duck back into the shop, but he had been seen, and so, with far too much embarrassment, he stood transfixed to the spot.

As soon as she disappeared out of view, however, David heard a familiar click. Louis had been trying for some minutes to catch his attention, so David reluctantly closed the door and walked back into the shop.

"Are you alright?" Louis asked.

"Yes, fine, thanks."

"You're blushing. I've never seen you blush before."

"I'm fine," David insisted, "I have to get back. Don't be late for those interviews," he shot back at his brother, excused himself abruptly from the warehouse, and made a hasty beeline for the rear door.

That evening, the interviews at the warehouse went exceptionally well. Brian Loxton was immediately and formally engaged to manage the Fife Street store, where Louis had undertaken to train him as soon as he commenced, which would be in a fortnight. Michael Johnson, an intelligent gentleman with a quick mind and piercing eyes, was engaged to manage the Abercorn warehouse, and a lady, Ivy Collier, whom Brian had invited to come along for an interview, was likewise engaged immediately.

Ivy Collier was an Irish lass with a dominant Irish accent. She had the curious ability to find quite naturally a slightly humorous slant on most things she spoke about, which had the brothers giggling through the better part of the interview. Her position would be a bookkeeper for both shops, as she seemed to have an affinity for numbers. It suited the boys hugely, and they viewed her immediate appointment with much relief.

Brian waited outside the warehouse until Ivy's interview was over so that he could walk her home, because it was by then quite dark. As David bid them a pleasant evening at the door and thanked them once again, he asked Brian to put the word out that they were looking for more salespeople, at least another two, perhaps three. Brian agreed to send those whom he felt would be most suitable and then departed with Ivy.

"Well, that was quite a day." Harry shuffled some papers as he tidied up his desk.

"Very positive," Louis chirped, "I feel good now that we will get some help. The three of us are not doing the business any favours at this level of strain."

David entered the office and sat heavily on a chair. "Well, that was fun," he chuckled.

Louis and Harry glanced at each other with a knowing look.

"What?" David asked, having caught their exchange.

"You've been a bit out of sorts today," Louis ventured.

"No, I haven't," David dismissed the idea out of hand. "What makes you think that?"

"You acted all strange when you met Mrs Rubinstein's daughter."

"I did not!" he objected.

"You've got yourself a girlfriend!" Harry teased.

"I have not!" David protested, just a little too vigorously.

"We'll see," Louis almost sang. "I heard them talking about you when you went out the back to check on something. She likes you, Brother. She likes you a lot."

"She does?" David asked with unmistaken excitement in his voice.

"You see," Harry smirked. "David's got a girlfriend," he sang.

"Oh shut up." David stood and tried to change the subject.

"Harry," he said, "have we got time to get some dinner? I'm starving."

Harry promptly consulted his watch. "Not at the Charter Hotel," he replied, "but we can get something to eat at the bar of the Maxim Hotel if we hurry."

The brothers left without delay, although they didn't much like the Maxim Hotel. It was frequented by the BSAP personnel and could get a little rowdy at times, especially on Friday nights. Yet all was calm on this particular evening, and they ate their fill on a simple, but tasty beef stew. As they leaned back in their chairs after the meal, contemplating the events of the day, David's thoughts were only about Hanna. He was interrupted by Harry.

"David, who was that Ndebele in the odd uniform who popped into the warehouse this morning?"

"Oh heavens!" David sat bolt upright, "he was from the Post Office with a telegram."

"What did it say?" Harry pressed.

"I didn't open it. In fact, I don't know what I did with it. No sooner had I signed for it, I ran to Fife to see Mrs Rubinstein." David was very concerned.

"Check your pockets," Louis said calmly.

David patted his shirt pockets and then his trouser pockets, but found nothing. He immediately stood up and patted the pockets on the seat of his pants and felt something on the right. He whipped it out and held the elusive envelope.

"Whew..." David sighed, and sat down again. "That was close; I thought I had dropped it on the street as I ran."

"It would seem that Miss Rubinstein has had quite an effect on you, Brother," Harry mocked. "Go on, read it."

**TO: LANGBRO
RHODESIA**

MONDAY 10ᵗʰ JULY 1899

**ARRIVED SAFELY STOP FAMILY WELL STOP HAVE PURCHASED O'CONNOR'S FARM FOR LANCOE £800 STOP LANCOE TO BE BASED IN BEN STOP PROCEEDING TO BEN TOMORROW STOP BEGIN TO PREPARE LANGBJB THREE MONTHS HENSE STOP
LION**

The brothers sat in silence, digesting what Morris had coded into their telegram, then glanced at each other in confusion.

Louis broke the silence. "I'm sorry," he said, "read that again in English."

"He bought a farm?" Harry asked, utterly perplexed.

"That's what it says," David mumbled, studying the telegram.

"That cannot be right. Read it again," Louis insisted.

"It says the family are well, so that's good news, and he says he bought O'Connor's farm for us, well, for Langbourne Coetsee, which is us," David quickly pointed to the three of them, himself included, "for £100."

"He bought the farm off the man who treated him like a slave?" Louis looked horrified.

"For £100?" Harry questioned. "For us? I don't want to pay for a farm I don't want. Is he mad?"

"Well," David shrugged, "I've seen that farm and I think £100 is a bargain, an outstanding bargain. There is a homestead as well as a couple of barns already built on the farm, along with other infrastructure.

Perhaps he wants to resell it for a profit later."

"Go on," Louis pressed impatiently.

"For some reason, he wants to set up Langbourne Coetsee in London now, and not in Dublin. How strange is that?"

"Sometimes I wonder about Morris," Louis complained. "So we own a farm in Ireland now, which we – all of us – have paid for, and on which we cannot live. Instead, we have to live in a warehouse and sleep on the floor!"

For a moment they sat in silence until David and Harry burst out laughing simultaneously. It didn't take long for Louis to join in.

"Yes," David continued as he took a breath between the laughter, "we do have an odd brother. What affects us most, though, is the last sentence; he wants us to have the Johannesburg plan operational in three months. That means we need to get our new staff running at full competency as quickly as possible. Are you ready for this? Things will change radically from now on."

Both younger brothers were confident that they and their staff would meet the deadline.

"Good. Therefore, Harry, from today you will become the General Manager of Langbourne Brothers, Bulawayo; and Louis, you will become the General Manager of Langbourne Coetsee, Johannesburg."

"Looks like our recruitment exercise came at just the right time," Harry suggested.

"Perfect timing," David concurred.

The following month flashed by a great deal faster than anyone could have imagined. The staff numbers proliferated from just the three brothers to a complement of nine men and women, including some Matabele men that Michael Johnson engaged to handle the loading and packing for their wagon traders. Through his direction and management, the receiving and restocking of the wagons that came in from the bush were efficiently streamlined. A wagon could be turned around, fully stocked and the goods accounted for within two hours, a vast improvement from the full day it had taken previously and, as was often the case, well into the night for the Langbourne boys.

Brian Loxton used his experience of working in retail stores in London to improve the displays of the Fife Street store, making the shop more exciting. He moved the checkout counter closer to the front door to keep a tighter control on potential shrinkage, and – more importantly, he stressed – to greet his customers the moment they walked in. His cheerful and pleasant demeanour, developed during his time in the hospitality industry, was welcomed by the public and helped to ensure that a large number of customers repeatedly returned for further purchases.

Ivy Collier, in her constantly jolly, but thoroughly efficient ways, began producing daily and weekly figures for the boys, who now had time to study them during normal working hours. This allowed the boys to make changes to pre-empt potential problems before they arose. It was Harry who took charge of the sales figures and interpreted their meanings for his older brothers. David would often sit back during one of these financial discussions and marvel at how similar Harry was to Morris. Although Harry was good with numbers, David had to admit that Morris was still in a class of his own.

"Fellows," Harry announced one afternoon after a meeting, closing the ledger with a thump, "these figures tell me that our sales in the last month alone have increased by over 80%."

"Terrific!" Louis exclaimed. "Employing the right people has been very beneficial for the business."

"And," Harry leaned back and smiled, "we are not working as hard as we were; nor for such outrageously long hours. I actually feel we have a tighter grip on the company now. We can efficiently control the business, and don't have to spend our entire day just solving one problem after another."

David smiled as he looked at Harry; he reminded him so much of Morris. As complicated as Morris was, he missed his brother. "I'm glad to hear that, Harry," David commented, "because, in about one month, you will have to take over all of this on your own."

"I'm ready," Harry said with confidence.

"Louis, are you prepared for Johannesburg?"

"Well, I was hoping to buy a piece of land in the suburbs of Bulawayo and build a home there, but it seems unlikely I will do that now. It looks like I'll have to settle for a farm somewhere in Ireland."

The brothers laughed at Morris' expense. David lent over the desk and retrieved Harry's ledger, turning it to face him and opening it to the last page. "Is that what we have in the bank?" he asked Harry.

Harry glanced over and checked the number against David's index finger. "Yup," he replied casually.

"You say the properties in Suburbs are going quite cheaply at the moment, Louis?"

"Yes, cheaper than a farm in Ireland," he grumbled.

"What do you say we pop down to the Administration tomorrow and see if we can secure three properties at a reasonable price, and, dividends permitting, we can each build a house of our own? We may as well secure these properties before they go up in price, and as our postings are to be on five-yearly rotations, you may as well build a house here regardless, Louis."

Louis and Harry were elated and agreed instantaneously.

"Why wait?" Louis grinned. "There's no better time than the present,"

"Agreed," Harry enthused. "May I suggest we go down to the Charter Hotel and have a celebratory dinner?"

"Oh, I can't," David apologised sheepishly, "I am going to the Rubinstein's for dinner tonight."

"That's the fourth time this week!" Harry complained.

"He's in love with Hanna," Louis mocked his older brother.

"I am not!" David objected firmly.

David was correct; he was not merely in love with Hanna; he was madly in love with her, and she was just as hopelessly in love with him.

Chapter Six

London 1899

Morris stepped out from the underground railway station and stood on the pavement, looking around in bewilderment. He had no idea where he was, and – since it was overcast and drizzling – he could not tell which way was north, or even west for that matter. After asking several passers-by, who were extremely helpful, he found his way to Berkeley Square, and finally to the imposing black front door of Yoni Goldberg's flat. Having knocked quite soundly, he took a moment to look up and down the street.

Appearing mostly to have been constructed of stone, the buildings had common, adjacent walls, which prohibited any access to the rear. It looked as though one could get to the backyards only by entering the front door and exiting the back door. The front of the buildings were separated from the pavements by sturdy, wrought-iron fences, which were punctuated in turn by gates that led down narrow stone or concrete steps to a lower level.

Right beside Morris was one of these stairways, and he peered over the edge to see where they led. He saw a front door similar to Yoni's and a kitchen window draped with a delicate, lace curtain behind which lay a bar of white soap on the windowsill inside. Having never seen a dwelling below ground-level before, he raised an eyebrow in surprise. On the other side of the street was an oval-shaped park, surrounded by further terraced buildings. Since they were no taller than a man, the trees in the park, apparently, had been planted only recently, while a few benches had been scattered about for the convenience of the residents. Morris noticed that, unlike what he had become used to in Africa, no birds seemed to be occupying these young trees.

Morris' thoughts were interrupted when he heard the rattle of a latch, and the door opened. Wearing a black dress with a white apron, an attractive young lady greeted him with rosy cheeks and a friendly smile.

"How may I help you, sir?" she asked.

Morris quickly removed his hat. "Good day, Madam," he replied, "I'm looking for the home of Mr Yoni Goldberg."

"Mr Goldberg is not in, sir, but if you would kindly step inside, I will call Mrs Goldberg."

After allowing Morris inside, the maidservant gently closed the door and excused herself politely in order to locate Yoni's wife. Morris duly waited in the hallway, relieved that he had found the home of this influential man.

A graceful lady with her long, black hair tied in a bun appeared and greeted Morris kindly. Her exquisite dress immediately caught his attention.

"I'm sorry to intrude, Madam, my name is Morris Langbourne. I'm looking for Mr Yoni Goldberg."

"Ahh…" The elegant lady smiled warmly. "Please do come in. We were expecting you. I'm Ruth Goldberg,"

The Goldberg residence was opulent. Luxurious Persian carpets adorned the floorboards, and large oil paintings hung boldly from every wall. Intricate ornaments had been placed tastefully on various shelves and occasional, inlaid tables – just enough to draw one's eye, but not so many as to look too cluttered. An exotic, indoor plant stood in a wooden tub by a window. Morris had never seen such opulence and immediately went into raptures about their beautiful flat.

"Your home is magnificent," Morris gushed, then leaned in for a closer view of a painting of a beautiful woman with a soft smile and a pink ribbon in her long, flowing hair. She reminded him of his mother.

"That's a self-portrait by Marie-Geneviéve Bouliard. It's just over 100 years old," Ruth smiled.

Morris looked at her in disbelief. "I didn't know artists could paint to such perfection 100 years ago."

"Oh, artists have been painting for centuries, and each one has a particular style. Yoni and I appreciate a certain type of art, such as this painting, and so we have quite a collection. Please," she waved her arm gently towards the lounge, "have a look around while I organise a pot of tea. Yoni will be here very shortly."

Morris thanked Ruth and carefully worked his way around their lounge, studying the masterpieces and ornaments with fascination. Everything appeared to be of exceptional quality, even the furniture. The walls were painted a pastel green, with a pale-rose dado rail circumnavigating the entire room. Intricate white cornices separated the walls from the ceiling, from which hung a very extravagant crystal chandelier. It was fairly obvious that the Goldbergs were wealthy. Morris had never imagined that anyone could live in such luxury, and decided there and then he wanted to live in a place just like this. It would take some doing to get to the Goldbergs status, he was sure of that, but he was determined to try. Living in a warehouse in the middle of Africa had suddenly lost its appeal.

Yoni arrived just as the maid brought a tray of tea to the lounge. Hanging his thick woollen overcoat and hat on a stand in the hallway, he bustled through to the living area and greeted Morris heartily.

"I'm so pleased to have you in our home," Yoni said, as he pumped his visitor's hand. "When did you get in?"

"Only just arrived," Morris smiled broadly. "You have a magnificent home."

"Thank you." Yoni was obviously proud of his abode. "Please feel free to stay with us for as long as it takes to settle yourself."

Morris didn't hesitate to accept this invitation but was careful not to sound over-enthusiastic. It would serve his immediate purposes perfectly, and Yoni was just the person to help him get started in both his business and accommodation. In any case, Morris liked the man; he understood him, and they seemed to share the same ideals. Morris was very grateful that his father had introduced him to Yoni: this was going to make a significant difference to his life.

Within two days, Morris had found a suitable place to rent that would double as both a warehouse and for sleeping accommodation. It was in a small industrial area called Charing Cross, about half an hour's walk from Yoni and Ruth's apartment, close to both a railway station and a wharf on the River Thames. The nearest Post Office was just a five-minute walk away, convenient for sending telegrams.

The unit itself was simple, with a small storage area with access from the front and the rear. It had a tiny nook at the back, which Morris decided would be put to use as his sleeping quarters. It also boasted a closed-off area that contained a water closet and wash-basin with hot-and-cold, running water. A mirror had been attached to the wall above the sink, but it was cracked in half, and a previous tenant had also installed a bathtub. The 'Heath-Robinson' attempt at plumbing made it obvious that all this had been an afterthought carried out by an amateur. Nevertheless, it worked, and this was far more comfortable and convenient than Morris had been accustomed to in the warehouse in Rhodesia.

Having signed a lease agreement for a one-year period, to take effect in one calendar month's time, Morris gave himself a month to secure his agencies and suppliers. It would entail some travelling to nearby towns, as suggested by Yoni, so he wouldn't need to intrude on the Goldbergs hospitality for the full month, something that had concerned Morris a great deal. Nevertheless, both Yoni and Ruth appeared pleased with his company and made Morris feel more than comfortable.

Never wanting to waste time, Morris took his leave the day after he had signed his lease in order to depart for Manchester and Liverpool in the north, where he secured agencies for a vast range of fabrics. In Sheffield, he signed agreements for luxury goods, especially silver-cutlery sets; in Scotland's Glasgow, he tied up contracts with two whisky-distilling companies and found a business that made precision brass scales, the type he had seen used in Post Offices to weigh letters. He found factories that made items from copper, brass, and glass, and signed exclusive agencies with them for distribution in Africa.

On his return journey from Scotland, he stopped in a town called Nottingham. It didn't seem a very important place, especially on the rudimentary map he had acquired before his departure from London, but he thought he would give it a try, regardless. Securing one night's accommodation and checking into a room above a very traditional drinking establishment, Morris set off on foot to explore the business opportunities. Before leaving, however, Morris stopped in at the bar to see if the publican would give him information that might save him some time.

"Excuse me, sir," Morris asked the burly man, "what would the biggest factories in Nottingham be?"

"Bicycles, lad," the man responded with a knowing smile.

"Bicycles?" Morris reflected, "Mmm... Where might I find this bicycle factory?"

"It's the Raleigh Bicycle Company, not far from here, actually. Walk out the door and turn right, then keep walking for about twenty minutes and you'll see it on the left. Can't miss it."

"Thank you, sir," Morris nodded appreciatively and headed out the door.

Just as the publican had said, he found the Raleigh Bicycle Company 20 minutes up the road, and it was certainly impossible to miss. Covering several acres of land, the massive brick structure had a saw-tooth roof with a tall chimney, which spewed forth copious plumes of smoke. Morris noticed that a railway line passed right by the building. So big was the factory that, for the first time in his life, Morris felt strangely insignificant and almost intimidated as he walked through the massive front doors.

He was greeted by a sizeable desk at which two men sat. One of the men was tapping incessantly at a typewriter, a slight echo of the clicks reverberating off the bare walls. The other man seemed intensely occupied with some paperwork, and both ignored Morris. As he stood patiently waiting for one of them to acknowledge his presence, Morris glanced around the spacious area, which now seemed cold and uninviting. A large painting of a man in a business suit, his arms folded and a contented smile playing on his lips, hung on the wall to the right. He was slightly greying and looked to be in his early to mid-50s. The name, attached to the frame on a small brass plaque, was Frank Bowden.

"Yes?" the man at the paperwork rudely interrupted Morris as he studied the painting.

Morris politely took one step closer to the desk and smiled, "I have an appointment with Mr Bowden at two o'clock," he deliberately misinformed him. "I apologise, I'm a little early, but I have just arrived from London - lost track of time in my haste."

"Name please?" he asked without much enthusiasm.

"Morris Langbourne."

He pressed a button on a box-like apparatus and spoke into it. "Mr Langbourne for Mr Bowden," he barked.

Amazingly, the box spoke back in a scratchy voice. "Send him up, please."

Morris stared at the contraption in awe; he had never seen anything like it.

"Upstairs, second door on the right," the receptionist directed him abruptly, before returning immediately to his indifferent paperwork.

Morris thanked the man and made his way up the stairs to the right, giving his jacket lapels a cursory dusting down with his fingers. When he entered the second door on the right, he was confronted by a slender and somewhat insipid young man, who greeted him with a strained smile.

"I'm sorry, sir, I didn't catch your name."

"Morris Langbourne, from London," he smiled back pleasantly. The office was a little more welcoming, and definitely a far cry from the bland reception area.

"I don't seem to have you in Mr Bowden's appointment book," he said apologetically, flipping furiously through some pages of a book on his desk.

"Oh," Morris looked unhappy, "this appointment was made some two weeks ago."

"Oh dear." Now the secretary was concerned. "I'll see if Mr Bowden can see you presently. What are you selling?"

"I'm not selling," Morris pumped out his chest, "I'm buying."

"Oh, in that case, I am sure he will see you very shortly. Excuse me for a moment, Mr Langbourne." He smiled very sweetly and walked through another door, his polished leather shoes accentuating his stride.

A moment later he returned and ushered Morris into the side office, and Morris nodded his appreciation as he passed him.

Although Mr Bowden owned the factory outright and was as perpetually busy as one might expect, he remained very courteous and showed Morris a good deal of respect by standing up and walking around his desk, shaking Morris' hand firmly and shuffling one of the two chairs near his desk for Morris to sit upon. To bring himself close to Morris, Bowden then sat in the other guest chair, a move which Morris noted and appreciated.

"Jim tells me you've come all the way from London to buy one of our bicycles. A good choice, Mr Langbourne."

"Not exactly, sir. I'd like to obtain many of your bicycles, and represent you and your company in the Southern African region," Morris stated.

Bowden started to wave one finger in the air as if he were looking for an elusive word. "How exactly do you intend to do that?"

"My three brothers and I have a very substantial and well-established warehouse and retail business operation in Southern Africa... Three warehouses, actually," Morris corrected himself, "one in Rhodesia, one in Johannesburg, and one in London. We also have a comprehensive distribution system, utilising about forty wagon traders throughout the new country of Rhodesia."

"And you want to buy my bicycles to ship to Africa?"

"No, actually I don't." Morris relaxed slightly and leaned back in his seat, casually crossing his legs with a confident air about him. "I want to be your agent, your exclusive agent, for all of Southern Africa. I want to sell your bicycles, not buy them."

"Have you been to Africa, Mr Langbourne?" Bowden looked very suspicious.

"Yes," Morris said nonchalantly, "I've lived there for eight years, since 1891. Have you been there yourself?" he shot back at Bowden. That question seemed to unnerve the powerful industrialist.

Frank Bowden cocked his head slightly and smiled, leant back in his chair, and crossed one leg over the other, in imitation of Morris. "No, Mr Langbourne. Actually, I haven't."

"A lot of business is going on there, Mr Bowden. The continent is opening up at a cracking pace."

"And do they not sell bicycles there?"

"They do, but they are very hard to come across. I must admit I have never seen a Raleigh bicycle there. Can I assume you are not established in Africa yet?"

"What's the population like?"

Morris inwardly smiled; he knew he had Bowden when he answered his question with another question. "They found gold in Johannesburg, diamonds in Kimberley, Rhodesia is opening up to the north. People are flocking in there by the thousand, and hardly anyone imports bicycles."

"And you say you have three warehouses and a retail outlet?"

"Yes, including a network of wagon traders who service the outlying towns and settlements of Rhodesia."

"So my understanding is that you want me to supply you with some bicycles, at no cost, which you will send to Africa? How do I know you will ever pay me?"

Morris shuffled and sat upright. "You don't. You would have to take me at my word."

"I don't take many people at their word, Mr Langbourne. Perhaps you have some references from people who might vouch for you and your business?"

Morris gave this some thought. "Mr Goldberg from Lloyds of London could vouch for my credentials."

"Never heard of him," Bowden smiled smugly.

Morris scratched his head. "If you are looking for someone you have heard of, I might suggest Dr Leander Starr Jameson. Ever heard of him?"

Bowden cocked his head, his blue eyes boring into Morris. "Yes," he said cautiously, "he's been in the papers. Didn't he attempt to overthrow the South African Republic's Government or something to that effect?"

"Yes," a flash of annoyance crossed Morris forehead momentarily. "He was the administrator of Rhodesia at the time, and he was, and his administration still is, one of our biggest customers. Thanks to his folly, he left the settlement practically defenceless, and we nearly lost our entire business in an uprising. We were on the verge of starvation and nearly killed."

Bowden seemed suddenly curious. "What was the name of the town?"

"Bulawayo."

"That's right, in Rhodesia," said Bowden as he stared out the window for a brief moment. "I remember reading something about a native rebellion. So you were there when it happened?"

"Yes, unfortunately. The town was under siege by tens of thousands of Matabele warriors. Nonetheless, we survived," said Morris brushing the issue off casually, "but now I want to do business with you. I'll try and locate Dr Jameson to get a reference. I believe he is currently in London somewhere and he should not be too difficult to find. He owes my brothers and me a huge favour after the damage he caused."

"No, no ..." Bowden held up his hand to interrupt the conversation, before standing up and walking back to sit in his customary chair behind his desk. "No, sir, that won't be necessary," he smiled and shook his head as if in disbelief. Opening a drawer to take out a sheet of white paper, he placed it on his desk, picked up a very expensive fountain pen, and took off the cap. Pausing for a moment, he stared at Morris.

"What is it exactly that you want from me?"

Morris smiled openly; he knew this was going to be a lucrative deal. For the next hour, the two men discussed the terms and conditions of the proposed business arrangement. Bowden realised from the ensuing level of discussion that Morris was an extraordinarily shrewd negotiator and had a thorough grasp of all the subtleties of business. The structure of his organisation appeared ingenious, and that which Morris demanded, appeared challenging, despite Bowden's long experience in commerce and industry. In the end, Morris had convinced him beyond any doubt that a massive market was emerging in Africa, just ripe for his products, and that Bowden ought to capitalise on this market. Concessions were made and mutually agreed upon, and a formal business relationship was established almost immediately.

When he judged the discussion to be over, Frank Bowden looked at a clock on the wall and invited Morris to join him at a local hotel for lunch. Morris accepted, and the two men walked out of the office.

"Jim," Bowden passed his secretary the sheet of paper he had been making notes on, "I'm taking Mr Langbourne down to the usual for lunch. Please type up this agreement for us to sign when we return."

"Certainly," Jim agreed, and smiled at Morris, but there was a great deal of curiosity lurking behind his eyes.

While enjoying a steak-and-kidney pie in a traditional public-house environment, the two men talked incessantly. Although Morris didn't particularly like the taste of beer, he politely joined Frank in one when he insisted. The conversation shifted to their pending business deal and Africa. Morris wanted 100 bicycles delivered to his London warehouse in precisely six weeks, flat-packed in order to save space. All parts had to be contained in separate boxes and clearly labelled to avoid confusion, so that, for example, one box contained 100 left pedals, another, 100 right pedals, yet another, 100 handle-bars, and so on. Frank Bowden agreed to all of Morris' requirements, and when all was said and done, Morris turned the conversation to Bowden himself.

"Tell me, Mr Bowden, what made you decide to manufacture bicycles?"

"Interesting question," Bowden reflected as he leaned back and dabbed his lips with a pale blue serviette. "I spent a lot of time in Hong Kong, bought a lot of property and made an awful lot of money there, mind you.

But then I became ill. The doctors didn't know what was wrong with me, so I came back to England and saw some of the top doctors on Harley Street. I was so ill they gave me about six to eight months to live. Then one doctor told me to start riding a bicycle every day."

"A bicycle?" Morris repeated in surprise.

"Yes, he believed in the medicinal properties of exercise, fresh air, and the peace and quiet of the countryside. It worked, and here I am!" Frank smiled broadly, his blue eyes glinting. "I recovered fully, and now ride every day. So, about twelve years ago I approached three gentlemen who owned a small bicycle shop in Raleigh Street, here in Nottingham, and bought shares in their business. They were only making about two or three bicycles a week, which I found frustrating in the extreme, so I bought them out completely. Then I made some production changes and three years later I needed bigger premises, so I relocated here," he gestured in the direction of his factory. "I changed the name of the company to honour the name of the street the business was created on, and today I am the biggest bicycle manufacturer in the entire world."

Morris was fascinated by this man. He leant back in his chair and shook his head in awe. "I admire you, Mr Bowden. That is the most incredible story I have ever heard."

"Well, I must say I'm impressed by you. You have drive, ambition and foresight, and at such a young age. That's why I have decided to take a chance with you." He took a sip of his beer. "Have you ever considered going to Hong Kong?"

Morris looked at him curiously. "No, never, but the suggestion has been put to me. Why do you ask?"

Bowden waved a finger at him with a sly smile. "I think you would be quite taken with Hong Kong; the business opportunities over there are huge, and I think it's right up your alley."

"Thanks, Mr Bowden, but I am far too busy in England and Africa to even give it a fleeting thought right now. Another day, perhaps."

"I'm going to do you a favour, Mr Langbourne." Bowden straightened up, leaned forward and placed his elbows on the table, "I have made some interesting friends in Hong Kong, and I'm going to give you the contact of one particular man. He can act as your agent in Hong Kong, just as you are my agent in Africa, so you will not need to actually go there. Just mention I referred you, and you will be surprised at what you find."

By the time Morris returned to London, after some three weeks on the road, he had exclusive agencies with Nugget, who specialised in shoe polish, some whisky distillers, cigarette manufacturers, Milner's Safes and a host of other extremely interesting agencies, including Frank Bowden's Raleigh Bicycles. But his greatest catch was his new connection in the Far East.

Langbourne Coetsee had become truly global, and all very, very suddenly.

Chapter Seven

Rhodesia 1899

Louis entered the warehouse through the rear doors and walked into Harry's office, placing a dirty money bag on his desk before pulling up a chair and sitting on it heavily.

"How was your day?" Harry asked as he looked up from his ledger.

"Not bad. Mr Loxton is doing a fine job. Here are yesterday's takings." Louis pushed the grubby bag closer to Harry. "Where's David?"

"He went to see the bank manager. I expect he will be here shortly. We received another telegram from Morris this morning." Harry pulled a brown envelope from under a leather book and tossed it on the table.

"What does it say?" Louis didn't take his eyes off it.

"I don't know," Harry responded casually, "I haven't opened it, but it's probably Morris giving you your marching orders. We were expecting it, weren't we?"

"You don't mind if it's me that goes to Johannesburg?" Louis asked, with a little concern in his expression. "After all, it was you that Morris wanted there."

"Not at all," Harry smiled. "If the truth be known, I'm actually quite happy here, and – in any case – we will be swopping over in about five years' time. Besides, my house will be built before yours."

Louis laughed. "True. Well, at least we finally own some property. Why don't you open that telegram? It's not addressed to David."

Harry gave a sly smile, picked up the envelope, and while keeping his ironic gaze on Louis, tore the envelope open.

TO: LANGBRO
BULAWAYO
RHODESIA

FRIDAY 6ᵗʰ OCTOBER 1899

BADGER TO GOLD NOW TO PREPARE LANGBJB STOP
EAGLE PROCEED TO COPPER AND PREPARE CONSIGNMENT
ARRIVAL FROM SOUTHAMPTON STOP THEN PROCEED TO EGGS
AND PREPARE CONSIGNMENT ARRIVAL FROM HONG KONG STOP
LETTER WITH MANIFEST POSTED TO MANAGER STANDARD
BANK COPPER FOR COLLECTION STOP PSE INFORM MANAGER
OF IMMINENT ARRIVAL STOP
LION

Since the use of codes among the four brothers was an integral part of their communication, reading Morris' telegram was as easy as if he had written it in simple English. "Lion" was Morris; "Eagle" was David; and "Giraffe" was Louis. "Badger" was the code for Harry, who was instructed to go to Johannesburg (codenamed "Gold") to prepare the warehouse at 9 Railway Road. Of course, it had been agreed among them that it would be Louis who would go instead. The brothers had earlier decided that David would inform Morris of this change of plan.

David was to go to "Copper", the codename for Cape Town, and engage a shipping agent to send the stock that was arriving from Southampton to Johannesburg by rail. He was then to go to East London, affectionately known as "Eggs" and situated a little further north-east of Port Elizabeth, to do the same for a shipment that was arriving from Hong Kong. Morris had, in the meantime, posted a letter with the manifest and all details of the incoming stock to the Manager of The Standard Bank in Cape Town, which he was to hold until David collected it when he arrived there. David would need to inform the manager by telegram to expect both the letter and his arrival.

"Hong Kong?" Louis exclaimed in surprise. "Who on earth is that?"

"Hong Kong?" Harry repeated. "Never heard of him. What kind of name is that? Sounds very Chinese, or Japanese."

Once again, Morris and his antics had caught his brothers completely off guard. As they were staring at each other in confusion, David walked through the rear doors.

"Good news, Brothers," David called out as he entered the office, "everything with Mr Honey at the bank went smoothly." He stopped in his tracks as he saw the confusion on his brothers' faces.

"Who is Mr Hong Kong?" Louis questioned.

David laughed. "It's a place, not a person. Why?"

Harry handed David the telegram, which he read quickly, then re-read much more slowly.

"Well, I'll be..." David mumbled, "How the Dickens did he...?" David broke off with a fond smile; he had forgotten the how easy it was to underestimate his brother's initiative.

"You really need to tell him that I'm going to Gold, and not Badger," Louis was concerned Morris might not like that change in plan. He, for one, was not going to tell Morris for fear of reprisal.

"Yes," David replied, still reading the telegram, "No, yes, I'll telegram him tomorrow. Well, it looks like it's all happening now, fellows. It's time to pull up our socks, shake a leg, and get on with it." David put the telegram down and smiled at his brothers.

"So, when are you gentlemen planning to go?" Harry asked, leaning back in his chair and locking his hands behind his head, a trait that very much reminded David of Morris.

"Let's enjoy the weekend, and then leave on Monday," David mulled. "I need to tell Hanna I'll be away for a couple of weeks." Having intended to take Hanna on the following Sunday for a picnic among the nearby Matopos Hills, he had already hired a buggy.

Louis and Harry glanced at each other, a furtive smile lurking at the corners of their mouths, a gesture which David didn't miss but rather chose to ignore.

"Louis," David quickly interrupted, "please go down to the railway station and buy two tickets to Mafeking for Monday. We should get there on Tuesday night, and we will book our onward tickets to Johannesburg and Cape Town on Wednesday."

"Sure thing, Brother." Louis stood and stole another knowing glance at

Harry before heading down to the station on Railway Avenue.

Little did the brothers know that the following Wednesday would have such a profound impact on their lives, in a way they could never have imagined, nor ever forget.

Sunday arrived on a pristine October morning, promising a sweltering day to come. Nevertheless, the anticipated heat could not spoil the excitement and joy evident in the young couple's faces when David pulled the buggy to a stop outside the Rubinstein residence on Livingstone Road in Suburbs.

David would have preferred to travel to the Matopos Hills on horseback as he was very proficient on a horse, and it would have given him greater mobility to explore the hundreds of secret passage-ways created by the massive, granite boulders. A journey on horseback, however, would not have been appropriate for his beautiful Hanna because he wanted to make her day into the rugged countryside as comfortable and as memorable as possible. Although driving a buggy had not been as simple as David had imagined, he had begun to master the reins after the short drive from Abercorn Street to Livingstone Road and to understand the horses' behaviour a little better.

When he arrived at the Rubenstein residence, he found the entire family waiting for his arrival. Mr and Mrs Rubinstein were plainly delighted that one of Bulawayo's most eligible bachelors had taken such a keen interest in their daughter. As David alighted from the buggy and politely kissed her hand, Mr and Mrs Rubinstein both thought that they made a very enchanting couple.

The family had previously enjoyed David's company when he had visited their home for meals; he had engaged with them freely, and his manners had been considered impeccable. Furthermore, they had never seen their Hanna happier.

David's descriptions of the Matopos over dinner one night – particularly of the few days he had spent out there with his friend "Major Bob" and another American scout – had prompted him to invite Hanna for a Sunday picnic. Mr Rubinstein had been concerned initially for their safety since their destination appeared to consist of a good three hours' drive by buggy, and the former site of fierce encounters between the BSAC and the Matabele not that long ago. David had patiently assured him, however, that many Bulawayo residents had continued quite happily to visit the site every weekend in order to enjoy the sights and the majesty of the imposing boulders. With some further persuasion from Mrs Rubinstein and Hanna herself, he had grudgingly relented.

David arrived at the appointed time of seven o'clock, dressed in beige longs and a white, long-sleeved shirt with a thin, black tie neatly knotted under his starched collars. He had specifically purchased for the occasion a straw boater hat with a red and black hatband which made him look particularly dapper, and very much in fashion with the semi-formal gentry of Rhodesia at the time.

Hanna, on the other hand, was dressed in a tight-fitting and frilly white blouse and billowing pink skirt. Her outfit so enhanced her beautiful figure that it caused David's heart to skip a beat once again when he saw her. She remained impossibly beautiful in his estimation with her liquid eyes and generous smile, a perfect complement to her sweet and loving character.

Hanna had prepared a straw picnic basket filled with homemade cakes and biscuits and a host of other enticing dainties that Mrs Rubinstein had insisted they would need for a full day out in the Matopos. When David lifted the basket, he momentarily wondered about the weight of it and tried to guess how much food she had packed in there. He thought it best not to question their provisions and hoisted the generous container into the buggy without comment.

After some hasty farewells, and several warnings from the parents to be good, to stay safe, not to be too late, and – above all – to be careful, they were eventually wished a lovely day and waved off. Hanna sat as proudly as could be by David's side, leaning slightly towards him and allowing their shoulders to touch ever so lightly. In one hand she held a delicate parasol over her head to keep off the fierce sun. Quite ecstatic by this time, she offered a quick prayer of thanks to her Lord for blessing her with such a man. David was equally happy because he had not known it was possible to love and be loved as deeply as Hanna loved him.

It took a good three hours to get to the Matopos Hills, and by then the October heat was upon them. They stopped at a place where they found seven other buggies and some horses that were attended to by a half-dozen Matabele youths and arranged with them that they care for their transport as well. Taking the heavy picnic basket and walking arm in arm, they wandered up a gentle slope to the top of one of the giant boulders. A dusty path had been worn in the dry grass by many others walking along it, and they followed it to where they knew other sightseers would be.

The view from the summit of the boulder was impressive and almost took their breath away. A huge grey rock curved away under their feet in all directions, littered with lichen of every imaginable colour. Placed precariously on top of this massive boulder, as if by a supernatural force, were still more rocks, equally enormous in their own right, but appearing small in comparison to the grandeur around them. A young family with two young boys, who had been sitting in the shade of one of the smaller boulders, packed their picnic basket and began their descent down the granite slope. David led Hanna to the same shady spot and laid out a blanket, upon which she set out their picnic provisions. The day could not have been more perfect, and David fell in love with Hanna all over again.

After a bit of exploring, and much eating, David lay with his head in Hanna's lap, chatting lazily about his life and family.

"Tell me about Morris," Hanna asked. She had never met him, but David often talked about him.

"Morris?" David chuckled. "He's quite a character: exceptionally smart and very perceptive. He can sniff out a business deal a mile away, and always thinks five steps ahead of everyone else. I'm sure he dreams about business in his sleep. Never try to argue a mathematical problem with him as you will surely come undone; he has a strange and uncanny ability to understand numbers and money on a level I have never seen before. But he has a very short temper, and that's his downfall."

"He doesn't sound like a nice person."

"Oh, he is, funnily enough. If he likes you, then he has a lot of time for you; but he doesn't suffer fools, not one bit."

"Do you two get along?" Hanna asked nervously.

"Well, that's the strange thing, we get on exceptionally well, and we almost need each other. We can speak in codes, and we understand ourselves just by looking at each other. It's almost as if we can talk without speaking. I do miss him terribly."

Hanna was silent for a moment. "I'd like to meet him one day," she said softly.

"Oh, you will." David sat up and turned to face her, "if I have anything to do with it, you most certainly shall."

"Then I can't wait," she smiled, her eyes sparkling.

Beside her was a dry and brittle scrubby bush that was trying desperately to cling to life among the ragged cracks in the rock. David reached over and snapped off a twig with its dry, gnarled leaves. "Do you see this stick?" David handed it to her.

"What about it?" Hanna said, taking it and smiling at David's sudden change in subject, and his curious way of looking at the nature around him.

"It grows all over these rocks, and when it rains, it bursts into life almost instantly, green and beautiful. The entire Matopos changes its look radically within a day or two. When I came exploring with my friend, Colonel Bob, it had been raining, and this place looked very different. I took some of these plants home and left them on a shelf, and they dried and shrivelled out till they looked like this," he pointed to the twig Hanna was holding.

"One day I spilt some water on the dead twig, and it sprang to life the next day!"

"How can that be? It is bone dry," Hanna marvelled and took a closer look at the plant between her fingers.

"I have no idea, but I spoke to a good friend of mine, Phil Innes. He has that hardware shop on Abercorn Street, and he knew all about it. He said it was called the 'Resurrection Plant', and that's what it does. Take that stick home with you and put it in a glass of water and see what happens."

"Well, then I shall," Hanna laughed. "It's beautiful up here, David. Thank you for bringing me."

"And we shall often return, darling Hanna." The word 'darling' slipped out unintentionally, and David suddenly blushed with embarrassment. To his relief, she didn't seem to notice; or if she did, she hid it well.

"I would like that," Hanna sighed as she looked out over the majestic rocks and boulders.

"Cecil John Rhodes loves it so much up here he calls this place 'View of the World', and he wants to be buried here in this rock when he dies."

"Here?" Hanna exclaimed. "How can you be buried in solid rock?"

"I have no idea, but that's what he said - right here." David thumped his fist on the rock. It hurt, but he pretended it didn't.

"He is a brilliant man, Mr Rhodes, but I think he has lost his mind wanting to be entombed in solid rock," she giggled.

"Hanna," David changed the subject, "I have to go away for a couple of weeks."

"Oh no…" Hanna squealed painfully.

"Just a couple of weeks. Morris needs me to go to Cape Town and East London to sort out some logistical problems," he said, quickly shifting the blame on to his older brother.

"When do you leave?" Hurt punctuated her voice.

"Tomorrow morning. I'm taking Louis with me to Mafeking. We will get there on Tuesday night. Then on Wednesday, he will go to Johannesburg, and I will go to Cape Town. From there I will travel to East London and then back home. Morris is moving our business to the next level now."

"So when will you be back?"

"In about two weeks. What I have to do won't take too long. Louis, sadly, will be away for a few years. He is going to take over the Johannesburg warehouse."

"My word…" Hanna looked over the landscape again, deep in thought. "I don't like the thought of you going away for so long." She looked into David's eyes forlornly, "I'm getting quite used to you being around."

"Hanna," David took her hand and smiled lovingly, "I can't bear to be away from you either. Two weeks is all."

The train left the Bulawayo station promptly at 10 o'clock the next day, the steam and shrill howl of the whistle enveloping several people on the platform who were trying to hold back their tears. One of these was David, distraught at having to say goodbye to his precious Hanna; the other was Harry, knowing he would not be seeing his older brother and confidant, Louis, for many years to come.

Restraining his emotions was not easy for David and his normally masculine identity was being sorely tested in front of his brothers. Yet for Hanna, the tears were flowing in abundance. Mrs Rubinstein also struggled to hold back her tears while watching her daughter's reaction to David's departure. Once the passengers had embarked, however, and the train finally left the station, life began to return to normal for all concerned.

Since it was a long way down to Mafeking, David and Louis settled in for the journey. When they had been well underway for about an hour,

David took Louis to the dining car to find some refreshment and to meet some of the passengers. David found that a little socialising was always uplifting when good friendships were forged and time seemed to slip away miraculously. The train was frustratingly delayed at a place called Palapye for five hours the following morning, and later again for two hours in the middle of nowhere. The brothers thus disembarked late in Mafeking and found lodgings only after 11 o'clock that night.

Nevertheless, on the following morning, David woke early and swung his legs out of bed, while observing Louis' lengthy shape under the blankets on the narrow bed beside his own.

David shook his brother gently. "Louis," he urged, "time to get up. We have to get to the station."

Louis groaned and rolled onto his back. He couldn't understand why travelling made him so tired when all he did was sit or socialise with fellow passengers.

"Can't we stay in Mafeking for another night?" he grumbled through a yawn.

"I promise you: you don't want to spend time here. No, we need to stick to the plan. Let's get to the station and book our passage and then find somewhere to have breakfast. If time permits, and I'm sure it will, we need to call in on Julian Weil and pay our respects."

Louis reluctantly peeled himself out of his blankets. Following David's lead, he washed his face and put on a casual day suit, omitting the tie, before taking the short walk down to the railway station. An elderly gentleman with masses of grey hair was in charge of selling tickets. He sat behind a small opening in a red-brick wall with heavy wrought iron bars cemented across it.

"Where to, Gentlemen?" he chirped happily.

"One ticket to Johannesburg, first class, one way, please, sir," David smiled back at the teller, "and one ticket to Cape Town, first class, also one way."

"Certainly," he obliged.

It transpired that the only train of the day would be arriving at 10 o'clock, and departing at 2 o'clock that afternoon. Louis would have to change trains in Kimberley, but David would ride the same train all the way to Cape Town. Necessities concluded, the Langbourne brothers walked to a local hotel, from where the welcome aroma of breakfast had escaped when the boys had stridden past a little earlier. Having eaten well, the boys walked across the street to Julian Weil's place of work and caught up with him there, spending a good few hours exchanging news and discussing business.

"How is that brother of yours, Morris?" Julian enquired, having a great respect for Morris' business and accounting skills.

"He has returned to Ireland," David told their old friend and mentor. "He wants to open a purchasing office there."

David knew that Julian would see this move as potential competition for his own business and it didn't take long for the penny to drop.

Julian's eyebrows rose in concern. "He wishes to cut me out of your business?"

"Absolutely not," David reassured him. "We will continue to buy from you, that is certain, but we have identified many products that would sell well in the Rhodesia area that you do not stock, and neither, it seems, does anyone else. Morris only wants to buy items that wholesalers here don't supply."

Julian nodded slowly, suspicion still burning behind his eyes. "Fair enough." He managed to flash a very brief smile, "I might become a customer of yours, too, then."

"Perhaps," Davis smiled, pleased that this awkward conversation was now behind them.

David and Louis spent the remainder of the morning walking around the settlement, popping their heads into other wholesalers and retailers and checking their stock and various prices, as savvy businessmen would naturally do. It didn't take long for the two boys to reach the end of town, where the hospital and cemetery were located. David stood on a mound of earth and stared out at the flat, empty landscape, thrusting his hands deep into his pockets. He found two coins in one of them and started jingling the metal discs unconsciously.

Louis stood next to his older brother and also stared into the grassy veld, the harsh, dry grasses swaying gently to the commands of the wind. After a brief pause, he looked over at David.

"Do you know you always jingle coins in your pocket when you are deep in thought?"

David stopped instantly. "I didn't know that," he chuckled, somewhat embarrassed. "I've been reflecting on when Morris and I stood on this very mound about eight years ago and made the decision to go to Rhodesia; it was called Matabeleland then. I was pondering how our lives, yours included, all changed with that one decision."

"I know. Morris brought me to this spot to see Daluxolo off, when those 30 wagons went up north. He told me about your decisions."

Both boys returned their gaze to the African bush and stood in silence.

Louis broke the stillness, looking across at his brother once again. "It took you three months to walk from here to Bulawayo?"

"Yes," David replied, "it feels like a lifetime ago. There's a place out there," he nodded in a direction ahead of him, "in the middle of nowhere, about halfway to Rhodesia, where there is an old log on the ground and a little pile of rocks. Under the rocks are some coins and other odd trinkets that I have placed there. It's a little secret of mine. I have shown Harry where it is, and he has also put a piece of his clothing there, well, more like a piece of leather from his shoe."

"Most curious," Louis frowned. "Why did you do that?"

"I don't know, it was just my way of thanking Africa, and showing my respect to her for allowing me to be here. I love this continent."

"Will you ever be able to find it again?"

"Oh yes. It is quite strange, but I know exactly how to go back there – from either direction, from here or from Bulawayo. It's as if the map to Nomandudwane is etched into my brain."

"Nomandudwane?" Louis turned to face his brother.

"I gave it that name. It means 'The Place of Scorpions'. It is the spot where I got stung on my finger by a scorpion. I'd like to be buried there when I die."

"You want to be buried in the middle of nowhere, where you experienced the most severe pain in your life?"

David laughed and shrugged. "That's Africa for you, I guess."

"So, is there a grand view, or does it overlook a trickling stream?"

"There's nothing there: flat ground, dry grasses, a thorny tree and an old log: just pure Africa."

Louis sighed and looked at his pocketwatch. "And I thought Morris was the crazy brother," he mumbled. "Come on; we need to get to the station, the train leaves in about an hour."

As they turned and strolled back into town, David scanned the low dusty roofs of the settlement. Something suddenly caught his attention.

"That's odd," he muttered, almost to himself.

"What?" Louis asked, but kept his eyes ahead.

"The train was supposed to arrive at 10 o'clock, but it is now almost time for it to depart and there is no sign of a train in the station."

"Looks like yet another delay," Louis groaned.

"That's not all, though. Look over at the BSAP camp," David pointed slightly off to the left, "there's a hell of a lot of activity going on there."

"Yes, you're right," Louis agreed, and pointed slightly off to the right, "and there, too, soldiers all over the place. It's been like this all day. Even when we got in late last night, there was constant activity going on. Didn't you notice?"

"Come on," David picked up his pace, "something's wrong."

As they walked down the main street of the settlement, everyone appeared to be excited. In a town usually regarded as one notch above cemetery status, this day was alive with activity. Entering the drab railway station and confirming that there were no trains, the brothers strode quickly to the ticket office. They found the grey-haired teller with ease.

"Excuse me, sir," David asked politely. "Is there a delay with the Kimberley train?"

"Oh dear," the man sounded almost distraught, "I don't even know if it will arrive today. Excuse me," he turned in a fluster and walked out the rear door.

"What's going on?" Louis wondered, confusion evident in his voice.

"I have no idea. Let's get back to Julian. He knows everything that goes on here."

In no time at all, they were back in Weil's sample room and noticed that even he was not his usual imperturbable self. He seemed to pace up and down without direction, shuffling papers, walking through a doorway and returning instantly without reason.

"Mr Weil," David called nervously, catching his attention, "What's going on?"

"Haven't you heard?" Fear was evident in his eyes.

"No?" David sounded equally anxious.

"The Government of the South African Republic in Pretoria has declared war on the British!"

"War?" both brothers exclaimed in shock.

"I'm afraid so." There wasn't much colour in Weil's face. "The Boers and the British have been at each other's throats for quite some time now; lots of sabre-rattling and ultimatums, but I didn't think it meant anything. None of us did, for that matter."

"So what do we do now?" Louis spoke up, asking the obvious.

"I have no idea." Weil pulled up a chair and sat down heavily, causing it to squeak loudly in protest. "This is very troubling. Even my contact in the BSAP can't tell me much, and he's their leader."

David looked at Louis and saw fear etched on his face. They had been through a brutal uprising in Rhodesia less than three years before, and now they had inadvertently walked into another war. All this before Louis turned eighteen. David's concerns quickly returned to the business. Rhodesia would be safe from this conflict, but all their supplies would have to come through the South African states to get to them, and, knowing Morris, there was already a tremendous amount of stock on board ships, steaming towards South Africa from England and the Far East.

"We've got a huge problem," David said to himself, but Louis and Julian heard him quite clearly.

"*You* have a problem?" Julian thrust a back-handed wave at David. "Your business is in Rhodesia, a long way from here, in another country. What about me, what will happen to me? I've taken some big risks, and I'm over-committed to the banks; this could spell disaster for me."

David tried to soothe the man. "I'm sure it will all be fine," he murmured, "this is exactly what happened to Morris, remember? And we came through it alright."

Julian was not convinced and stood up suddenly, walking towards the door. "Excuse me, gentlemen, I must speak to Baden-Powell."

"Major Bob?" David exclaimed in surprise, before quickly correcting himself. "I mean, is Major Baden-Powell here?"

"You know him?" Julian stopped in his tracks, a little perplexed, and looked back at David.

"Yes," David suddenly felt embarrassed, "we befriended each other in Rhodesia."

"Come," Weil barked as he strode out the door, "I'll take you to him. You should know that he has been promoted: his rank is now that of a colonel."

The thought of meeting with his old friend was somewhat of a comfort for David. Although the colonel was extraordinarily busy, he did make time to have a quick chat with David and reassured him that everything was fine and under control. He seemed in a reasonably jovial mood, despite the circumstances, and was also happy to take the time to soothe Julian Weil's concerns, although he deftly kept the conversation short and to the point.

David's initial anxiety was about getting Louis safely to Johannesburg and himself to Cape Town, but Colonel Bob was unable to help in that regard. He noted that the last train to depart Mafeking had left the previous day, loaded to the hilt with women and children whom he had ordered to evacuate to Kimberley. He suggested that if the train had not arrived by sunset, and in all probability it would not, now that war had been declared the brothers might find accommodation at Dixon's Hotel until things settled down. Weil offered, almost insisted, that the boys stay with him and his wife, an invitation they hurriedly and gratefully accepted.

Colonel Bob excused himself, and the trio made their way back down the street, feeling somewhat dejected since nothing new had been discovered. Julian seemed to spiral further down into such a nervous depression, that – by the time they reached his home – he was in no mood to talk to anyone.

David had stayed with the Weils before and liked the company of the pleasant and slightly rounded Mrs Weil. Louis also enjoyed her company and felt very at ease with her, but the ensuing dinner was a sombre affair, since Julian remained in a dark mood and did not say very much, leaving the conversation to David, Louis, and Mrs Weil herself. Their loyal cook, Langton, also remembered David, the cook's perfect smile showing that he was very pleased to see him. When he brought the meal through, he politely and respectfully asked after Morris. By the time Langton had cleared the table after the exceptionally delicious dinner, the young Langbourne boys could not wait to adjourn to their bedroom.

As David lay back on his bed, hands locked behind his head, contemplating the day's events, Louis rummaged through his tote bag.

"Do you think this war will affect us and our business?" Louis asked, speaking to no-one in particular.

"I don't know," David sighed, "it's hard to tell. We've been through that rebellion in Matabeleland, which was unfairly one-sided: machine guns against spears. Both sides will fight with much the same weapons this time; it could be very different."

"Mr Weil is certainly worried. What will we do tomorrow? What if the train doesn't come?"

David stared unblinkingly at the ceiling. "I have no idea," he said. "If the train is not there in the morning then we should go back and talk to Colonel Bob again. I have a feeling he will be a bit more forthcoming when Weil is not in his presence; I had the feeling that he was uncomfortable with Julian."

"That doesn't surprise me." Louis lay back on his bed, "Julian is a grumpy old bugger."

David gave a short laugh. He was surprised to hear Louis use such language, especially at his age. "Ease up there, Brother." He tried to sound offended, but a chuckle escaped him.

Louis closed his eyes and grinned, and then both boys gently slipped into a deep sleep.

David and Louis didn't have to find Colonel Bob the next day; he found them.

The morning saw the brothers anxiously waiting at the railway station dressed for travel with leather tote bags at their sides, among a small gathering of hopeful passengers. No hissing steam could be heard from the valves and pipes of the silent train, brooding alongside the platform, while the doors to the carriages remained firmly shut. No passenger could be seen inside, and nobody seemed to want to board her at all.

David boldly accosted a passing conductor all the same.

"Excuse me, sir," he asked, "is this train going to Kimberley?"

"I'm afraid not," the man answered forlornly, "this was to have been the last train to Kimberley, but it was turned back yesterday. The Boers have sabotaged the line halfway between here and Kimberley. All the passengers that were on it yesterday have had to disembark in Mafeking again. Nobody is leaving today, I'm afraid."

Suddenly, complete strangers were seen talking freely to one another, trying desperately to find other options for leaving, or discussing various possibilities as to how they thought the newly declared war might unfold. Soon after David became equally involved in an earnest discussion with a tall man in a Bowler hat, he felt a tap on his right shoulder.

"Excuse me, sir, are you Mr Langbourne?" a soldier asked formally.

"Yes," David responded, concern evident in his eyes.

"Come with me, please, sir," the military man politely insisted and turned sharply to exit the station.

David gripped Louis lightly on the shoulder and nodded in the direction of the serviceman. The brothers picked up their bags and followed him out. Once clear of the anxiously expectant passengers, the soldier advised David that Colonel Baden-Powell wished to see him in his office at the Dixon Hotel. Agog with curiosity, the boys obliged and promptly quickened their pace to keep up with the soldier, who was clearly in a hurry.

When entering the makeshift war office at the Dixon, the colonel greeted the young brothers warmly, without a care showing in his demeanour. It looked as if it was just another day at the office for him, a far cry from the anxiety evident in the civilian population. Three other officers in the room were busy poring over a series of maps that had been strewn hastily across a small collection of tables. Bob led the brothers into a side room and closed the door behind him.

"Thanks for coming, chaps," Bob smiled, "I hope you had a pleasant night?"

"Indeed," David nodded. "Unfortunately, however, we seemed to have made an early start in vain to catch the train to Kimberley."

"Yes, I'm afraid the train will not be departing, since the Boers appear to have disabled the line somewhere between here and Kimberley. Regretfully, it looks as if you may have to hunker down in Mafeking for a while, or at least until this mess is sorted out."

"Well," Louis looked at David nervously, "perhaps we should head north and go back to Bulawayo."

"I'm afraid the line north has been severed as well. We are rather cut off," Baden-Powell sighed, and indicated some rudimentary chairs for them to sit on.

The trio pulled up the chairs and took their seats, David now more concerned than ever.

"I'll have to get a message to Morris in London," David frowned, "he is expecting that I will arrive in Cape Town soon."

Bob scratched his head briefly. "All the telegraph wires have been cut, too. We have absolutely no communications with anyone outside

Mafeking."

David looked horrified. When Bulawayo had been under siege by the Matabele, they had not cut the telegraph lines because they had not known what the wires had been for, and so a relief force could be co-ordinated from the north and the south. This was different - very different. Realising that he needed to leave Mafeking as soon as possible, David quickly resolved to purchase two horses and ride north immediately. Having done it twice before, he knew the way. Louis might struggle in the saddle at first, he thought, but he could show Louis where Nomandudwane was situated, not that it was a big deal.

"Why did you want to see us?" David asked cautiously as the severity of the situation dawned on him.

"I need to take you two into my strictest confidence. I believe you and me, David, have forged a special relationship with the African bush, and with each other, and I believe we can trust each other implicitly."

David nodded cautiously; he did not like the direction in which this conversation was going. He felt as if he was about to be asked to do something illegal or extremely dangerous. "You can depend on me, Bob, on both of us," he nodded, if somewhat reluctantly.

"Good show," the colonel beamed, relief exuding from his face. "I knew I could count on you! What I am about to tell you is top secret, you understand, top secret." He looked at each of the brothers waiting for their confirmation.

David and Louis nodded at each other, then back to the colonel without saying a word, intrigue now replacing concern, albeit temporarily.

"It appears that the British were expecting hostilities from the Boer government, but not quite so soon. When the Boers declared war, the Brits were caught with their pants down and didn't have enough soldiers on African soil to secure a victory. A frenzied mobilisation of troops has begun from all the colonies around the world - Australia, New Zealand, India, Canada, and the like.

"The Boers are confident of a swift victory, their Transvaal President, Paul Kruger has been goading the British on. 'Bring ten thousand troops, bring twenty thousand, why, bring on fifty thousand troops', he said," the colonel gesticulated theatrically, putting on a false accent to try to imitate the president. " 'We will drive the British into the sea', the man boasted. The reality is, it is going to take months to get an army to South Africa, and by then the Boers would have all but won the war."

"How many soldiers have the Boers got?" David asked.

"We estimate about fifty thousand, scattered around the country."

"How many British soldiers are coming?" Louis asked nervously.

"About five hundred thousand," Bob smiled confidently, "and they are on their way right now. Soldiers, horses, food, medicine, weapons and ammunition; we can win this war easily with half a million people, but we need time. We have to use our heads."

"Half a million!" David exclaimed incredulously. "Are the Boers aware of this?"

"No, but they will soon find out," Bob almost chuckled.

Bob's tone quickly changed, however, and he became serious once more. He explained that he was tasked to distract the Boer army in order to give the existing British troops in the Cape and Natal provinces a fighting chance to hold them at bay until the reinforcements arrived.

"I have been misleading them," the colonel confided. "I have allowed some 'secret' messages to slip into their hands. They think I have stockpiled a large force here because they think I am going to attack Johannesburg from the north as soon as war is declared, just like your friend Dr Jameson attempted to do."

David lent back in his chair, somewhat confused by this conversation. "But that's a bit odd, don't you think?" he mused aloud. "There's nothing here at all, and we're a very long way from Johannesburg."

"I know!" Bob confirmed. "But because of the failed Jameson Raid, I know the Boers are obsessive about this town. They have an emotional issue with Mafeking, and they want control of it, come hell or high water. By enticing a large part of their army to come here, we split them up and make it a little easier for our chaps down south to handle them."

"Have you got enough men to hold them off if they come?" There was a slight tremble in Louis' voice which didn't go unnoticed by his brother.

"We have seven hundred men and two big guns, with lots of ammunition."

David gave the conversation some thought. He was intrigued that Bob would be sharing this top secret information; after all, he and Louis were strictly civilians. He wasn't quite sure where this conversation was going. The colonel was, in his opinion, an exceptionally intelligent person and a distinguished leader. He was a brilliant tracker, as David had discovered when they had once spent a few days in the Matopos Hills and had exchanged a lot of useful and interesting information.

"So," David said slowly, scratching a spot on his chin, "how do Louis and I fit into this picture?"

"I'd like you to run some secret errands for me if you don't mind,"

"If we can," David assented, cocking an eyebrow at his brother.

"I have my hands full, and my soldiers are working round the clock fortifying this town; they are fully occupied. We're trenching like crazy, laying barbed wire, securing forts, allocating ammunition, setting up a medical centre; it's hell out there. We will have our hands full when the Boers arrive."

"When they arrive?" Louis picked up on what Bob said.

"They are coming. Over six thousand of them, according to my scouts, and they will be here tomorrow."

"Tomorrow?" both brothers exclaimed in unison, David sitting bolt upright in shock. "You have seven hundred men against their six thousand?" The reality of war had struck.

"I don't have the resources or the time, chaps, but I need to ask if you would mind finding two shovels somewhere. I don't mind where you get them. Then I need you to slip unnoticed into Weil's Number 4 shed. There you will find about forty, green-metal trunks. They are empty, but I need you to fill them all with sand. Are you able to do that for me?"

After David had nodded in assent for the both of them, David and Louis were bundled out of the war office by the colonel with further tactful smiles of encouragement and reaffirmations of total secrecy. Although questioning the wisdom of this exercise between them, and nervously discussing the impending bloodbath which was inevitably going to commence the next day, the two brothers did as was asked of them. Soon after completing their task, they strode back towards the colonel's war office, sweating profusely.

"I need to get a message out of here," David mumbled to Louis while trying to catch his breath.

"That's going to be impossible. What would you tell Morris if you could?"

"I need to get a message to Hanna too," David grumbled, not listening to Louis.

"Ahh..." Louis sighed but left the conversation at that. He had forgotten that David would have had other issues on his mind, and he could see a worry in his older brother's face that he had not seen before.

As soon as Colonel Baden-Powell saw the boys enter the hotel reception area, he leapt to his feet and confronted them.

"All done, chaps?" he asked cheerfully.

"Yes, sir." David wiped the sweat from his brow, still trying to catch his breath. The exercise had been done with such urgency that his energy was all but drained.

"Excellent, thank you. Lids closed? Did you close the lids?"

"Yes," Louis confirmed.

"No-one saw you?"

"Nobody."

"Perfect, thank you, thank you," Colonel Bob repeated. "Not a word of this to anyone, you hear?" He waved a warning finger at them.

The boys nodded, and then the colonel turned on his heel and walked out onto the street. Standing with his legs slightly apart and arms folded across his chest, he let out a loud and forceful bellow.

"Captain Rudge!"

David cast a knowing look at Louis, since they knew Captain Rudge. In the distance, they heard Charles Rudge acknowledge his name.

"Operation Ant Bear!" Bob thundered. "Now!"

Colonel Baden-Powell walked back into the hotel, and, as he passed the Langbourne brothers, he leaned slightly over to them and lowered his voice. "Enjoy the show, chaps," and then he was gone.

More confused than ever, David and Louis sauntered out the hotel into the bright light of the mid-day sun. The bell from the Market Square began to ring, and the remaining civilian residents of Mafeking, all of about three hundred of them, emerged from their places of work or residence. Even the local African people from the village near the town started to assemble and mill about, waiting for any announcement that might be made.

Captain Rudge appeared and took to a crude podium. As he stood at attention, waiting for the crowd to settle and the noise to abate, he noticed David standing not too far from him, and gave an indiscernible nod of recognition when their eyes locked. David returned the inclination just as discreetly. This brought back fearful memories of the two rebellions he had endured in Bulawayo, where once before Charles Rudge, with his voluminous and clear voice, had been the spokesman for the military in charge.

Rudge's message was precise: the Boers were arriving tomorrow and would launch an attack on the town. Residents were to utilise the new trenches closest to their positions if hostilities erupted. A few other standard instructions followed, such as what to do if injured and who to report to should something untoward happen; where a notice board would be located (which it was mandatory to read every day); and how food supplies would be rationed if the attack was prolonged.

He ended his address by warning the residents that soldiers would now be carrying high explosives, called "landmines", from Weil Storeroom Number 4 to be buried in strategic holes that had been dug around the town. These "landmines" were highly dangerous and very sensitive; they could be detonated simply by someone walking too close to them. Everyone was instructed to give the approaching soldiers a wide berth in case of an unexpected detonation.

Just then two soldiers appeared from the doorway of Storeroom Number 4 carrying a green metal box between them. It had a handle on each side, and it was clear that the soldiers were straining under its weight. They walked carefully, concentration etched deeply on their faces.

"Careful!" Captain Rudge exploded at the two soldiers, giving the assembled crowd a fright. "Do not jostle that mine," he pointed menacingly at them.

The citizens began to murmur nervously, then, almost as if against their will, backed away, slowly at first, and then more rapidly as the soldiers approached. The scraping sound of shoes on gravel filled the air. Two more soldiers appeared behind the first pair carrying yet another container between them. The convoy of forty "landmines", carried two-by-two, began the journey to strategic locations around the town's perimeter.

"Go back to your homes in a calm and quiet manner," Rudge bellowed as the assembly began to break up nervously. "We will be testing one of these landmines at eighteen hundred hours this evening. Do not be alarmed."

"There's nothing but sand..." Louis whispered to David, with a perplexed frown.

David held a finger to his lips and hissed quietly, but he was smiling.

"I think the man has gone crazy," at which Louis began to smile, too.

"I think he will pull it off," David began to chuckle. "I'll give him one thing, though, he's not stupid. If I didn't know, I would have been completely fooled."

For a few hours that afternoon, many curious townsfolk took time to watch the forty pairs of soldiers bury the boxes of sand in the near distance. Once their jobs had been completed, they scampered back to the town limits, looking very relieved, and then immediately commenced with other urgent fortification and technical tasks.

One team of men knocked together a lookout platform atop the roof of a house within the Market Square. Because Colonel B-P, as many called him, had realised that he would be spending a great deal of time up there, he had had a "speaking tube" attached to the top. The tube poked through the roof and ended at a makeshift communication exchange directly below, consisting of wires and speakers, and that connected half a dozen of the defensive forts located a short distance from the town. The tower resembled an upright ladder held in position by some supporting planks of varying length.

To complete the lookout tower, a flat piece of wood was nailed to the top rung to serve as the colonel's desk, and a bent nail was used as the hook on which to hang his field glasses. In the event that he became a target of sniper fire, which he most certainly would, the colonel had some sandbags placed on the roof at the base of his ladder to protect him if the firing became a little heavy. Because the bags were assembled in the shape of a square, he affectionately called it his "pepper-box".

For the forts that were too distant for wires and speakers to be connected, the colonel commissioned a Mr Fordisch, a stately resident of the isolated town, to manufacture some megaphones. He used an intricate wire system within the conical monstrosities which vibrated well and helped carry voices a respectable distance, especially in the fresh night air.

At precisely six o'clock that evening, about a dozen soldiers trotted through the town, calling out loudly that one of the mines would be tested, and that the citizens should not be unduly alarmed. Oddly, however, the soldiers also encouraged the residents to wander down to the bridge near the railway line and watch from a safe distance, if they so wished. Needless to say, apart from satisfying simple curiosity, the population were very keen to see what the army had put in place to protect them from the impending war.

David and Louis stood shoulder to shoulder with Julian Weil and watched with anticipation as Colonel Bob – wearing his wide-brimmed, felt hat with four rounded indentations in the crown – walked cautiously to a spot in the open bush with a man he referred to as "Moffat". In absolute silence, the gathered mass watched as the two men seemed to study the 'landmine' intently, getting down on their haunches and appearing to hold a brief conference. They pointed occasionally, out into the bush, making arches and circles with their outstretched arms, before walking very carefully backwards, away from the mine site, while continuously scanning the open land around them with exaggerated stares.

"They are certainly making a good show of it." Louis whispered into David's ear, a sly grin on his face.

David allowed a soft chuckle to escape, but did not take his eyes off the spectacle in the distance. He had to admit that if he had not known that the tins were filled with sand, he would have quite readily believed that a deadly "landmine" lay concealed in the soil.

Bob and Moffat stopped about 50 yards from the gathered crowd, whispering among themselves and completely ignoring all the people who stood anxiously at some distance behind them. Some of the men started mumbling, and a muffled complaint about the thing not working was overheard. In the distance, a slight movement in the dim evening glow caught David's attention. His experience in the African bush had made him acutely aware of any movement, or, for that matter, any colour that seemed out of place.

"Over there," David whispered, nudging Louis and discretely twitching his chin in the relevant direction.

"What?" Louis scanned the veld but couldn't see anything out of place.

"Ahh... nothing," David relaxed, "just an African man running up the path, likely heading for home."

Louis saw the man jogging hard, and thinking nothing more of it, turned his attention to the two men in the field discussing their failed "landmine".

Suddenly Colonel Baden-Powell saw the pedestrian and began to get edgy as he rapidly approached their position. Bob started shouting and flailing his arms to warn the hapless man to go back, but nothing seemed to make the approaching man slow down. The closer he got, the more animated Baden-Powell became, and even Moffat joined in with frantic warnings. By the time the man was about 100 yards from the mine site even the citizens had begun to join in the warning chorus. The man saw and heard the commotion, but, not understanding what was going on, ran all the faster. At 50 yards, the fresh twilight of the early evening was loudly interrupted.

Whoomp! The landmine exploded and hurled tons of dirt, stones and rock high in the air. A shockwave followed almost instantaneously, causing the assembled residents to duck involuntarily. It blasted the poor unsuspecting man clean off his feet. He flew a good two yards backwards through the air and landed heavily on his back. Pebbles and dirt rained down on the onlookers and dust floated majestically in the air, blocking out all signs of the purple and pink sunset. When a gentle easterly breeze brushed the murky atmosphere clean, over 300 men, women and children remained crouched in shock and disbelief.

A terrifying scream suddenly erupted from the runner, who stood up and, like a crazed man, bolted for his village, arms flailing and eyes wide in pure terror. It appeared that the man was not injured, but thoroughly shocked. Baden-Powell turned to face the onlookers and spoke calmly and clearly to his audience, standing with his legs slightly apart and arms folded high across his chest.

"We have forty of these landmines planted in secret locations around the perimeter of the town. Whatever you do, do not deviate from any road or track. These mines are highly sensitive. Please note how closely that man came to being injured. Stay well clear!" he warned sternly.

"Tomorrow we are expecting the Boer army to arrive. We will hold them off until reinforcements join us from Kimberley and Rhodesia. I strongly discourage you from leaving town. If you do, I cannot guarantee your safety. For now, your point of contact will be Captain Rudge, and I will maintain a notice board on the wall outside the Dixon Hotel which you are to please regularly read to keep appraised of any developing situation. Please return to your homes now. Thank you," he ended his announcement.

As the group of shocked civilians gradually dispersed, David made his way to Bob, drawing Louis along with him but deliberately leaving Julian behind.

"Colonel Bob," David caught his friend's attention as he reached him, "I desperately need to get a message out to Bulawayo. How can I do that?" The need to communicate with any of his family was fast becoming an obsession. If he could only get a message to Harry, he would be able to raise the alarm with Morris and pass a message to Hanna.

"Impossible right now, David," Baden-Powell frowned, but took him by the shoulder and walked with him towards town. Louis followed at a respectable distance.

"All communications are down, and we are truly isolated. In time, if I figure out a way to communicate with others, I'll let you know. I can only apologise for the disruption to your plans. Good work, by the way," he whispered, casting an eye around to make sure nobody heard him.

"I'm glad we could help," David forced a smile, "but I'm curious, how do you get a box full of sand to explode?"

"It's what you call a bluff," Baden-Powell laughed heartily. "You see, Moffat and I planted several sticks of dynamite in an ant-bear hole near one of those fake landmines. Now everyone thinks we have forty lethal mines around the town. There are Boer sympathisers in the settlement; we know who they are, and you can be sure that they will get a message to the advancing Boers to stay well clear of the bush around here."

"How did that jogger detonate the dynamite?" David scratched his head in confusion. "Surely you would need to ignite a fuse?"

"Indeed," the colonel chuckled, "we lit a long fuse and backed away. We used the cover of twilight to hide the smoke from the fuse. The poor pedestrian was a most fortunate and opportune occurrence. He didn't trigger it; his timing was totally coincidental, so I just capitalised on the event. As far as you, me, Moffat and Rudge are concerned, we have just buried a bunch of harmless boxes of sand; but to everyone else, the enemy included, we have some very powerful and sophisticated landmines protecting the town."

"That's pretty clever," David had to admit.

"I have a lot of games of bluff I have organised for our friends when they arrive. If you have any good ideas, though, please do let me know. Now, try to get a good night's sleep, for tomorrow our war begins."

Baden-Powell's scouts were quite correct in predicting the arrival of the enemy, but they had underestimated how many would come. A contingent of over 7,000 Boer combatants surrounded Mafeking, and immediately began to dig in and open fire on the settlement. The British responded, and the vigorous fighting continued until dusk. Mafeking was isolated, and well and truly under siege.

It was a pattern of fighting that persisted for many weeks, and it was a game of wits between the two belligerent commanders. Because Baden-Powell was severely outnumbered, he depended on his skills of deception, trickery and bluff to a very effective degree. He teased the Boers almost every day, in what he called giving them a "kick".

From his perch on his lookout tower, and through his field glasses, he could see their movements and noticed their barbed-wire defences. One day he observed that what he could actually see were the stakes holding up the barbed wire, but not the metal strands of wire, because they were too distant. He had depleted his inadequate supply of protective wire, but based on what he saw, or rather couldn't see, he had his men hammer stakes in vulnerable positions around the settlement and act as if they were stringing wire across the posts. They were also instructed to pretend to step over the invisible strands of wire or crawl under them every time they walked past a stake. The ruse was perfectly successful.

Other ploys were to throw improvised bombs at the Boers using very flexible fishing rods and to conduct fake raids on the Boer camp late at night, using the megaphone. An officer would launch an imaginary assault on the western front, directing his troops to attack and "flank left". He would then pass the megaphone to a runner, who would rush across the town so that another officer might instruct another platoon to "advance right and charge", or whatever military jargon he preferred on that night. The result would be a sleepless night for the Boers, and much wasted ammunition as they fired at their imaginary opponents. For the Brits, it became something of a game, resulting in raucous laughter the next day over breakfast with their comrades, and the planning of another form of trickery, which Baden-Powell thoroughly encouraged.

They made mannequins of soldier's torsos mounted on sticks, some holding fake guns or field glasses, which they bobbed up and down from trenches, trying to make the enemy think there were more of them, and drawing fire away from artillerymen. One of the residents manufactured an acetylene lamp using a cake tin as the reflector that was effectively used as a spotlight at night. They attached it to a long stick and shone it about the battlefield for a few minutes, then, extinguishing it, a runner bolted to another side of the town and re-lit it. After a few minutes, the process was repeated by a fresh runner, tricking the Boers into believing they had many of these spotlights and thereby lessening the enemy's attempt at night raids. Sadly, the gas didn't last too long, and that bluff ended abruptly.

Although the Boers were exceptional marksmen and superior in numbers, the British, particularly Colonel Bob, were ingenious at war games and thus kept the enemy at bay, thwarting every attempt they made to take Mafeking. When the Boers realised it would not be an easy task, they resorted to shelling the town with their big guns, but the principal objective was to lay siege and literally starve the population into surrender.

Within the first two weeks, a large number of soldiers on both sides had been either killed or injured, while the terrified citizens cowered for cover during the day, only venturing out into the streets when there was a brief lull in the artillery fire. Once the first fortnight had passed, however, people unexpectedly began to accept the noise and blasts and robust shouts and skirmishes designed to repel an attack. They started to go out to the bars and hotels to meet and socialise, and children would gaily play in the open fields - always mindful, though, to stay close to the safety of a trench. As had been seen before during the siege of Bulawayo, humour began to play a significant part in the daily lives of both civilians and soldiers in the town. Colonel Baden-Powell, in a subtle but effective way, managed to keep spirits high, using nicknames for forts, soldiers, buildings and places, and of course, for the Boers and their generals.

David, though, was not having a good time of it at all. His concerns were four-fold: survival among the shells, bombs and bullets; the safety of his younger brother; the concern for the ships that needed his urgent attention in Cape Town and East London; and – most important of all – the love of his life in Bulawayo, who had no idea where he was. He honestly believed that Hanna would be fretting, and he was at a total loss as to how to let her know he was alright. David desperately wanted to let her know how much he loved and missed her.

Finally, there was a breakthrough. As David was walking towards Julian Weil's store in the hopes of gleaning some information from him, the Boers let loose a shell from "Old Creechy", the nickname Baden-

Powell had given the Pom-Pom that fired 94-pound shells at the town. The boom and the screeching sound of the speeding missile heading towards the settlement had citizens scampering for the nearest trench like disturbed rats in a kitchen. Old-fashioned, gentlemanly manners went out the window in times like these; the first to reach a dugout was the first one in. From the corner of his eye, David caught the movement of a soldier bolting for the same ditch he was aiming toward but dared not hesitate to look to see who it was or what rank he held. At a time like this, the slower man may not live. David dived headlong into the welcome cool of the earthen protection, followed immediately by the man behind who tumbled in clumsily after him. He landed right on top of David with a solid grunt, only a fraction of a second before the shell exploded close by.

"Sorry about that, old chap," the soldier apologised as he untangled his limbs from David's. "That was frightfully close. The damn Boers are starting to perfect their aim a little."

David had soil in his ears and mouth, and the soldier had knocked the wind out of his lungs.

"Heavens above!" David wheezed after managing to get some air in his lungs while spitting out dirt and bits of dried grass.

"You alright there, lad?" the soldier asked when the falling dirt and dust had subsided. Although the trench was a little narrow, he began to help David up.

"Yes, yes," David said, swivelling onto his backside, "all well. How about you?"

"David!" the soldier exclaimed in surprise. "Fancy meeting you here," the man chuckled and squatted beside David, facing him square on.

"Colonel Bob," David grinned as the light spread out around them. He was pleased to share a trench with his old friend. "Yes, that was a bit too close for comfort."

"Damn Boers." Baden-Powell laughed but tried to sound serious as he dusted his shoulders off.

"How's the war going?" David chuckled at his own question, rapidly running his fingers through his hair and creating his personal dust cloud.

"Very good, actually. It won't be long now," the colonel said confidently.

"Bob," David asked with all sincerity, "I honestly need to get a message to Rhodesia, to Harry. He must alert Morris that Louis and I have a problem and can't deal with the business. I also need to let Hanna know

I'm alright."

"Hanna?" Baden-Powell cocked an eyebrow. He realised now why David had not seemed himself. "Yes, of course," he scratched his chin, avoiding David any embarrassment.

"I could make a run for it, at night in a storm; the Boers won't see me," David almost pleaded.

"No!" Baden-Powell was firm, "I know you probably would give them the slip. Good Lord, I know full well that you are very capable of it, but I can't risk it. It's far too dangerous. If they catch you, they will kill you, make no mistake, and I can't have that hanging over my head."

David sighed; he was at a total loss and felt completely helpless. "Honestly, how long do you think we will be detained here?"

Another one of Old Creechy's shells shrieked towards them. The two friends sat quietly waiting for the explosion and yet another shower of debris. This time it was a little further off, and they both relaxed visibly.

"It all depends on how quickly the British can get a relieving force up here," Baden-Powell sighed, shuffling onto his rear end and locking his arms around his knees. "You see, General Plumer of the BSAP, and his men up north, who were protecting Rhodesia, attempted to come down here to help but ran into some Boers heading for Rhodesia. He got quite a hiding, sadly. He lost a lot of men, and now his numbers are too few to be helpful. I understand the Boers have also locked up Ladysmith, in Natal, and they're giving the Brits there a bit of a knock, too. Even Kimberley is under siege. Until we can sort out Natal and build up a sizeable force in the Cape, we have to simply wait. What we are accomplishing, though, is that about eight thousand Boers are tied up here and so cannot fight in Natal. Think about it, if they have fifty thousand men in total, and eight thousand of them were deployed to Mafeking, a mere handful of us have been tying up a good fifteen percent of their fighting force."

David cocked his head and looked at the colonel sternly. "So, how do you know all this, Bob?"

"Ahh... You don't miss a trick," Bob winked. "I have a runner or two - African men from the village. The Boers don't pay much attention to them as their concern is with us British. I pay them to take coded messages to Plumer, and he sends very brief messages back to me. He is about fifty miles north of us, so this is not an overnight thing. Moreover, it's dangerous, because – if the Boers catch one of my men and find a note on him – they will kill him, so I don't do this often."

"Please, may I send a coded message to Harry with your next runner?" David pleaded. "It will consist of only half a dozen coded words."

Baden-Powell laughed. "Sure David, get it to me before nightfall, and don't mention this discussion to anyone."

David's spirits soared despite Old Creechy sending him another complimentary shower of dirt. He knew precisely what he would say to Harry, and for the first time in ages, his heartache eased.

Chapter Eight

London 1899

Since a distinct chill hung in the air and it was drizzling outside, Morris shrugged into his black overcoat and placed his felt Derby hat carefully on his head, as he surveyed his rather gloomy warehouse in the fading light of the day. About six weeks previously, it had been packed to the ceiling with all his purchases, while transporters and labourers had bustled about, carrying boxes down to the nearby wharf, where they had been loaded aboard a ship bound for Africa. Now it was empty, the bare, grey-concrete floor exposing a few potholes, while the matching, windowless walls expressed an air of loneliness and despair. Even more depressing was the small stack of empty, cardboard boxes in a vacant area, behind which lay a thin and grubby mattress. This was his bedroom and living quarters, all in one.

Although it had been a busy time, Morris had been in his element: negotiating with shipping lines, transporters, rail managers, bankers, lawyers, insurance agents, and accountants. Some negotiations had turned into robust discussions, while others had degenerated into verbal tirades. Since it was the very stuff that Morris had been made of, he had been mightily pleased with the way things had worked out. He was in business, this was his life, and he had arrived with a vengeance. Morris understood that he was not the most popular businessman in town, but those who made a deal with him invariably made good money from him.

As he reflected on some of his more notorious meetings from time to time, when his sparring partner believed he had got the better of him, Morris would smile to himself, because he knew that he had been the actual winner and he always relished a victory in business.

Covering the oil lantern with his hand and blowing the flame out, Morris stepped out of the wooden door and turned a large, iron key in the lock. Having been invited to dine with Yoni Goldberg and his lovely wife Ruth at their opulent home, he had been holding back all day for this hour to arrive. He was starving, therefore, and in sore need of some good, homely company. The Goldbergs would provide him with all of this and more.

As he strode towards Berkeley Square, his concern for David and Louis began to overwhelm his thoughts, as it had done for the previous two months. News of the Boer War in South Africa had remained a constant, front-page headline, and the "Siege of Mafeking" always had been included, probably because the son of the Prime Minister of England was in Mafeking at the time. Morris was certain that both his brothers had long passed through Mafeking before the war had been declared, and that they had arrived safely in Johannesburg and Cape Town respectively, but the fact that neither of them had sent him a telegram bothered him terribly. Even Harry, who kept in good telegraphic contact with Morris, had not received a word from his brothers.

According to the newspapers, moreover, the death toll had been horrific on both sides. The Boers had captured one of the top war correspondents in South Africa by the name of Winston Churchill. It was not looking good for the British whatsoever. Morris needed reassurance from Yoni, who by this time had become almost a father-figure to Morris.

Arriving at the Goldberg residence, Morris bounded up the short flight of steps and knocked on the door, pulling his collar up against the drizzle and the cold. He turned to watch a man with a small flame on top of a long pole lighting a gas street-lamp across the road.

Shortly thereafter, Ruth Goldberg opened the door. "Come in, Morris," she urged, bustling Morris inside. "Good to see you again. Come in, come in," she fussed, "my word, it's freezing out there."

"It is, rather," Morris agreed, enjoying the ambient warmth of the Goldbergs opulent apartment, as Ruth took his hat and coat and hung them on a carved, wooden hat-stand.

"Come through to the lounge, I have made a fire that will warm you up. Yoni will be here shortly. I fear he has been held up at work again, which is quite normal."

Morris always admired the welcoming feel of his hostess' home, and once again he resolved to move out of the cold and dank warehouse and set himself up with an apartment in their vicinity. He also committed to the idea of filling his home with pictures, carpets, statues, and ornaments, so that he, too, could live an equally lavish lifestyle. After all, he believed he had earned it.

"Have you found a place to live yet?" Ruth interrupted his dreams as if she had read his mind.

"Not yet, Mrs Goldberg, although I have made myself quite comfortable at the warehouse," he lied, "as a temporary measure, of course. I'm just waiting to hear confirmation that my consignments of stock have arrived safely in Africa. Once I know that for certain, I will quickly work out what my budgets are and begin looking for a decent place to live."

"Very prudent, Morris," she smiled, pouring him a shot of sherry in a delicate, crystal-cut goblet. "Drink this, and it will warm you up."

Morris accepted the sherry gracefully, and took a small sip of the warm liquid, enjoying not only the sweet flavour but also the feel of the fine-quality crystal. He looked around the room again and admired the richness of his surrounds.

"Any news from your brothers?" Ruth asked, jerking Morris back to reality once more.

"No. Over two months now, and not a word. The telegraph system seems to work in Johannesburg and Cape Town because my brother Harry is able to keep in touch with me from Bulawayo, but nothing from David or Louis. The last place we knew of them was in Mafeking, but – as you may have read in the papers – the town is totally under siege, and there have been many deaths there. I'm beginning to fear the worst."

Ruth tried to ease Morris' concerns. "The local papers are saying that the commander of the British forces in Mafeking is doing a fine job in keeping those Boers at bay,"

"Major Baden-Powell, or rather Colonel Baden-Powell, as the newspapers are calling him now, yes, I know him. David is particularly friendly with him."

"You've met him?" Ruth exclaimed in surprise. Morris' stories from his time in Africa always fascinated her.

"Oh yes," he smiled, "David is very good at tracking in the bush and even better at – how would you call it? – counter-tracking? He can cover his tracks so well that nobody can follow him. It saved him from a very nasty spot of bother one day when he had been hunted down by a murderous band of Matabele warriors. When Colonel Bob heard of this, he befriended David, and they would spend a fair amount of time in the bush tracking, or anti-tracking, studying animals and trees, bird-watching, and the like, the sort of stuff that doesn't interest me much.

"Well, I never!" Ruth marvelled in disbelief, "I don't think I will ever truly appreciate what you boys must have experienced in Africa."

"Oh, I'm not a big friend of the bush, Mrs Goldberg. Neither are any of my brothers, come to think of it, except David; he is truly one of a kind. Not only does he enjoy the bush and all the creatures and plants within it, but he can also lay bricks and build a structure as good as any builder I know. He is brilliant at business, has a very sharp mind, and is loved by everyone he comes into contact with. He understands people, and most importantly, he understands me!" he laughed.

"I'd love to meet him one day." There was genuine compassion in her voice, and she fumbled for a tissue under her sleeve, also beginning to fear the worst.

Just then the sound of a key rattled in the hallway.

"Yoni has arrived," Ruth smiled, pleased to escape the emotions arising from the subject. "I'll be right back."

Ruth quickly disappeared out of the lounge to welcome her husband home, and Morris took the opportunity to step closer to the fire and sip more of his sherry. The images of his two brothers having been captured by the Boers, or lying dead or injured in the Mafeking area, filled him with anxiety. If his multiple shipments became lost or were requisitioned by the war effort in Africa, it could also mean the total demise of his business. He was at a complete loss as to what to do, or how to salvage the situation. Once again, a war had intervened with his business, and once more, it had sent him to the very precipice of financial ruin.

"Morris!" Yoni Goldberg greeted him as he bound into the lounge, thrusting his bushy black beard forward. "My apologies: I was delayed at the office."

"No apologies necessary, Mr Goldberg," Morris managed to smile in reply, raising his half-full glass of sherry. "Your lovely wife has been looking after me exceptionally well,"

"Excellent. I received another telegram from Harry today," he said as he reached into his pocket and retrieved a mustard-coloured envelope, which he handed to Morris.

A great deal of tension was felt in the air as Morris tore the envelope open. As with all the previous telegrams Harry had sent, Morris was fairly sure that the latest would contain no further news.

Y GOLDBERG
LLOYDS LONDON
LONDON
16 December 1899

NOTE RECEIVED TODAY VIA BSAP AS FOLLOWS STOP ADVISE LION EAGLE AND GIRAFFE IN TIN RESIDING AT HAPPY STOP GOLD AND COPPER IMPOSSIBLE STOP CANNOT LEAVE TIN STOP ADVISE LION URGENT STOP MESSAGE ENDS STOP ESTIMATE L MONTHS OF STOCK AVAILABLE STOP PLEASE ADVISE STOP
BADGER

"Thank the Lord God Almighty!" Morris exclaimed and gave an audible sigh of relief, before collapsing heavily on a plush sofa.

"That made no sense to me whatsoever." Yoni pulled at his bushy beard.

"It's in code," Morris frowned. " 'Badger' is Harry, David is 'Eagle', and 'Giraffe' is Louis. They are well but pinned down in Mafeking. It seems they are staying in Julian Weil's home. What a relief!"

Yoni was intrigued. "What made you boys design a code?"

"Yoni," Ruth chuckled as she entered the room, "you have little idea of just how clever these boys are, or of what they have had to endure."

Yoni looked at her inquisitively; he was not quite sure what she meant but knew he would receive an explanation soon enough.

" 'Tin' is our code for Mafeking because all the houses there have old, rusty-tin roofs," Morris continued, not just to explain to the Goldbergs, but to reassure himself that what he had read was as he understood it. "Johannesburg is 'Gold', for obvious reasons, and Cape Town is 'Copper', only because both start with the letter 'C'. Then there is 'Happy'; that is the code name we give for Julian Weil because he is always grumpy and hardly ever smiles."

Ruth burst into laughter which induced Yoni to chuckle and soon even Morris had joined in with the hilarity. With the relief of knowing David and Louis were alive, the evening suddenly took on a festive air, which prompted Yoni to open an expensive bottle of Bordeaux from France in order to celebrate the good news over dinner.

Almost as soon as the evening meal began, Morris was serious again. His most significant concern now was the safety of his consignments heading to Africa, not having anyone there to arrange their safe onward journey to Rhodesia.

"Badger, I mean Harry, said he had about two months' worth of stock left in the warehouse. That is not good."

"Oh?" Yoni asked, as he took a sip of his wine and briefly savoured its tang, "I'm presuming 'L' means two months."

"We have a code for numbers too: 'Black Rhino' is a series of words that have ten letters in them that do not repeat, so 'B' equals one, 'L' equals two, and so on."

Yoni was impressed. "Intriguing," he murmured, while he took another sip of wine, then placed his glass on the table with a studied deliberation. "I may be able to help you with your shipment, Morris," he said. "As you know, since I am quite well connected in the marine and shipping industry, I have a lot of influence in this field. Lloyds, for example, has an office in Cape Town and the agent over there is a friend of mine. Tomorrow morning, I will send him a telegram in which I shall ask him to track your shipments and take good care of them until this awful war is over. He also will have his own contacts in East London and Port Elizabeth, so I will ask him to get the word out and rescue your stock."

"Mr Goldberg," Morris put his knife and fork down and looked him straight in the eye, "you have no idea what this means to me. I would be indebted to you for life if you were to be so kind as to do this for us."

"It would be my pleasure indeed, Morris. But you would be required to come into the office tomorrow with all your waybill numbers, ship registrations, packing information, and every other detailed information you have that might help in identifying your goods."

Morris smiled because he knew he had everything that Yoni needed and more. Thanks to Harry's telegram and Yoni's influence, Morris felt as if his barely suppressed desperation had flipped on its head. He realised at once that this was yet another turning point in his life. He lifted his glass of wine and stared intensely into the dark-red liquid before taking a sip. David and Louis were alive, and that was the most important thing of all.

Chapter Nine

Mafeking 1899

As the siege continued, with no sign of an imminent relief force, food rationing was a reality, and the threat of starvation became a genuine concern for the townsfolk. The logistics of avoiding starvation was a vital and time-consuming part of Baden-Powell's war strategy. Not only did he have to hold the town for the British, thus effectively keeping almost eight thousand Republican soldiers out of the war, but he had to protect its inhabitants, feed them and keep their morale high. He knew that if the residents' spirits were not upheld, it would add a significant loss of morale among the defending forces themselves.

Through occasional exchanges of letters between the Boer commander and himself, a somewhat unusual truce became established. The Boers, having a firm Christian faith, preferred not to fight on a Sunday. Baden-Powell, therefore, agreed that the British would also refrain from fighting on a Sunday, and so, once a week, the soldiers on both sides took a day off.

The residents of Mafeking had fêtes and picnics on the outskirts of town and also played Polo, lawn tennis or cricket while the Boers lounged about their fortified embankments watching in amusement. Baden-Powell even held a baby show, to parade the infants that had been born during the siege, which was an event thoroughly enjoyed by all.

One Sunday a British private, while keeping a watchful eye on the

Boers, accidentally fired a shot from his rifle, causing the Boers to leap into action and take cover, loading their weapons, training a Pom-Pom cannon on the town and preparing to retaliate. Realising what had happened, the sergeant in charge of the private immediately put his rifle down and walked towards the Boer camp. Without even taking a white flag of truce, he stepped over the imaginary barbed wire and entered their territory. The Boers, albeit suspiciously, allowed him to approach, their sights trained firmly upon his torso. When he arrived, the sergeant apologised and gave some cigarettes to the Burghers. They accepted his apology and reciprocated by exchanging some newspapers. The soldiers shook hands briefly, and the sergeant returned to the town unharmed.

This exchange of cigarettes for newspapers became almost a Sunday ritual. Baden-Powell enjoyed getting the newspapers because it was the only news he received from the outside world. The paper, 'The Standard and Diggers News', was printed in the Transvaal and therefore had a bias on the war towards the Boer government, often describing the imminent taking and surrender of Mafeking, or the massive bombardment, loss of British life and damage inflicted upon the town. Baden-Powell soon realised that if the news was negative about Mafeking or the British involvement as a whole, the Boers were happy to exchange a newspaper for cigarettes, but sometimes they refused to hand over any papers. When this happened, Baden-Powell discerned that the British had inflicted some damage on the Boer army somewhere in the country, and therefore they preferred not to share the news. Thus, using this method, he correctly ascertained, how the course of the war in other parts of the country was proceeding.

One morning David found Julian Weil to be in exceptionally good spirits - uncharacteristically good spirits! Colonel Baden-Powell had earlier learned that Weil had a warehouse full of wheat, originally destined for Rhodesia thanks to a new and favourable tariff that had been imposed just before the outbreak of the war. Weil had offered to sell the entire consignment to the army, but at grossly inflated prices, despite the fact that the population was on the brink of starvation. Negotiations had broken down, but Weil had stood his ground. Weil's store manager, Ian Taylor, had that morning informed David that a well-known and respected Lord in England had now agreed to fund the purchase from his personal pocket to the tune of £50,000 sterling. With this agreement securely in place, Weil had released the wheat, becoming a very wealthy man almost overnight.

Later that morning David met up with Louis and found a shady spot behind a damaged building, about three yards from a trench, that they could dive into for safety if necessary.

"Weil is going to make about £50,000 out of this war," David mumbled.

"I'd call that profiteering at the expense of the civilians," Louis shook his head, "out of you and me, and our hunger. It doesn't seem fair."

"No," David agreed, "it doesn't. I'll bet Baden-Powell is not impressed with him either."

Both brothers ducked their heads as a volley of shots rang out around them. When they realised they were in no immediate danger, they relaxed a little, leaning against the building.

"I guess you could say we profited out of the Matabele war in Bulawayo," Louis continued, ignoring a high pitched whine as a bullet ricocheted past them a little way off.

"Indeed we did, but not at the expense of others' health and safety. We dealt in luxury goods, and we sold them at the going price of the day. In fact, Morris kept our prices slightly cheaper than the opposition, which made us more attractive to the general population. The fact that Morris bought thirty wagons of goods at normal prices and then stupidly lost the wagons for a year while prices increased obscenely, worked in our favour. But I think using food as a bargaining tool, at the possible expense of peoples' health or even lives, is foul play."

"I must say I have lost a lot of respect for Weil after today's dealings," Louis muttered.

"When word gets out, I'm sure that will be the general feeling amongst the citizens."

"And the military," Louis added.

"I want to break out of here and get back to Bulawayo," David changed the subject suddenly. "It has been three months now, and I can't see this siege ending anytime soon. Each of us has almost taken a bullet or two already. The British are taking a severe beating in Natal, and there is no sign of a relieving force. The Brits haven't even started moving north yet."

"I'm with you," Louis said quietly without shifting his eyes.

"I've been surveying the Boer trenches with my telescope for days now, and they have us well and truly covered. There's no way out."

"So, do you have a plan?" Louis asked tentatively.

"No, not yet," David sighed.

Louis suddenly stiffened and grabbed David's arm. "Look! Over there! That African man."

David looked in the direction Louis pointed. A solid African man stood with his back to a wall, looking cautiously left and right. He wore nothing but a loincloth around his waist, his brown skin shimmering in the sunlight under a thin sheen of sweat. The muscles of his torso were finely honed.

David squinted his eyes. "Nguni?" he whispered.

"It looks like him, doesn't it?" Louis replied softly.

"How on earth...?" David began, then carefully stood up, taking one step into the dirt street to see if the man would notice him.

He did! He crouched slightly to start running towards him, but David dropped his hands, palms towards the ground, to signal him to slow down, and then motioned him to walk.

Nguni understood, and casually, though nervously, began to saunter towards David and Louis. David retreated to the shady spot and sat down beside Louis again.

"How did he get in here?" Louis was astounded. "How did he know we were here?"

"We'll find out soon enough," David answered, joy evident in his voice.

When Nguni was upon them, the boys broke from their shady spot and stood to greet him.

"I see you Nguni," David grinned and gripped his right forearm tightly, slapping his shoulder with his left hand, a little too hard in his excitement.

"I see you, Boss David," Nguni boomed with his baritone voice, his brilliant white teeth flashing his joy.

"I see you." Louis clasped Nguni's right hand in a traditional Xhosa grip, also ecstatic to see a familiar face.

"I see you, Boss Rooie," Nguni beamed, "You have seen much rain as you are as tall as the maize crops now," he chuckled heartily.

"Come sit here." David led them back into the protection of the wall and shade and sat them down in the dirt. "If the guns start, we must jump into that hole." He pointed to the trench nearby.

"What are you doing here?" Louis asked.

"I was coming to find the Rangbon brothers," the big Xhosa man smiled, "to find you. My cousin from the village over there came to visit me and said he had seen you here. He said the white men were fighting amongst themselves with big guns. I have come to help my bosses."

"Thank you, Nguni," David smiled and gave his broad shoulder a squeeze, "but it was very dangerous. How did you get in here? We can't get out." He spoke in English so that Louis could understand the conversation.

"I have been outside for five days. I have found a way."

"Five days?" David exclaimed in a forced whisper, "You must be hungry, Nguni."

"No, Boss David, I have been eating the food from those men around the town," he chuckled.

"Nguni!" David scolded, "they could have killed you."

According to Nguni, the entire perimeter of the town was heavily guarded by the Boers, but just fifty yards behind the fortifications there was no-one, only their sleeping tents and cooking areas. Once an assault group moved away from the lines of attack, they were quite relaxed and carefree. Nguni would help himself to cooked leftovers in their camps under cover of darkness, and keep a watchful eye on their tactics and movements during the day.

He had found a small gap in their defences, and, in the blackness of night, he had sneaked into Mafeking. His biggest problem had been Colonel Baden-Powell's defences, as they were far superior to that of the Boer's siege lines.

"Can you lead Louis and me out of here?" David asked Nguni, "We want to return to Bulawayo."

"That is why I have come," he grinned, "but there is one problem, Boss David and Boss Rooie, you are not African like me; your skin is not black. We must fix with mud."

"Can we go tonight?" Louis asked anxiously.

"No, not tonight," David raised a hand, "tomorrow night. I need to speak to Colonel Bob first. But we shall leave tomorrow night," David grinned and winked at Nguni.

An hour before sunset David jogged over to the house where Baden-Powell had his lookout platform. As always, he stood on the top rung with his field glasses, relentlessly scanning the battlefield.

"Bob," David called from across the street in a suppressed voice.

It caught the colonel's attention, and he looked down. When he recognised who it was, he signalled him to enter the building and find his way up. David wasted no time and, walking through the communication centre on the ground floor while casually greeting the officers on duty, he made his way up the stairs to the ladder contraption to the roof. Above him, on top of the wooden structure, Baden-Powell stood in silence, seemingly glued to his field glasses.

"Bob," David repeated.

"Come on up." The colonel glanced down briefly before returning to his observation and sidled to his right slightly.

David gingerly clambered up the ladder and joined his friend. He had his trusted telescope over his shoulder and retrieved it, scanning the area in front of him. The view was magnificent, and he could now well understand why Baden-Powell spent so much time up there.

"You know," David broke the silence without taking his eye off the landscape, "they call you 'The Wolf' down there?"

"So I've heard," Baden-Powell chuckled, "because I never sleep."

"Do you ever get any?"

"I don't need much. Yesterday I only managed four hours before a bullet shot through the bedpan under my bed. Made a hell of a racket it did," he laughed aloud.

"Do you remember that man, Nguni, who looked after our wagons up in Rhodesia?"

"Yes, that big Xhosa chap. I remember him well," Bob mused, shifting his view slightly to the right.

"He arrived in Mafeking today."

The colonel put his field glasses down and stared at David. "How did he manage to get past the Boers?"

"How did he manage to get past *your* defences is more the question," David grinned. "Oh look, I see some Boers at eleven o'clock."

"Yes," Baden-Powell raised his field glasses again, "I've been watching them. They have been looking at digging a new trench over there. I think they have identified that bare patch of soil, where you see that lone stick pegged in the ground, and will return in the morning with shovels. That's a real bugger as it will throw my defences out. I had hoped to dig in there myself, but I simply ran out of time. How did he get past my men?" he asked David, still keeping a wary eye on the enemy.

"He's a brilliant tracker - came in at night, not difficult for him. But he surveyed the Boer positions for five days before he made his move. That stick you say is a peg in the ground; it's not a stick. It's a meerkat. Look carefully, and you will see its head move. He is catching the last warm rays of the sun before he goes to sleep. He's the last sentry of the day."

"Five days in Boer territory?" Baden-Powell continued the conversation as both men kept their eyes trained on the distant landscape. "Oh yes, I see it now. A meerkat. Funny little creatures, those. I wonder if I could have a chat with Nguni?"

"That's why I came looking for you. He could tell you a thing or two about the Boers, I'm sure. Oh look, the meerkat has gone to bed, cute little thing. You say you would like to dig a trench over there?"

"Yes," Baden-Powell lowered his field glasses for the second time and stared at David, turning slightly on the flimsy step of the ladder.

"The meerkat lair is a warren of tunnels in soft soil, spread over about half an acre of land." David lowered his telescope. "But you knew that, didn't you?"

"Yes," Baden-Powell repeated, looking curious.

"I reckon you could dig a trench in soft soil, riddled with thousands of little tunnels, in, say, about three hours?"

"Two hours, actually," the Colonel smirked.

"The moment you start digging, they'll scamper away very smartly. I'd like to leave tomorrow night with my brother. Nguni has found a way for us to get past the Boers without any problem. It's your blokes that worry me."

"I cannot condone this, and you know that, but I cannot stop you. This is on your head, you understand?"

"I understand, Bob. But I do think you need to have a chat with Nguni before we go."

"Right-o," the Colonel nodded his agreement, "tomorrow at lunchtime; let's meet in Weil's Warehouse Number 4, now that it's empty. Tonight I have a trench to dig, and tomorrow we will give those Boers a surprise kick when they come back to try and dig in themselves. Do you have that compass I gave you in Bulawayo?"

"I never leave town without it." David rummaged in his pocket and withdrew the intricate brass compass, placing it on the makeshift desktop in front of him.

Baden-Powell studied it for a moment as the needle swung gently, as if a horizontal pendulum, searching for magnetic north. "If I had known how beautiful this piece of engineering was I probably would not have parted with it," he mumbled just loudly enough for David to hear.

"If you used the telescope I gave you, you probably would have spotted that meerkat ages ago," David retorted with a grin.

"Touché," Baden-Powell continued the banter without taking his eyes off the compass, the needle gently slowing down to a fixed point. A bullet from a Boer sniper cracked overhead, but BP didn't flinch. David, on the other hand, jerked in surprise, causing the compass needle to wobble.

"Doesn't that worry you?" David asked nervously.

"Oh, the Boers take pot-shots at me all day long. That one came from behind us and I know that chap is a useless shot. If a shot comes from about two o'clock, well that shooter is pretty sharp, so I casually clamber down; I don't want him to know how accurate he is. There! That's north," he announced calmly as the needle in the compass stabilised.

David gently took hold of the compass and turned it carefully until the 'N' lined up precisely with the red tip of the needle. Baden-Powell then lowered his nose to just an inch above the device and peered in the direction the meerkat had last been seen. Another bullet cracked overhead, but this time it sounded a lot closer. Again, the Colonel did not flinch. As hard as David tried to keep his composure, though, he jerked slightly in surprise, causing the needle in the compass to wobble again.

"I make that 121° East. What do you think, dear boy?" Baden-Powell calmly asked for confirmation.

David slid the compass across until it was directly in front of his face, and once the needle settled down, he gauged the direction to where he had last seen the meerkat.

"Give or take a degree or two, I'd agree with you, Bob."

"Splendid!" Baden-Powell exclaimed. "Distance?"

David looked across at the patch of ground in question. He had no idea but guessed it was about six hundred yards. Bob disagreed, and said he felt it was more like five hundred yards, but was happy to accept David's guess. David knew, however, that Baden-Powell was just saying that to humour him; Baden-Powell was far more experienced in matters of distance, trajectory, velocities and the capabilities of well-trained soldiers than he was.

There was another crack of a bullet, this time coming from slightly behind and to the right of them, and it unquestionably passed underneath their feet.

"The little bastard," Baden-Powell muttered, "he's a new one. Time to get down as I don't know his marksmanship abilities. Climb down casually if you don't mind, we don't want them to think we are worried."

David quickly pocketed his compass and began to climb down the ladder, pausing briefly near the bottom to scratch the seat of his pants in a somewhat exaggerated fashion. Baden-Powell also clambered down a few steps before going back up to collect a journal that he had deliberately 'forgotten', and then came down again. In that time three other bullets cracked about their heads. Once within the safety of the pepper-pot David sighed in relief and shook his head in awe at his friend's ability to accept being shot at, seemingly without a worry in the world. His admiration for Baden-Powell magnified tenfold.

"Thanks for the information." Baden-Powell gripped David's shoulder when he crouched below the sandbags, "I look forward to talking to Nguni. If you let me know which part of town you would like to exit, I'll ask my men to give you safe passage out of the defence lines."

"Thanks, Bob. I believe Mafeking will be well cared for under your command." David gave him a quick slap on the back of his shoulder. They exchanged a few hurried words before David crouched to leave.

"If you get the chance, do send me a message to let me know you got to Bulawayo safe and sound." Bob gave David a stern look, "My heart will rest easier if I know you made it home unscathed."

"Will do, my friend," David readily agreed.

"Keep it in code, will you?" Bob withdrew a well-worn notebook from his breast pocket and thumbed through the pages. As the pages flashed by, David watched curiously, but couldn't help notice several sketches, notes, diagrams and scribbles on just about every page.

"There!" Baden-Powell tilted the open book towards David with his index finger planted firmly alongside an ink diagram of a perfect circle, with a black dot slap bang in the middle of it. "That's my code for 'home'. Depending on the context, you can use this to say 'I've gone home', or 'let's go home', or 'come home'."

"You have a lot of codes in there," David nodded at the notebook, somewhat intrigued.

"Oh yes, my boy. Codes are everything in a war. This one I designed myself, and I must say, it is my favourite. Unless you know what it means, no-one could ever decipher it."

David smiled knowingly. "Well, Bob," he said, and then tapped the dot twice with his index finger, "I'm going home."

"Go well, David. Please send my regards to Hanna," he mocked.

David waved a naughty finger at him, but laughed all the same, then swiftly made his way out the building.

For the last hour of daylight, David sat with Louis and Nguni behind the same building alongside the trench and discussed their plan of escape. It was an exciting time for the boys; the prospect of capture, torture or death was the least of their worries, although it did cross their minds occasionally. For Louis, the chance to get back to Bulawayo and take over his shop once again, and to involve himself with civilised and stimulating conversations in the Charter Hotel dining room, was heady stuff. The prospect of building his home on the piece of land that he had recently bought in Suburbs was also a huge drawcard. He longed to leave the war-torn, hungry and distressing town of Mafeking. As for David, his thoughts were solely and firmly on Hanna.

Nguni had found a tin bucket, dented and pock-marked with bullet holes, which he had half filled with black, wet mud he had discovered down by the river. Just before their escape, he told them, they were to strip down to their underpants and smear themselves completely with the mud.

"Your skin must be like me," he said sternly, then began to laugh.

David laughed too and was quite happy to do this, but Louis didn't look too pleased. The reality and dangers of their escape were beginning to dawn on him, and suddenly he was getting butterflies in his stomach.

"I'm worried, David," Louis confessed. "How will we survive out in the wild if we make it out of here? Have you thought about that?"

"It will be tough, Louis, I must be honest. We will have to hunt for food in the traditional way, but Nguni will help us."

"We find villages," Nguni's deep voice rumbled. "They give food. They share."

"What does worry me is that we have no guns for protection from wild animals." Louis was notably anxious.

"How many you want?" Nguni asked casually in his broken English.

"You can get guns?" David cocked an inquisitive eyebrow.

"Those people have many. They sleep at night as the hippopotamus sleeps in the day."

"That's dangerous," David warned.

"It is not difficult to take from someone who snores."

David and Louis began to chuckle. David decided that they needed three rifles, one each, and whatever food Nguni could safely pilfer, but Nguni declined point blank to use a weapon. They scared him, and, in any case, he preferred to use a spear to defend himself and to hunt, just as his father had done, and his father before him.

The following day they continued their planning in the shade of the tree, tumbling into the trench four times before lunch to avoid Old Creechy's projectiles. At one o'clock they carefully made their way to Warehouse Number 4 and entered the gloom of the empty storage area. The corrugated iron roof made it unbearably hot inside. When David closed the door behind them random shafts of sunlight, created by bullet holes in the thin iron walls, streaked happily inside, illuminating the room with an eerie and forbidding ambience.

David shuddered as a nervous chill ran down his spine, and Louis regretted not relieving himself before this meeting. Nguni stood in silence, casting suspicious looks at the walls and roof. A moment later the flimsy corrugated iron door was noisily flung open, and Colonel Baden-Powell stepped in, looking quite jolly and full of smiles.

"Afternoon, Gentlemen," he greeted the trio, "thanks for meeting me here. I see you, Nguni," he politely welcomed the large man in his Xhosa tongue.

"I see you, Boss Colonel," Nguni beamed, pleased with the officer's respectful greeting.

Baden-Powell pushed through the pleasantries very smartly and got straight down to business. He ascertained that Nguni had been sneaking in and around the Boer camps at night for the last few nights and his questioning seemed to concentrate on numbers of Boers and heavy weapons. Nguni's responses appeared to satisfy the Colonel, probably, David assumed, because he already knew the answers.

Nguni suddenly got down on his haunches and dusted the earthen floor with his hand, and began to draw a rough map on the ground with his finger. It held Baden-Powell's full attention, and the colonel started to add to the schematic that was unfolding with his finger. BP had given many of the Boer positions silly nicknames, like Snyman's Ditch, and Botha's Bog, and indicated where they were in the dust. Even Old Creechy's position had been accurately identified by Nguni. When the basic map of Mafeking had been drawn in the dirt, and the Boer positions and trenches identified, the colonel stood up and commended Nguni for his work, and for giving him the information.

Then Nguni did something most extraordinary. He put his finger on the end of the railway line and started extending it in gentle curves, away towards the north. When he reached the extent of his reach, he shuffled on his haunches and continued the line a little more, forcing Baden-Powell to step aside, and there he stopped. Standing up, he placed his heel on the right side of the line and scuffed the ground, then, putting his heel on the left, made another scuff.

"Camp," Nguni declared, his deep voice rumbling off the metal walls.

"Well I'll be!" the Colonel exclaimed, "how many men?"

"Many," was the simple, but meaningful answer.

Baden-Powell studied the ground in deep thought for a long while, and the onlookers dared not interrupt.

In the distance, Old Creechy boomed into life. David and Louis jerked, looking over their shoulders nervously.

"Should we run for a trench?" Louis couldn't hold his tongue.

"No," Baden-Powell replied calmly, not moving his eyes from the sketch on the ground, "I saw them move Old Creechy's aim towards the hospital area a moment ago. We are safe here. Nguni," he continued, totally oblivious to an explosion off to his right, "is the railway line working? Have the Boers damaged it?"

"No Boss Colonel," Nguni smiled, his perfect white teeth glinting in a thin shaft of sunlight.

"Splendid. Thanks to you I'm going to give these fools a kick they won't forget."

Boom… Another one of Old Creechy's shells was on its way.

"Blast and damnation!" Baden-Powell almost shouted.

"What?" David reacted, concerned. He had never seen Baden-Powell look so angry, nor lose his temper like that.

"I specifically asked the Boer commander…" he paused as another explosion erupted, "I specifically asked him not to target the hospital. I'm going to move our Boer prisoners into the hospital, then let's see what they do! I have to go. Nguni," he addressed the big Xhosa man in his language, "take care of my two young friends. May you travel safely, my friend," and with that, he turned on his heel and disappeared out the door in a frantic hurry as Old Creechy spoke once more.

Later that evening, just as Mrs Weil served a meagre dinner at the table, David confided in them that he and Louis were escaping. Julian was unmistakably shocked to hear this, and both Weils tried to discourage them in this possibly suicidal folly. When the couple realised that nothing was going to stop the brothers from carrying out their plan they grudgingly relented. They agreed to look after the few possessions in the tote bags until the boys, hopefully, returned to collect them once the war was over. Gracious farewells and thanks were exchanged after dinner, and, at nine-thirty precisely, David and Louis slipped out the back door, and melted into the darkness.

The brothers met Nguni by the arranged spot at the anthill beside the cemetery on the north side of town. They stripped down to their underpants and plastered black mud all over their bodies. With that done, Nguni took the bucket and completed the disguise by roughly smearing mud in their ears, on their eyelids and, to their indignation, mixed with ribald amusement, in their armpits.

"You must be like me, black, all over," he grumbled.

"I'm worried about this," Louis said nervously to his older brother, "are you sure you want to do it?"

"I don't want to put you in any danger, Louis, but I fear if we stay here the chance of being killed is far higher than if we attempted an escape. Just stay right behind me and do exactly as I tell you."

Half an hour later Captain Rudge walked towards them from the direction of town. The boys were already well concealed in the dry grass, and they could see he was having trouble spotting them. Rudge paused and looked about nervously. David blew a soft whistle that caught his attention, and he moved closer to where they hid. He stopped only feet from David and continued casting a cautious eye into the pitch black landscape, not looking in their direction for a moment.

"Can you hear me?" the captain whispered without averting his stare.

"Yes, right here, Captain Rudge," David hissed from his hiding place almost at his feet.

"My men will stand down for five minutes as soon as I scratch my head and walk back."

David looked at Nguni, almost invisible in the grass just inches from him. Nguni nodded.

"Thank you, Captain. That will be perfect."

"Please give Colonel Plumer my best regards. God speed you on your way, Gentlemen." Rudge frowned into the dark, then, abruptly turning on his heel, scratched his head casually, and then marched stiffly back into town.

"Colonel Plumer?" Louis whispered.

"Long story, I'll tell you on the other side. Alright, Nguni, let's go. We have five minutes." David abruptly ended the conversation.

Nguni stood silently and looked around briefly, then signalled the two boys to follow him. Clad only in underpants, they fell into line as if Nguni's double shadow, mimicking him step for step. Each of the brothers carried a blanket rolled up tightly and slung over a shoulder with a piece of string, the twine also blackened by mud. Within the blanket roll was a single change of clothing, a pair of bush shoes and a khaki cloth hat. David's bundle had one extra item: a sheath knife.

Clouds had rolled in that afternoon and blocked out the starry night, and with a waning moon barely on the horizon, the night was almost pitch black. The glow from Mafeking behind them and from the occasional fire the Boers had lit around their fortifications were all Nguni had to guide him, but even without that assistance, he knew exactly where he was going. His only concern was an unpredictable flash of lightning that might give his presence away.

Like ghosts, the trio walked silently along old bush paths, Nguni occasionally cutting off one track only to join another; sometimes dropping suddenly to his haunches, the two boys reacted in full synchronicity, then, without a word, moving off again with absolute stealth. David marvelled at the deftness of Nguni's movements, unexpected in such a large man; he reminded David of a leopard stalking its prey.

After what seemed like ages, Nguni stopped and faced David. "We are past," he whispered very quietly. "Wait. I fetch guns."

Before David could say a word, Nguni melted into the darkness, again in absolute silence. David took his brother by the shoulder and gently forced him down onto his haunches, and, without a word, Louis complied. When their legs began to cramp, David carefully shuffled onto his backside, and Louis followed suit. Time was dragging, and David started to sense fear and danger. It became a massive struggle within him to not stand up and go looking for Nguni, but he knew that would be a deadly move. He began to wonder if Nguni had been captured himself, and then tortured into leading the Boers to them. He decided that if Nguni did not return within one hour, he would start walking north with Louis regardless; then again, he could not leave his friend behind. His mind was in turmoil, and he began to regret ever asking Nguni to help them escape.

"We go!" Nguni suddenly spoke quietly into David's ear, and he nearly leapt out of his skin. Louis, too, almost let out a startled squeal.

Very much relieved, the Langbourne brothers smartly got to their feet and fell in with Nguni once more, not stopping for a solid half an hour. When they halted, Nguni handed David and Louis a rifle each, along with a small square carton of bullets.

"We walk until the sun greets us, then we sleep," Nguni spoke softly in Xhosa.

David nodded and explained to Louis what would happen while they quickly unrolled their blankets and put on some clothing; the shoes were a welcome relief as they both had small, painful cuts on their soft soles, earned on the silent, barefoot march.

Just as the sky over their right shoulder began to show hues of mauve and pink, Nguni, to the boys' heartfelt relief, stopped by a thicket of dark bushes. The big Xhosa man prodded the foliage with his spear, making sure that no creature had beaten them to the natural haven, and then summoned the boys into the dense thicket. They spoke easily now in soft tones, unravelling their respective blankets and curling up for a much-needed sleep.

When David opened his eyes, the sun was high, and he assumed it was getting close to mid-day. Louis was fast asleep and had not moved since David had last seen him at dawn. Nguni, however, was not there. Desperate to relieve himself, David dared not expose himself outside the protective shelter of the thicket until Nguni returned; he assumed the man was scouting the area, so he lay still, trying not to think about his bladder. About two minutes later, Louis stirred and stiffly lifted his head off the ground.

"Morning Brother," David greeted him in a soothing voice, "sleep well?"

"I don't know what hurts more, my feet, my back or my head. Man, I need the loo," he grumbled.

David smiled, he knew exactly how Louis felt. Taking a chance, he propped himself up on his elbow and craned his neck, hoping to see enough beyond the green leaves to ascertain if the coast was clear. A soft rustle of leaves behind him made David freeze.

"Molweni," Nguni greeted the boys from outside the bush, "it is safe."

David and Louis struggled out of their blankets and crawled through their leafy sanctuary on all fours. When they stood up and looked at Nguni to greet him, the large man burst into uncontrollable laughter. Both brothers stared at him in total confusion, until they looked at each other, and then they too erupted into raucous laughter. Both boys were dressed in long khaki trousers, a smart khaki open-necked cotton shirt with short sleeves, but every inch of exposed skin on their arms, face and chest was smeared thickly with black mud. Even their hair was plastered with dried mud.

It was a sight that had the three men almost rolling on the ground in fits of laughter - almost, because David and Louis could not control their bladders a moment longer, and, standing back to back, relieved themselves on the dry earth, laughing their heads off. For Nguni, this was the funniest thing he had ever seen; he collapsed on the ground and roared like a crazed hyena, tears streaming down his face and holding his belly, gasping for air, only to burst out laughing again. Every time the brothers looked at themselves, they too burst into fits of laughter once more.

When sanity finally prevailed, the trio sat in the shade and discussed their strategy to get to Bulawayo without any roving Boer patrol spotting them. Nguni had been for a walk around the immediate area and had not come across any military men. Because he was a black African, and this war had been classified as a "white man's war", he could roam around the bush in relative safety, only because he wore his traditional clothing and was unarmed. There were many African men, however, that helped the British in the war, but they were distinct in their uniforms, and were armed with modern weapons.

The walk to Bulawayo would take a good six to eight weeks, but the journey on horseback would be a lot quicker, more like two weeks, and David was impatient. Furthermore, the men would be a lot safer on a horse, not just because they would have a fighting chance of outrunning a Boer patrol, but also any predators, such as lions. Such predators would commonly leave a horse and rider alone as they would appear to be a single massive beast, whereas a human walking as an individual was extremely vulnerable to attack.

"We should pass a British camp about halfway to the Limpopo River." David scratched a line in the sand with a dry stick, indicating the river that formed the border with Rhodesia, "the commander there is Colonel Plumer. I have a message Colonel Bob wants me to give to him."

"What's that?" Louis asked curiously.

"He believes the British are not making progress against the Boers and the siege will go on for another six months or more. He thinks the Boer's tactic now is to starve them into submission, and he only has two months left in rations."

"Even with Weil's £50 000 worth of wheat?" Louis was surprised.

David shrugged, even he could see how much Weil was profiteering. "A lot of money for such a small amount of wheat," he sighed, "so yes, Bob wants Plumer to stock up on food, urgently."

"I know the camp," Nguni mused, "it is far."

"It would be a lot better if we had horses," Louis stated the obvious as he tended to some cuts on his feet.

"Tomorrow, that way," Nguni pointed to the east, "there is a small camp for those bad people. They have horses. We can take some."

"Can you ride a horse?" David asked Nguni.

"Yes Boss," came the simple reply, which incorporated a mischievous smile.

"Then I guess Louis and I will have to keep our black skin on until then," David chuckled and gave his brother a playful nudge.

Chapter Ten

London 1899

When Morris walked up to the second floor of the Lloyds of London building and introduced himself to the receptionist, he found that he had been expected, and was politely asked to take a seat while Mr Goldberg was called.

A moment later Morris was invited to "please come through, Mr Langbourne. Mr Goldberg will see you now."

He followed the receptionist through a short corridor and entered Yoni's domain, the door closing discretely behind him. Morris was impressed with his host's office. Elegant and regal, the decor of the office reflected the same loving hand as that of the Goldberg's home. Intricate statuettes carved from a dark marbled stone graced a deep reddish-brown sideboard, and two brass and glass ornaments gracefully enhanced the leather inlay of Yoni's generous desk. On the walls were magnificent oil-on-canvas paintings set in intricate frames with a rustic gold finish. The Cartier fountain pen that lay on the desk in front of Yoni was certainly very expensive and crafted with exquisite precision.

"You have a lovely office," Morris marvelled in awe.

"Ruth's niece, Rose Bertha, helped me decorate it," Yoni chuckled. "She did most of our home too. She has a flair for this sort of thing."

"I can see that," Morris agreed, taking a closer look at the name on one of the paintings. "When I move into an office I would like her to help me decorate it."

"I will introduce you to Rose Bertha." Yoni indicated a chair for Morris to sit upon. "Incidentally, Lloyds own a building on Finsbury Pavement. The entire top floor came up for rent this morning. I think it would be perfect for you; three bedrooms, a lounge and dining area, and an office. Our property manager will be looking for a quality tenant. I would be delighted to vouch for you if you would like that."

"It all depends on the cost," Morris frowned, but, secretly, all he wanted now was a home and an office like Yoni's, and he was ready to jump at the deal regardless of the price. The Finsbury Pavement lease sounded perfect; a comfortable home, room for his family when they visited, and an office all wrapped up in one.

"I'll introduce you to the property manager later. Now, let's have a look at your paperwork."

For the next hour, the two men waded through the wads of paper that Morris had accumulated over the previous months, listing suppliers, delivery dates, destinations, wharfs, ship numbers, cargo numbers, and a host of notes, names, places and routes. That was just for the England and Scotland purchases; Hong Kong was another matter altogether. When Morris finished explaining all that he had done, Yoni was rather confused and felt a little overwhelmed, but, as was his way, methodically made notes on a jotter and worked out what he would say in the telegram he would be sending to his friend in Cape Town.

"I would hazard a guess that your goods are already in Cape Town, but where? That is the question. Let's hope my friend can resolve that problem. As for the consignments from Hong Kong, well, they may still be on the water, but again, let's see what we can do. It will take about two weeks before I get an answer."

"I would offer to send Harry from Bulawayo, but I think Rhodesia is cut off from South Africa, going by the newspapers, that is. In any case, I need him there to keep the shops operational. My partner in Johannesburg, Danie Coetsee, could help store the goods if necessary."

"No," Yoni objected, "Johannesburg is Boer territory, and Cape Town, Port Elizabeth and East London are British. You will have to store your goods, when we find them, in those respective towns until the war is over, no matter who wins."

"Oh, this is so stressful. I see in the papers today that the death toll in

Mafeking is estimated at over 100 with nearly 300 injured. I worry so much about my brothers."

"The Boer death toll is at least double that, they say. I read an interesting article today that your friend, Colonel Baden-Powell, had a train carriage fitted with heavy armour by a local coachbuilder, and had the train steam up the railway line right through the middle of a Boer camp, killing dozens of their soldiers."

"Good grief!" Morris was surprised at the extent of the war. "I wonder if the coachbuilder was Mr Geran?"

"That's the name, Geran." Yoni looked at Morris curiously, "You know him too?"

"Of course. We bought a large number of ox-wagons from his business. In fact, his wagons now form a vital part of our business in Rhodesia. We have traders who buy from us and then rent these wagons to ply their trade around the countryside. We call them wagon traders. We make money from their sales, and from the wagon rentals too. On top of that, they rent our oxen; thus when they are out of town doing their business we don't need to feed the beasts nor do we have to employ men to look after them. If an ox becomes lame or dies, the trader is obliged to return a healthy one to us. It's a great business deal."

"Do you have a plot of land to care for your oxen when a trader returns to town?"

"We don't need to; the traders are never in town for more than one night."

Yoni just shook his head in disbelief. "Is this your main business? I thought you had a wholesale business."

"Wagon trading forms a tiny part of the business. The wholesale and retail business is our mainstay." Morris suddenly frowned. "But if I lose these consignments the wagon business will become the core business, and I can't allow that to happen."

"Leave this with me, Morris." Yoni became serious again. "In the meantime come with me, and I will leave you in the hands of our property manager. He will show you the apartment in Finsbury Pavement. Let's meet this evening at my home for dinner. Ruth would be delighted to see you again."

Morris met with a nondescript man in a grey business suit with a large, red nose that he kept blowing noisily into a handkerchief. Mr Edwards was the property manager for all of Lloyds' properties in London, and it appeared they had many. The apartment in question was on the fourth floor of a drab building sandwiched tightly between two other buildings of equal non-beauty. As they trudged up the four flights of stairs, illuminated only by some windows encrusted on the outside with tangled spider webs, Morris was beginning to have some doubts about the place.

"There is a gentleman in America," Edwards made idle chit-chat with his young charge, "a Mr Otis, I believe, who has invented a type of compartment that lifts people from one floor to another using all manner of levers and cables. They call it an 'elevator' as it automatically elevates people from one floor to the next. I could certainly use them in London, what with all the buildings I have to manage on a daily basis."

"They lift people, so they don't have to walk?" Morris questioned.

"Yes, these Americans are always up to something new with all their fancy inventions and names. They can't simply call them 'lifts'; no, it has to be an 'elevator'," he said in a mock irony so common in England.

"Well," Morris shrugged, "it sounds like a marvellous idea to me."

"Here we are, Mr Langbourne," Edwards stopped at a door painted black with the number 12 screwed on in brass numerals. He inserted the key and pushed it open. Morris stepped into the small hallway, still slightly hesitant about the idea of paying rent for a place to live when he really could manage with a thin mattress on the floor of his warehouse. That notion changed in a heartbeat, however, when the apartment opened up into an empty, spacious lounge and dining area.

Morris allowed his eyes, and his imagination, to roam eagerly over the walls, floor and ceiling of the room. There was a black fireplace against a side wall, encompassed by an intricate design of white stucco (the uppermost area of which was stained with light grey soot), and a generous mantelpiece completed the look. An elaborate brass and crystal chandelier hung expectantly from the ceiling, four half-burnt candles perched precariously in their holders. Mr Edwards was saying something behind him, his voice echoing off the bare white walls, but Morris was not listening. There was a row of windows along one wall of the lounge area, and, as Morris approached them, he looked down to street level. A brief wave of vertigo overtook him; he had never been so high in his life! Daily life was bustling about below him, entirely oblivious to his presence. He imagined a plush leather armchair by the window where he would sit and contemplate his business ventures, or maybe a lounge suite for his guests to enjoy the view of the street and buildings on the other side of the road. No, he thought, perhaps his office would be better suited for this spot, where he could let his business imagination run free all day, or maybe he could put the dining table here instead? His thoughts were overwhelming!

He turned to tell Mr Edwards he would take it, but Edwards was still talking.

"There are three bedrooms, Mr Langbourne. Follow me," he droned on.

Taking himself firmly in hand, Morris nodded politely as the two men walked through the remainder of the apartment. In his mind, he claimed his bedroom, a spacious area with another fireplace, and a water closet with private bath, just like his room at the Fitzgerald Guest House in Dublin. He discovered a second communal bathroom that serviced the other two bedrooms, and a significant amount of wardrobe space in every room, including the passageways. An old pale yellow Aga stove graced the small kitchen. It was so perfect in every respect that Morris could barely contain his excitement.

"What is the rental of this flat?" Morris asked his guide.

"We require £45 per month, plus a bond of equal amount," he responded matter of factly.

"That's acceptable," Morris demurred. "When may I take possession?"

"As soon as you deposit the requisite amount of £90 into our bank account, sir."

"I can arrange that," Morris smiled and extended his hand in a handshake, "consider that a deal."

Mr Edwards shook hands with Morris, sealing the arrangement, and the men made their way back to the Lloyds office (but not before Morris took another hurried tour of the flat and a second heady view at the street below him).

The paperwork for the lease agreement was quite simple and quickly completed, and the rental payment went through smoothly. Before lunchtime, on that same day, Morris was the proud occupant of an upmarket apartment in a prestigious suburb of London. He was concerned, however, that his brothers were sleeping on blankets on the floor in Africa somewhere (except, that was, for David and Louis at present, as they were under Julian Weil's hospitality), but he would decorate the spare bedrooms lavishly for when they visited - one day.

The idea of his brothers staying with him naturally turned Morris' thoughts to his family in Ireland. How he would love it if Bloomy could visit him. He made a mental note to invite her to London once established in his new home. Oh, the excitement was almost overwhelming. As for his father, well, he was a little wary of him because he would also have to invite Helena and her brood of children. *'No, that would never do,'* he thought to himself and immediately put it out of his mind. He then thought of Bloomy's husband and their infants and put the idea of inviting her out of his mind just as quickly.

At six o'clock that evening he donned his coat and hat and strode off to Yoni and Ruth's home for the arranged dinner. Morris was in excellent spirits; he had a beautiful place in which to live, although presently without furnishings, and his brothers were alive and well. Not only that, Yoni had his contacts in Africa running around locating his consignments and making arrangements for their safekeeping. All he had to do was wait. Waiting, however, was just about the most difficult thing in the world for Morris; he needed to work. He was a businessman, and that was a great motivator in his life. He needed to buy, sell, negotiate, deal and increase his wealth, more especially now that he was paying rent on two properties. Waiting was definitely not acceptable.

As always, Morris was warmly welcomed into the Goldbergs home, but this time they had other guests: Mr and Mrs Friedlander and their daughter, Rose Bertha. Morris enjoyed the family's company, especially that of Mr Friedlander as he was a very astute businessman and Morris found that they had a lot in common. Mr Friedlander was a commodity broker who specialised in procuring spices and fragrances. He had a warehouse in London, a similar concept to that which Morris had in Bulawayo, where he stored his purchases. He would then export his wares to other traders, most of whom were in the United States of America and Continental Europe.

What intrigued Morris was Mr Friedlander's ability to understand world prices for particular commodities, and then to most efficiently buy when prices were low and sell when they were high. He watched political and world events, including weather trends that might affect a country's agriculture, and seemed to predict when there might be shortages of certain crops. He had made a lot of money this way and spent a great deal of time reading newspapers and talking to captains of industry and commerce, particularly those who were from foreign lands.

Rose Bertha, a few years younger than Morris, looked a bit like her father; her facial features were quite hard and she had a fairly solid build. Morris didn't find her particularly attractive, but he appreciated her artistic flair and asked her to decorate his new apartment for him, which she shyly, but readily agreed to do. Morris confirmed that he enjoyed the look and feel of the Goldberg residence, but that he obviously didn't have the budget they had.

Rose, having decorated many of the homes of her parent's friends as a hobby, assured Morris that by visiting certain second-hand dealers in the back streets of London whom she had previously utilised, she could use her charm and bargaining skills to procure outstanding items at reasonable prices. She was confident she could do an absolute treat on his new home for a minimal outlay. Pleased with this, Morris gave her a budget which she accepted with obvious excitement.

Morris was on top form that night; everything was falling into place quite perfectly.

Chapter Eleven

Somewhere in Bechuanaland, February 1900

When an unexpected streak of lightning tore through the night sky and rain began pelting down, the plan of stealing three Boer horses took an unexpectedly dangerous turn. Not only was their cover of darkness compromised, but also the improvised black make-up of the two European boys began to wash off, thereby dislodging their nocturnal camouflage.

David signalled Nguni and Louis to backtrack, and just as they had arrived unnoticed at the perimeter of the Boer camp, so they slunk almost invisibly back into the darkness of the surrounding grasslands.

"We have to make another plan," David whispered, wiping streaks of rain and mud that stung his eyes, "the lightning will give us away, and with our disguise washed off we are too white now, too easily visible."

Nguni lifted his head above the height of the grass and waited for the next flash of lightning, then crouched back into the huddle. There was no cover for a good four hundred yards; the first tree line was a little too distant for comfort.

"You and Boss Rooie go to the trees. I fetch horses," Nguni insisted.

"You can't do it on your own," David objected.

"Go. I do it," Nguni ordered.

David sighed, he didn't have a better plan. "Alright, but be careful. If there is any problem, stop and come back to the trees. We will make another plan. You understand?"

"I understand," Nguni nodded. "Give me knife."

David unbuckled his belt and slid his sheath knife off, handing Nguni the knife complete with scabbard.

"Be careful, Nguni," David demanded in a forced whisper.

"Go," Nguni instructed.

Another flash of lightning announced an even fiercer downpour of rain. When the flickering dance of lightning stopped momentarily, Nguni, like magic, disappeared. David tapped Louis on the shoulder, and crouching low, the boys made their way to the distant tree line where their rifles and now sodden blankets lay waiting.

Louis was trembling, both in fear and from the cold. "I'm scared for Nguni, David," he whispered.

"I'm not happy with this either," David agreed. He did not like the idea that Nguni was risking his life for them.

"He's a very loyal person, Nguni," Louis spoke into the darkness, "Why is he doing this for us?"

"I don't know. He's an extraordinary person. He has no reason to."

After what seemed like a very tense hour, a brilliant flash of lightning gave the boys a snapshot of a distant burly man walking three horses towards them. Because the burst of light was so suddenly over, it resembled a single image from the new art of photography: just a man in mid-stride, holding the reigns of three horses.

"That's Nguni!" Louis trembled.

"Yes," David said calmly, "the problem is if we can see him, so can they. Let's hope they are all in tents keeping out of the rain," he said, referring to the besieging army.

With mounting tension, they waited for the next flash. The storm was subsiding, and the streaks of lightning were lessening; the rain was now a gentle, steady cascade of heavy drops.

"We should go and meet him halfway," Louis suggested.

"Yes, David agreed, "but I don't want to miss him in the dark."

Another flash of brilliant light revealed that Nguni had already covered much more ground than they had expected.

"Let's go!" David relented and leapt from concealment with Louis on his heels. In no time they had reached Nguni, and each quickly gathered the reigns of a horse, leading it back to the safety of the trees. Only once they were behind the protection of the branches and leaves did they relax.

"No problems, Nguni?" David asked tentatively.

"No problems, Boss David," Nguni replied grimly. In a shimmer of distant lightning, David didn't like the scowl on his face.

"Do you think we must ride fast?" David questioned the large man, fearing the answer.

"Yes, Boss. We go fast." Something had saddened him.

David's heart sank; he didn't want to know what had happened in the camp, but he was certain that it was not good.

"We need saddles," Louis interrupted the exchange. "We can't ride far and hard without saddles."

David sighed, knowing Louis to be right. He was in a quandary; he wanted to leave immediately, but also knew saddles were essential if they were to have any hope of outrunning a search party. Nguni read his mind.

"I go," he said, handing his reigns to David.

"I'll come with you this time. You can't carry three saddles on your own. Louis, wait here!" he demanded.

Louis led the horses to the relative safety of the tree-line while Nguni and David took off at a half walk, half jog, back towards the Boer camp, David allowing Nguni to take the lead. As they approached the tents, Nguni dropped to his haunches and surveyed the area, then, despite his size, bounced forward and sprinted in total silence towards a small cluster of bushes. David kept up with him but feared he could not maintain the same stealth and secrecy as his friend. When Nguni stopped, he was standing by a neat pile of leather saddles, covered by a coarse tarpaulin.

Carefully lifting the protective sheet, the two very gently removed three saddles, desperately trying to ensure that the metal stirrups and buckles didn't clink together and alert the Boers. The rain had just about stopped and the effective cover for any noise that they might make had gone with it. David's fair skin was also very vulnerable to the flashes of lightning, and so, despite the cold and wet, he was flushed with apprehension. He helped Nguni lift two of the saddles on to his shoulders, then picked up one of his own. As David turned to leave, a fork of lightning lit the sky and exposed to his sight, lying on the ground at his feet, a Boer. His throat was slit from ear to ear, the fresh blood washed clean by the rain and leaving a ghastly open gash across his throat.

David gasped in shock, but Nguni, aware that this might happen, calmly and forcefully gripped David's shoulder with a free hand.

"Go," he said softly but firmly in his baritone.

David looked Nguni in the eye, nodded, and stepped over the Boer soldier. Suddenly the tree-line, where Louis stood expectantly with the horses, seemed a thousand miles away. David's heart pounded violently in his chest, and all he could think of was getting to the safety of the horses and mounting up. With the saddles balanced on their shoulders, the two ran awkwardly back to Louis. When they were barely ten yards from the safety of the trees, their luck ran out; a bullet cracked over David's head.

"Run!" David yelled, all need for stealth abandoned in that instant.

As they reached Louis, gasping desperately for oxygen, the crack of passing bullets increased dramatically, some bullets even thudding into the wet ground at their feet. The horses, being accustomed to all the noise and chaos caused by their human owners, waited calmly. This helped David to compose himself.

"Wait," he exclaimed. "Put the saddles on - quickly!" He realised that the Boers wouldn't charge blindly into the dark after them as they didn't know how many of their invaders lay in the tree-line waiting for them to approach. They would, David guessed correctly, fire random volleys in their general direction and then give chase at first light. David's prime urgency now was to get a significant distance between themselves and the Boer soldiers as quickly as possible, and they could only do that with correctly saddled horses.

In very short order the saddles were fitted, buckled up and the horses mounted, while life threatening crackles of flying .303 copper-coated, lead bullets continued to pass all too closely around them. No further instruction needed to be given; as soon as a man was in the saddle, he kicked his horse into action, and thus they bolted to safety. Once over a slight rise, and in a safe zone, David brought the trio to a walk to give the horses a breather, and, more importantly, to check if everyone was alright.

"Anyone hit? Any bleeding?" he panted, adrenaline searing through his veins.

When Nguni and Louis confirmed they were unhurt, he asked them to feel around in the dark to see if there was any blood on the horses. Miraculously they too were unharmed.

"We need to ride through the night, fellows," David sighed, "but at a fast walk. No galloping or the beasts will be exhausted if we need to take evasive action. Nguni, can you lead us to the British camp?"

"Yes Boss," he rumbled, a sly smile on his lips, "we go where the ground is rock."

"Excellent," David took a deep sigh. That would hamper the Boers tracking attempts.

"How far?" Louis spoke between gasps of air; he was shaking from the shock of their encounter.

"By horse, near-near," Nguni chuckled and smiled at David.

David laughed, "Alright Nguni, you lead. *Masihambe!*" He waved ahead letting Nguni proceed before them.

"What's so funny?" Louis asked, confused at the laughter.

" 'Near-near' means anything between now and approximately three days time," David giggled. Nguni looked over his shoulder and smiled knowingly.

Over the next two days, the Boers made significant gains on their quarry, determined to outpace them and exact revenge for the loss of one of their Burghers. It was only because of Nguni's anti-tracking skills that they kept ahead of them, misleading the enemy, laying false clues and deceiving them. Louis, all the while, watched David and Nguni in fascination as they occasionally crouched and studied soils and stone samples, broke twigs and leaves, chuckled at some antic or another, and had a bit of fun in the process.

By mid-afternoon, on the second day, Nguni saw a plume of smoke ahead of them. He nudged Louis heavily with his elbow, pointing to the smoke.

"Near-near," he rumbled and then started to chuckle.

Colonel Plumer's camp was at hand, and they had outsmarted, outrun and survived the Boer hunting party. The three men stopped and looked back in the direction they had come, certain that the Boers were now far behind them. They had laid many anti-tracks but had been surprised at the persistence of the enemy.

"Good job, Nguni," David nodded at his burly friend and smiled. "Now let's go get something to eat; I'm starving."

Colonel Plumer's camp was a pitiful sight to behold. The occasional tent was in shocking order, and the soldiers, although looking alert and well disciplined, had certainly seen better days. There were far fewer than the boys had expected to see. The trio was greeted cautiously at the edge of the east side of camp and escorted to the colonel's tent. Plumer, a very distinguished looking gentleman, with a white manicured moustache that drooped down his jowls, greeted them with smiles and offered them food and water when he saw their tattered clothes. He wanted to laugh when he saw how muddied and matted their hair was, knotted and tangled with bits of straw, grass and twigs. He also noticed how thoroughly streaked with mud and dirt they were, yet their African companion appeared pristinely clean and tidy.

"What the devil have you boys been up to?" he chuckled, eyeing them over while placing an unlit pipe between his lips, drawing on fresh air.

"We have been chased by some Boers out there, sir." David pointed over his shoulder with his thumb, oblivious to his state of presentation. "We out-ran them, but a word of warning, they are a very determined bunch, and sadly we may have led them to your position."

"Never fear," the colonel smiled, "they know exactly where we are; we are expecting them. What brings you this far north?"

"I have a message from Colonel Baden-Powell in Mafeking for you. Also, we are returning to Bulawayo."

"Good Lord!" Plumer exclaimed, a sharp frown creasing his brow. "Well, then, do come in." He ushered David into his tatty tent while Nguni and Louis tended to the horses, getting them much needed water and feed.

Colonel Plumer's tent was sparse: a stretcher with bedding, a chair and a small table lit by a lone candle of which he had melted the base and stuck directly to the desktop.

"Go ahead, lad, spill the beans." Plumer wasted no time in getting to the point.

"Colonel Baden-Powell believes he will run out of provisions before the British forces arrive to relieve Mafeking. The Boers are not allowing food, or anything for that matter, to enter the town, so he believes their strategy is to starve the town into submission. Already we are on rations. One way he believes he can eke out the food provisions is to allow some of the African population to leave; there are about one thousand of them in the village attached to the town. The Boers are not interested in them, only the British. He asks that you stock up on food from Rhodesia because you may have an influx of refugees."

"Good Lord," he muttered, "did he give you a letter for me?"

"No. The colonel felt that if I got caught trying to leave with written instructions from him, the Boers would regard me as a British soldier and capture or execute me. By having nothing on me, they might regard me as a civilian, giving me a chance to go free."

"I see," Plumer seemed lost in thought. "We are frightfully isolated here. The Boers disabled the railway line, and Bulawayo is a good twelve to fourteen days ride away. Furthermore, my troops have been seriously depleted by the Boers, took heavy losses in the first week of the campaign, I'm afraid. Indeed, food would have to come from Bulawayo."

"I am leaving for Bulawayo tomorrow, sir. I could take a message to Rhodesia for you if that helped."

"Indeed, indeed," he murmured. "Good show, that would be splendid, if you don't mind. I'll write you a note to give to the general up there."

"With due respect, Colonel Plumer, I would prefer a verbal message. One never knows where the Boers are likely to crop up."

"Of course, of course," Plumer frowned, picking up his empty pipe and going through the motions of drawing on some tobacco smoke while deep in thought. "You will be safe north and west of here. The Boers seem uninterested in Rhodesia. It seems they have enough headaches of their own down in Ladysmith and Colenso. And Baden-Powell is certainly giving them a hiding in Mafeking, I believe."

"Oh he is, I can confirm that. I actually think he is enjoying the fight," David smiled, catching Plumer's full attention.

"Is that a fact? Well, I'll be damned!" he smiled, and sucked some air through his pipe again.

"Colonel, we have very little on us, basically the shirts on our backs and a blanket. Would it be too much to ask you if we may borrow a jacket and some provisions for the journey?"

"Sadly, I can't offer you any form of clothing. All we have here are our military uniforms, and I certainly cannot give a civilian anything of any military significance. Why, do you know that if a Boer, or any enemy for that matter, wears his adversary's clothing or insignia, concerning the rules of war, that person may be summarily executed? No, no, we can't have that. I cannot put you in that predicament."

"I didn't know that," David admitted.

"The Boers don't have a uniform. You know that the word *'boer'* means 'farmer' in Dutch?"

"Yes, I know that," David smiled, "but if the Boers don't have a uniform, what would that make me as a civilian, also without uniform?"

Plumer thought about that for a moment and pulled on his imaginary tobacco. "Good question, but the Boers are rather distinctive, don't you think? Unruly, unshaven, wild hair, and all that sort of thing?"

"Right now I qualify as a Boer," David grimaced.

Plumer looked down his nose at David and frowned. "Indeed," he reluctantly concurred. "They are also armed, whereas you are not. I shall give you a pass, signed by me, that will identify you as a civilian. And food, yes, certainly I can help you there."

And so it was that at first light, armed with provisions and an official pass identifying the Langbourne brothers as civilians, the three young men pointed their horses to the north and headed for Bulawayo. Two days into the march, David pulled Louis and Nguni to a halt by a thorny, stunted acacia tree and dismounted. A dead log lay on the ground, and David sat on it, waving a hand to his companions to do likewise.

"We will rest for a while. Do you know this place?" David asked Nguni, passing a water container around.

"Yes Boss," he smiled, "It is the place the scorpion touched you."

David smiled sheepishly, "Yes, I call this place Nomandudwane."

Louis suddenly looked at David inquisitively. "This is the place you were telling me about? The Place of the Scorpion?"

"Yes," David said dreamily.

"This is where you want to be buried? There's nothing here for hundreds of miles around, for heaven's sake."

"That's why I am at peace here. This," he gestured with both arms outstretched, "is Africa. Nature at its best, how it should be. Even in a time of violent war, this place is at peace, and untouched by humankind."

Nguni looked at David, very confused. "You wish to die here?"

"No, Nguni. I don't wish to die here, but my soul," David looked into the bush, a very gentle and calm look on his face, "My spirit is at peace here."

Louis looked at the ground in front of him. A small pile of stones lay amongst the brittle grass. "You once said you and Harry left a part of yourselves here. Is that where you buried it?"

David stood up, taking a single stride over to the stones, and to the amazement of Nguni, turned them over carefully. A scorpion scurried out from beneath, causing David to jump back in fright, and making the others scramble off their seat on the log very smartly.

David laughed. "Well, I didn't expect that! It truly is the Place of the Scorpion."

Once David had ushered the scorpion out of harm's way with a dry twig, he continued removing the stones, exposing the old coins and bits of leather that he, on two occasions, and Harry only once, had hidden. Louis asked to add a piece of his clothing to the collection, which David agreed to do with mock ceremony, but Nguni politely declined.

"My spirit belongs in my ancestral village," Nguni announced, "but your spirits can stay where they are happy."

"You have two homes, Nguni," David looked confused, "one near Port Elizabeth, and one in Rhodesia, the one that you and Daluxolo made by the wagons. Where will your spirit rest?"

"Our ancestral home is in my village near Port Elizabeth," Nguni rumbled, and then sighed. "My brother and me," he pronounced in isiXhosa, "we have decided our job in Rhodesia is finished. Once we harvest our crops, we shall return to our homes. *Sizakugoduka.*"

David smiled sincerely at the large man. "That will be good," he replied in Nguni's language. "When you return to Port Elizabeth you must see Mrs Du Plessis, where our factory was. Morris and I have arranged for her to buy you fourteen oxen, and for Daluxolo, also fourteen oxen."

"Why?" Nguni asked, bewildered.

"My brothers and I wish to thank you and Daluxolo for protecting our wagons when they became lost. We know that European gold and silver is not important to you, but cattle are. Also, you and your brother must select the best oxen available at the time. Only the best," David reiterated.

Nguni stared silently at David, then reluctantly nodded his thanks. He spoke no words; everything that could be communicated was done through eye contact. David simply smiled as he understood that all was in order.

David was delighted that they had come upon Nomandudwane, as something told him it would be the last time he would visit this place. Five days later they reached the Limpopo River, and to David's mild amusement, the old wooden crate which he had used as a chair and had left on the south bank was still there. The Limpopo was flowing. It was the first time David had seen the rapid currents of the river, and, wary of crocodiles, the boys took the time to have a thorough wash in the fresh waters.

David and Nguni knew it would be only one more week before they arrived in Bulawayo, and for David, the arms of Hanna. After spending an uneventful night in the soft, cool sand of the south bank of the Limpopo River, the three men rolled up their blankets and mounted their horses.

"Shall we?" David smiled at Nguni, then stared across the river at Rhodesia's border.

Nguni grinned and waved his hand to the north, giving David the lead. *"Masihambe!"* he shouted in glee.

Chapter Twelve

London 1900

Morris bounded up the stairs to his new accommodation and arrived at the solid door slightly out of breath. It had been given several coats of paint in its time, the final finish being a glossy black making the brass numerals, lock and door handle stand out regally, the effect of which he rather liked.

Fumbling with the key, Morris entered his new home and closed the door behind him, taking in the hallway with a critical eye and then moving into the cavernous interior. His footfalls echoed slightly off the bare walls as his imagination ran riot with what he would, or could, do to make his home very comfortable with a luxuriousness he had never dreamed possible. Morris had arranged for Rose Bertha and Mrs Friedman to arrive at 8 o'clock so that he could explain to Rose Bertha what his expectations would be. Little did he know, then, that it would be Rose, rather, who would tell him what to do.

At precisely 8 o'clock a gentle knock was heard at the door, and the mother-and-daughter team greeted Morris, all smiles and filled with excitement at the prospect of throwing their artistic flair at a blank canvas, with a generous budget. As Morris walked about, gesticulating where he would like his desk or office, and which bedroom would be his, indicating sizes with his outstretched arms, or pointing a finger at a spot on the wall, the two ladies would occasionally steal a glance at each other with a wry smile and a wink. These secret exchanges went unnoticed by Morris, but when he finally felt he had covered all his requirements, Rose Bertha took over, going back to the lounge and reiterating what was discussed. She added in other options, indicating a bigger desk, repositioning it; the rejection of one of the four comfortable chairs Morris wanted, suggesting a more significant rug, and so on.

Although Morris hesitantly agreed with one or two of the suggestions, he disagreed with most of both Mrs Friedman and Rose Bertha's ideas and began to get very flustered. He was regretting asking Rose Bertha to help him and was frustrated with her mother's attendance and her almost intentional counter-suggestions to virtually everything that was discussed. Rose Bertha noticed Morris' mood change, including the colour of his flushed face, and tactfully gave her mother a stern look.

"I feel a lot has been covered," Mrs Friedman changed tack suddenly, understanding the look in her daughters' eye, and casually walking towards the hall. "Perhaps we should take a break now. Morris, I know you are a busy man and have work to do at your warehouse, and goodness me! I do so need a cup of tea. Perhaps we should meet again tomorrow and continue our discussions."

"Yes," Morris said bluntly, glaring at Rose Bertha, "I have a meeting to attend. Let's meet again tomorrow morning at 8 o'clock sharp."

"Splendid," Mrs Friedman chirped happily and winked at her daughter as Morris strode towards the door.

Morris didn't have a meeting to get to. There was very little he could achieve until he knew that his shipments were safe, and only then could he gauge sales in Bulawayo before he could decide if he needed to re-stock. He was at a loss, and became immensely frustrated. Having two women suddenly thrust upon him deciding what he should do, and not what he wanted to do, was quite exasperating. He let the ladies out, locking the door behind him, and walked down the four flights of stairs, a cloud of anguish floating ominously above his silent figure. Once on the pavement, he bid the ladies farewell and forced out a thanks.

"Oh, Morris?" Mrs Friedman almost sang as she caught him on his heel about to head off in the opposite direction, "I may come back this afternoon to measure up for your drapes. Would you mind if I have a key to get in?"

Morris grumbled to himself momentarily and then fumbled in his trouser pocket. "Here, look after it; it's the only one I have," he instructed ungraciously.

Mrs Friedman took the key and thanked him kindly as they parted company.

"Mother," Rose Bertha looked up at her with a frown, "he is quite a grumpy character. How will we ever decorate his apartment when he gets into a mood at the slightest disagreement?"

"Never fear, my little Rose," she smiled gently, "he is just like your father. I know how to deal with boys like him."

"Well I don't," Rose Bertha mumbled. "How are you going to handle him?"

"Simple. We send Morris out of town for a week or so, and while he is away, we get everything done. When the boy gets back, he will be over the moon."

"Mother! How on earth are you going to send him out of town?"

"Your father is going to Paris tomorrow for ten days. I'll get him to take Morris with him. You've seen how well those two get along, and I'm sure Morris would love to socialise with like-minded businessmen on the Continent. In any event, I have a key to his apartment," she grinned mockingly, holding the metal key lightly between two fingers.

Rose Bertha started to giggle. "Mother, you *are* naughty."

Mrs Friedman smiled back, "I do need that cup of tea, mind you. That boy can be awfully stressful."

Persuading her husband to take Morris on his trip to Paris the following day was simple enough. In fact, he delighted in the idea and Morris, who was bored out of his wits, leapt at the formal invitation that was delivered to him by hand later that afternoon. Not only would this trip provide him with unexpected options to increase his supplier base, but it would give him the commercial stimulation and business networking that he so desperately needed.

At the crack of dawn the following morning, Morris was standing side by side with Mr Friedman on the platform at Marylebone Station. Tote bag in hand, and wearing his pure wool overcoat and Derby hat, he was looking dapper and quite the expectant traveller, smiling profusely, the frustrations of the previous day all but forgotten.

"I have arranged that we will stay with an old friend of mine," Mr Friedman announced as they were about to board the train, "Monsieur

Follot. You will enjoy his company. He has a son about your age."

"I look forward to it, Mr Friedman. Thank you for including me on your trip." Morris was very grateful for the experience.

"Don't mention it, young man. There will be days that I leave you to your own devices, but there will be days that I will ask you to join me for meals with some of my colleagues. I do believe you will get quite a thrill out of the people you meet."

It took two days to finally arrive in Paris, employing a combination of trains, ferry and coach. As they neared their destination, Morris was struck by a massive iron latticework structure that soared high above the approaching city.

"What is that?" Morris asked his host in awe, unable to take his eyes off it.

"Ahh… That is the Tower of Eiffel. It is by far the tallest man-made structure this world has ever seen. Impressive, isn't it?"

"What's it for?"

"It was completed about ten years ago to showcase the Paris Universal Exposition in 1889. These expositions are basically international trade exhibits that showcase a country's industrial achievements."

"Well, I'll be…" Morris marvelled, "what a splendid idea. I wonder who thought of this?"

"Actually, it was Prince Albert, husband of Queen Victoria, who championed the idea back in the 1850s."

"When's the next exposition? I'd like to attend it," Morris quickly looked at Mr Friedman in anticipation.

"I think the next one will be in Glasgow, Scotland, in… 1901, I believe. You'll have to wait another two years I'm afraid."

Morris' heart sank; two years seemed an eternity for his overactive ambitions. "I suppose I have no choice but to wait," he sighed, causing Mr Friedman to smile inwardly.

Paris was truly exquisite at the end of the 19th Century, and Morris instantly fell in love with the city. Tradesmen and women plied their wares on the pavements selling all manner of goods, including a variety of food and snacks. A beautiful river graced the centre of the town, as did a curious thing he noticed immediately: the abundance of artists, mostly men in bérets sporting copious moustaches, sitting on stools along the banks and attentively scrutinising their canvasses perched precariously on three-legged easels. Fine art was indeed sold everywhere - in shop windows and from street-side carts.

Most of the women dressed impeccably, the fashion was delightful, and Morris couldn't stop admiring the womenfolk. They used makeup to subtly enhance their features, walked with pride and elegance, and wore the most magnificent jewellery. A tall lady, delicately holding an intricate parasol, smiled at Morris as she passed him, her liquid eyes speaking volumes into his. His heart skipped a beat, and a strange feeling rushed through his stomach. Morris couldn't help but beam back, childishly and lovingly, and as her fragrance gently caught him when she silently slid past him, his senses soared to a new and unknown level.

For the first time in his life, the femininity and sexuality of a woman became noticeable to him. He turned to look back at the beautiful woman, and, as he did so, she gracefully turned and locked eyes with him momentarily, flashing him a seductive wink. She smiled coyly, then continued on her way without missing a beat, never to be seen again, but forever remembered in Morris' thoroughly confused mind.

While Morris was still in this befuddled state, Mr Friedman led Morris to a six-story apartment in the centre of Paris and trudged up to the 5th floor, where he was introduced to a portly and welcoming Monsieur Follot. His wife, Madame Follot, was rather thin, making the couple seem a little mismatched. Like many of the ladies at street level, Madame Follot was certainly beautiful, wearing an elegant, and unmistakably expensive outfit. Her jewellery was overly ostentatious and her fragrance magnificent. Morris was utterly distracted; even her accent was captivating. He made a concerted effort to pull himself together and keep his eyes trained on Monsieur Follot and Mr Friedman. They all spoke in French, so, not understanding the conversation, Morris cast his eye over the luxurious apartment.

To his further amazement, the walls of the apartment were painted with the most intricate repetitive design of pale burgundy lines and shapes, and in amongst the patterns were subtle depictions of bunches of grapes. The conversations between his three hosts drifted into an indiscernible mumble as Morris walked slowly over to the wall and gently touched the designs with his index finger, a deep frown etched across his brow. He had never seen a wall painted with such a decoration, let alone in such fine detail. Morris noticed that the conversation behind him had stopped and silence enveloped the room. He looked over his shoulder; the three adults were staring at him, perplexed.

Morris cleared his throat, "I have never seen a wall painted like this. It is beautiful."

"It is not painted, Morris," Mr Friedman beamed, "it is printed wallpaper."

"Paper?" Morris exclaimed, turning to admire the designs again, and using a fingernail to gently scratch at the surface, just to check that it wasn't plaster.

"That is my forté, Monsieur Langbourne," Monsieur Follot smiled, "It is my, how you say... my business."

"Your business?"

"My... indus-rie," he tried to find the English word, throwing an expressive hand in the air, smiling at his accomplishment.

"Monsieur Follot designs and manufactures wallpaper, Morris," Friedman continued. "He has a very productive factory near here. They print designs on rolls of paper that are glued to the walls of a room. It finishes off a room very elegantly, don't you think?"

"Do you have different designs and colours?" Morris was intrigued.

"*Oui, oui, Monsieur!*" Follot exclaimed, "*quarante-deux*, err... forty-two combinations of colour and design. Thirty-two designed by me, and ten by my son, Paul."

"I can see a great use for this in Rhodesia," Morris mumbled as he returned his attention to the wall. "May I visit your factory Monsieur Follot? I believe I might like to purchase a quantity of your wallpaper."

"*Oui, oui*, of course. But now, we eat."

Paris, for Morris, was an experience on a grand scale. He discovered new and exciting industries and cultures: perfumeries, cosmetics, art, decor, fashion - the list went on and on. He met with numerous businessman and industrialists and made a new friend in Monsieur Follot's son, Paul. A tall and handsome man of his own age, Paul was artistic, studying sculpture, art and jewellery design. He had porcelain skin and flowing black hair. Dressing immaculately, as most young Parisians seemed to, Morris noticed that Paul caught the attention of many younger women. He also ascertained, with some frustration, that he had a fair way to go to bring himself up to Paul's level of couture. One afternoon, as they walked along the banks of the River Seine, Morris asked

Paul to take him to a store that sold French aftershave lotions with a particularly agreeable fragrance. Paul willingly obliged and took him to a large departmental store called Le Bon Marche, where he personally knew the manager, Monsieur Andre Hersh, a good friend of his father.

When Morris walked into the shop, he was flabbergasted, not only at the sheer size of the building but also at the vast array of products they sold. Staff and customers thronged the warehouse; business was incredibly brisk. Paul made some suggestions for Morris and he soon made a purchase. They then went to the top floor to see if they could find Monsieur Hersh.

After a very congenial meeting with the manager, punctuated by broken English with Paul filling in the gaps, Monsieur Hersh took a liking to Morris and his keen interest in the business along with his intelligent questions. He immediately offered to show Morris around the building and demonstrate the retail systems. Along the way, Morris was introduced to other departmental heads and made to feel important.

"I have never seen an operation of this magnitude," Morris admitted as they were about to depart. "I am somewhat amazed at how popular your business is."

"Many years ago our owner, Monsieur Aristide Boucicaut, decided to change our philosophy, putting our customers first and foremost," Hersh smiled and waved his arm at the hundreds of patrons milling about the store. "Boucicaut put tickets on the goods, thereby fixing the price and alleviating the need for our customers to haggle and negotiate a price. We made it easy for them to purchase from us. He created a library on the first floor where the husbands could sit quietly and enjoy a book or a newspaper while their wives shopped to their heart's content. If the wives brought their children a play area was made available for the youngsters; we continue to look after our customers in the best way we can.

"Boucicaut was the first man in France, and probably the world, to allow returns, refunds or exchanges. We look after our staff; we pay fair wages and employees who are single women are accommodated safely on the top floor of the building. Content staff make for a better shopping experience for the public. We advertise regularly, and even give out printed catalogues of our latest goods, with prices included, which keep our customers constantly informed about our products."

Morris was truly impressed. "I admire what has been achieved here, sir."

"You have a retail store in Africa, do you not? Perhaps one day you will expand to this level?" Hersh chuckled.

"I doubt it," Morris shook his head as he cast an eye over the magnitude of the business once again. "I have come to realise that my retail outlet in Bulawayo is not that profitable. You need displays, merchandising and lots of staff. Rent for retail space is costly. No, I prefer to be a wholesaler. Expenses are far less, and my wholesale side is much more profitable; we deal mostly with business owners, and not so much the general public. I would prefer you as my customer," Morris nodded at Hersh, "rather than the public."

"Perhaps we will one day be a customer, Monsieur Langbourne," Hersh smiled and shook Morris' hand.

"Perhaps," Morris returned the gesture with a sly grin.

The ten days in Paris gave Morris a new insight into commerce, industry, people and cultures. He returned to London a more mature man, filled with ideas, ambitions and a new and curious interest in the opposite sex.

"So, what did you take away from that?" Friedman asked Morris on the last leg of the train ride.

"A great deal, Mr Friedman." Morris frowned in concentration. "The French seem very passionate about what they do, and I can't believe how well they dress and groom themselves."

"Indeed, they are the world leaders in fashion, you know. I take my wife and Rose Bertha to Paris twice a year so that they can couture a new wardrobe."

Morris snapped a horrified look at him. "Truly, they only buy their clothes in Paris?"

Friedman shook his head slightly but smiled as he sank further into his seat. "Yes, expensive tastes my girls have."

Morris parted company with the older man at Marylebone Station, thanking him profusely for affording him such a valuable experience and including him in Monsieur Follot's hospitality.

It was only when he walked into his warehouse with the pockmarked bare concrete floor and dank walls that reality returned with a vengeance. Suddenly he didn't like London anymore, and a wave of loneliness washed over him. For a moment Morris seriously considered moving to

Paris, with its exciting atmosphere and well-dressed population. He locked the door and trudged to the back of the warehouse, dumping his tote bag unceremoniously on the ground and stared, mournfully, at his thin and lumpy mattress. For the first time in ten days, he suddenly remembered his brothers and the conditions they were living in.

"Things have to change," he muttered, "and the sooner, the better."

Chapter Thirteen

Rhodesia 1900

The trip from the Limpopo River to Bulawayo was much more relaxed than the last time David had traversed it. They followed the railway line, and along the way they came upon small settlements - previously forts, but now railway stations with water for the steam engines. Inhabited only by a handful of hardened men, there was very little reason to stay in these settlements, except to sleep under a rusted iron roof.

After two days on the march, Nguni broke away to reconnect with Daluxolo to the west, to harvest their crops and make ready to abandon their temporary village. Such partings were always emotionally hard for David, but the two friends planned to meet again when David was next in Port Elizabeth. David would have abandoned his horse for the luxury, speed and safety of a train, but as the Boers had disabled the line near Mafeking there was no point in running a service south of Bulawayo, so, reluctantly, the Langbourne brothers pushed on by horse.

Apart from a close call with a huge elephant bull, that was obviously frustrated with everything and everyone, the journey was quite uneventful. As was usually the case after a long stint in the wilderness the boys smelt civilisation long before they saw it.

"What do you smell?" David tested his brother.

"Coal? Smoke from a fire."

"Yes, me too. When I first rode into Bulawayo with Morris, I could smell fried onions."

"Thanks a lot!" Louis exclaimed. "Have you any idea how hungry I am? I'm about to fold in half from starvation, and now you remind me of fried onions."

David laughed; he had to admit he was ravenous himself. "Before nightfall, we should be there."

"I'm going to have a double-sized portion of steak at the Charter when we get there."

"If they are still open by the time we arrive," David teased.

As they passed through the residential area called Suburbs, David was tempted to call in on the Rubinstein residence and surprise Hanna, but his personal appearance and state of hygiene was less than acceptable and may have had an effect opposite to that which he was hoping for. With great willpower, he pulled gently on his reins and led his horse towards the centre of Bulawayo. The brothers stopped at a stable yard and handed their horses into the care of the owner before walking the rest of the way to Langbourne Brothers on Abercorn Street. They tactfully decided to enter the warehouse through the back door and found Harry in the office pouring frantically over a pile of papers.

Harry stopped dead still when he saw his brothers come through the door and stared with wild, disbelieving eyes.

"Greetings Brother," Louis broke the awkward silence.

"Good Lord!" Harry exclaimed in horror. "Just look at you."

"You've seen me with a beard." David scratched at his unruly growth feeling somewhat self-conscious.

"You, yes, but not him," he nodded at Louis, "nor have I seen you two so thin and emaciated."

"We are hungry, I'll confess to that." David announced.

Harry suddenly burst out laughing. "You look ridiculous, Louis. And look at your hair! When last did you two have a haircut?" He stood up and rounded his desk to shake their hands in welcome.

"About four months ago? I don't care what I look like," Louis objected painfully, "but I'm going to the Charter Hotel for supper forthwith."

"Oh no, you are not!" Harry spoke with authority. "There is no way on earth you two will be seen around town like this. We Langbournes have a reputation to uphold, for heaven's sake."

Harry was serious about their status in the community, and the brothers were left in no doubt about that. Despite being the youngest brother he was acting like their late mother, and both Louis and David were somewhat taken aback by his outburst. He took them by the shoulders and marched them straight out the door. There was a small bar of blue and white mottled soap on the concrete wash hand basin in the courtyard which he picked up and thrust into Louis' hand.

"Besides," he continued, "you two smell to high heaven, and you are stinking out the warehouse. No hotel in Bulawayo would ever let you in. Now get cleaned up, put on some smart clothes and then go down to Sharon's dress shop and have a haircut. Good Lord!" Harry threw his hands in the air in disgust as he stormed back into the warehouse and slammed the door behind him.

David and Louis stood in the relative silence and stared at each other in disbelief. They realised they must have been quite repulsive to have elicited that reaction from their brother.

"Well," David shrugged, "just as well we didn't call past Hanna's on the way in."

The laughter from this gentle comic relief completely took their minds off their hunger as the boys stripped off, splashed, lathered up and washed weeks, if not months of dirt and mud from their bodies and hair. Harry was the main object of their hilarity. Once they had finally removed the last of the grime from the pores of their skin, they realised that they had no towel to dry off. Giggling foolishly, they stood naked at the back door and knocked politely. Harry's stern glare when he opened the door did not last a second; seeing his two bedraggled brothers standing naked, dripping wet and smiling coyly, he burst out laughing, slapping his thighs and doubling over in glee.

Clean, dried and changed into business suits, the boys still looked awkward with their wild beards and woolly hair, but Sharon Alhadef made short work of their bedraggled locks and whiskers, and the boys soon looked like respectable businessmen again.

"You two go down to the Charter and order a meal," David instructed to his brothers. "Order whatever you are having for me too, Louis. I have to do something first."

"Going to see Hanna?" Louis enquired behind a grin.

"Err... No, I'll go after I've had something to eat. I have to see Major Seward and pass on to him some messages from Colonel Plumer. I think that's pretty important right now."

"Fair enough," Louis nodded, "but I'm starting without you."

The boys parted company and David hurried to the British South Africa Police camp, which was now located on the west side of town. Once there, he asked for Major David Seward. After a bit of running around and asking for directions, he finally found the correct office and asked the orderly for an urgent meeting with the officer. Seward heard the orderly mention his name as he stuck his head in the door, and David immediately caught the sound of a chair scrape the ground as the major leapt to his feet to personally usher him in.

"Good grief, good grief!" he almost shouted, even before he exited his office, "I can't believe you are here. Look at you; I've seen skeletons fatter than you. I heard you were caught up in Mafeking."

"I escaped," David said calmly over a vigorous handshake.

"You're probably the first insider to escape. How did you do it?" Seward shook his head in awe, guiding David into his office and pulling out a chair for him.

"It wasn't too difficult; I had help."

"What's it like in there? I hear it's hell on earth, but I also hear Colonel Baden-Powell is doing a sterling job defending the town. He's all over the news here and in London."

"It's a long story, Major Seward. Perhaps tomorrow we can meet up, and I'll tell you all about it, but for now, I have an urgent message for you from Colonel Plumer which I need you to pass on to the right person."

"You ran into Plumer?" Seward raised an eyebrow.

"Yes, Colonel Baden-Powell gave me a message to give to him if I made it out of the siege. Now Colonel Plumer has a message for you."

"Go ahead," Seward retrieved a notepad and a pencil from his desk.

"You won't need that, sir. It's pretty simple actually. Colonel Plumer needs food, urgently. Lots of food, and medicine. The Boers are starving Mafeking into submission, and sadly Baden-Powell is running low on provisions. He is talking about starting to eat horse flesh. Already they are collecting locusts, drying them out and mixing them into stocks of flour to make the bread go further."

"Good gracious!" Seward exclaimed in horror. "I didn't realise it was that bad."

"He is also going to ask the African population, about one thousand of them, to leave Mafeking because he simply can't feed them all. The Boers will let them leave as they claim this is a white mans war and they have no problem with the African population. Baden-Powell will be sending them to Plumer for protection, but Plumer needs food. Everything is either blocked or controlled by the Boers south of him, but he can receive food from Rhodesia."

"Yes, indeed. Right-o, I'll get on to that immediately."

"And talking of food, I haven't had a wholesome meal in almost three months, and I have a large juicy steak waiting for me down at the Charter, so if you would be so kind as to excuse me…"

"Of course," Seward interrupted him with a broad smile, "I quite understand, however I think you will find the steaks at the Charter less than juicy; boot leather comes to mind. Regardless, tomorrow, please, do come and see me. There is much we need to discuss." He stood and ushered David to the door.

"Oh!" David suddenly remembered something. "I would assume you will have a dispatch going to Colonel Plumer shortly?"

"Yes, indeed," Seward confirmed, "you want to send him something?"

"May I?" David asked, but he knew the answer already. "Could I borrow a pen and a piece of paper, please?"

Seward handed David a fountain pen and a clean sheet of paper, upon which he wrote 'The Wolf' near the top. In the middle, he carefully drew a circle, followed by a prominent dot in the centre. At the bottom of the page he wrote 'Shaya'nyoni', the nickname a Ndebele warrior gave David, thanks to a most unceremonious argument he once had with an ostrich.

"What in heaven's name does that mean?" Seward asked, perplexed.

"If Plumer gets this, he will know it needs to go to Colonel Baden-Powell. They call him 'The Wolf' down there. Baden Powell will understand the rest." David grinned knowingly as he folded the sheet of paper and handed it to Seward.

Having delivered his messages, David made his way directly to the Charter Hotel and sat down with his brothers, indulging in the first square meal he had had in several months. Yet David was impatient; he needed to satisfy his hunger, especially with all the savoury fragrances wafting from the kitchen, but he also felt an urgent need to visit Hanna - not only because he so longed to see her, but also because he needed her to know he was alive and well. Besides these personal concerns, David wanted a quick update on the state of their business from Harry.

"Louis was telling me what it was like in Mafeking," Harry leaned back casually in his chair, crossing his legs under the table.

"Mmm…" David responded as he savoured the delicious piece of sirloin in his mouth.

"Nasty stuff. I was very relieved to get your message," Harry added to allow David time to enjoy the mouthful and swallow.

"Morris?" David questioned, shooting a quick look at his brother.

"Arrangements made for someone in Cape Town and East London to secure the shipments."

"Good. Sales?"

"Strong, but stock getting low. Shortages are starting to bite everywhere."

"I expected that. Wagons?" David threw sharp single-worded questions at Harry, a trait they had developed in their hectic business life. Harry would always respond with the absolute basics; the brothers preferred and understood this abbreviated form of communication that they had developed between themselves.

"Going exceedingly well. Prices everywhere rocketing, so the traders are happy."

"Cash flow?"

"Good. Physical money is becoming a problem. Nothing is coming up from South Africa. But the new Administrator of Matabeleland, a chap called Hugh Marshall-Hole, has found a solution. He has printed special cards upon which he has stuck small denomination stamps, and then signed them making it legal tender. They call it the Marshall-Hole Currency, and it's supposed to last until the Boer War is over."

"Marshall-Hole?" Louis spoke with his mouth full. "What kind of name is that?"

"Yes, well," Harry shrugged, "I have a drawer full of these cards now, and they are pretty useless to us until the situation normalises. I can't see Morris paying for goods in Hong Kong with Marshall-Hole stamps. They might be valuable one day as a collectors item, but right now they are quite useless to us as foreign exchange."

David chuckled, "True. Daily sales?" The questions continued.

"About £300."

David stopped chewing, "£300 per day?" he repeated, swallowing hard.

"Between both stores," Harry smiled.

"Blimey," David retorted and continued eating, casting a quick glance at Louis and raising an eyebrow. Louis returned the gesture.

And so the rapid question and answer session continued, leaving both David and Louis confounded at the rapid increase in trade and the unprecedented increases in basic prices that had occurred in the mere three months they had been held captive in Mafeking.

"That's what wars will do, I suppose," Harry concluded, "but what is most frustrating is the shortage of money. It is the same thing that happened in the Matabele rebellion. There are people in the community who are actually selling their cash for an extra 10% of the value of the money."

It didn't take long for patrons to recognise David and Louis, and they soon surrounded the boys, which effectively ended their business meeting. Their unexpected companions started asking questions about Mafeking and the siege. Trying to talk through mouthfuls of food, the brothers made no effort to stop eating but did try to be accommodating in answering the incessant queries as best they could.

"Gentlemen," Harry finally stood up slowly with his hands raised slightly over his head, "my brothers have not eaten well in a long time. Please show some respect and let them finish their meal. May I suggest that we reconvene here tomorrow evening after they have rested? David and Louis will answer all your questions over a social beer or two."

"Bravo," a distinguished man responded, which was followed by a low rumble of mixed agreements and apologies from the others as they politely dispersed.

David winked at Harry. "Thanks, Brother," he mumbled as he shovelled another fork-load of steak into his mouth.

When they had finished their meal Louis ordered dessert, but David abstained; he was beginning to feel slightly queasy, he wanted to see Hanna, and it was starting to get dark.

"I'm off, fellows," David dabbed his lips with the white linen serviette.

"Off you go," Harry said sternly. "We'll talk in the morning."

David stood to leave and quickly looked Harry in the eye. He wanted to say thanks, thanks for understanding, for taking firm control of the family and business, and for his necessary authority in dealing with his elders, but, instead, he gave a very slight nod. Harry cocked his head very gently with a barely discernible smile at the corner of his lips; Harry had read the message, and David knew it. As it was between him and Morris, from that day on David knew he could communicate with Harry with just a look, a gesture or a faint click of the tongue. Harry had matured so fast that David found it quite intriguing. He made a mental note to tell Morris that he had chosen the right man for the Bulawayo side of the business.

He pushed his chair in and silently slipped out the door.

Chapter Fourteen

London 1900

Morris didn't sleep well that night. After ten days in what seemed to be the most luxurious bed in Paris, his thin, lumpy mattress on a concrete floor did him no favours. He awoke in a very unpleasant mood, and he knew it. Rolling onto all fours before standing, he stretched his back and neck, and then set about getting ready to face the day. The thought of the renovations and liveability of his proper accommodation being delayed another week because of his absence caused his mood to sink further.

As if by way of callous indifference, the day was equally gloomy, damp and cold. Locking the storeroom door behind him, he wandered the streets looking for a roadside stall that would sell him a cup of tea or coffee, and perhaps an egg on toast. He managed to find a dingy cafe not far off, but the sight of their unappetising fried eggs in the grease-streaked warming compartment was enough to make him decide to forgo his hunger. Instead, he headed to the only place he could think of: the Goldberg residence.

It was only about 7 o'clock, too early for him to knock on their door and invite himself in, so Morris meandered about the various streets in the suburb for almost an hour before returning to Yoni's home. Embarrassed to simply advertise his presence, Morris stood outside, hoping to catch Yoni as he commenced his short walk to his office. As he had anticipated, just a few minutes before eight o'clock, Mr Goldberg emerged from his front door and immediately saw Morris standing on the opposite side of the road.

"Are you back, Morris?" He excitedly crossed the street to greet him.

Morris walked over and shook his hand warmly. "Yes. It was a most incredible experience, Mr Goldberg. Paris is an amazing city."

"Yes, indeed it is," Yoni smiled, and took Morris by the shoulder. "Walk with me and tell me all about it."

"I've made some valuable connections. Have you ever heard of wallpaper?"

"Of course, becoming very fashionable these days. By the way," Yoni changed the subject excitedly, "your cargo in Cape Town and East London have been found and secured."

"Thank the good Lord!" Morris exclaimed loudly but immediately checked himself, half expecting residents on the upper floors to lean out the windows and reprimand him for disturbing the peace.

"You have to pay demurrage, which is expensive, so I was going to ask my friend to find a commercial warehouse for you until this war is over."

Morris thought about this and tried to figure out if there was a cheaper option. He had no idea how long this Boer War, as they were now calling it in London, would go on for. He was annoyed at himself for not thinking about demurrage costs; he was well aware that shippers would charge heavily if goods were not cleared from their warehouses, but argued that surely they would make concessions in the event of a war.

"Sadly not," Yoni shrugged, "business is business, war or not."

Morris suddenly looked up at Yoni. "I have an idea. I know someone in Port Elizabeth who lives in a house all on her own. I would far rather pay her to look after my goods than some commercial warehouse, and I'm sure she would appreciate the income. I will make some enquiries through my bank manager in Port Elizabeth, and see if she will do this for me."

Yoni's brow furrowed, "I can't fault that idea, Morris, but going by the manifests you showed me there is enough stock to fill two houses."

"I am sure it will work," Morris dismissed the concern. "Excuse me Mr Goldberg; I need to get to the post office and send an urgent telegram."

"Certainly, but do let me know your decision. Also, please call past your apartment. Mrs Friedman and Rose Bertha will be there at ten o'clock I believe."

"Most certainly," Morris called over his shoulder as he quickly strode off, headed for the Post Office.

His telegram to Jack Shiel at the Standard Bank in Port Elizabeth was simple enough. Morris asked him if he would talk to Sonja Du Plessis, his former landlady, and negotiate a monthly price to store enough goods to virtually fill her home from floor to ceiling. Satisfied that he had shortened his words to the absolute minimum and getting directly to the point, he paid the postmaster and sent the telegram on its way. Riding on a wave of excitement his mood lifted, but only slightly, so he treated himself to a light breakfast at a guesthouse across the road from the Post Office. He still had time to spare after the meal, but ten o'clock arrived at last, and he walked over to his flat on Finsbury Pavement. He was hoping beyond hope that his discussions with the Friedman ladies would be a great deal more successful than they had been during their first encounter.

Morris even began to consider how he would dismiss their services if they didn't agree with his stipulations. By the time he reached the building and started his trudge up the staircase, he was ready to dismiss them before they even commenced work. He patted his pocket for his key and realised that the women had it, his sense of frustration mounting all the more.

Although the door was closed and locked when he arrived, he could hear the two women inside chatting idly. He knocked and then waved a dismissive hand at the door, mumbling with frustration that he had to wait for someone else to give him access to his own home. He was, by now, in a very cantankerous mood.

"Morris!" Mrs Friedman sang out joyfully as she swung the door open, "welcome back."

"Thank you," Morris grumbled, but he was not looking at her. His gaze swept past her to a narrow writing desk standing on one side of the hallway. Upon it was a vase with a simple flower arrangement. The mirror attached to the wall above was showcased in an elaborate gold frame. The opposite wall sported a wooden plaque with three large hooks upon which to hang hats, overcoats or umbrellas. A luxurious rug, mostly burgundy with depictions of flowers embroidered into the weave, finished off the hallway.

For a brief moment, Morris thought he was on the wrong floor, and cast a quick glance at the numerals on the door.

"This is nice," Morris lied, because he secretly thought it was magnificent.

"Hello Morris," Rose Bertha murmured as she peeked around the corner.

"Oh, hello," Morris greeted her, looking perplexed as he stepped through the door. "This looks nice," he repeated as he ran his palm over the writing desk, feeling the texture of the wood.

"Come in and see what else we have done," Rose Bertha invited.

"Where did you get this?" Morris asked Mrs Friedman, ignoring Rose Bertha. He did not intend to be rude; it was just that his mind was totally occupied by the table.

"At a bric-a-brac store around the corner. It cost only £3/6d," she replied in her usual airy, flowery way.

Morris cocked his head in surprise. "Huh," he commented, not taking his eyes off the carpentry. "My apologies, Rose Bertha, you were saying?"

Rose Bertha smiled lightly and shrugged off the initial rudeness of Morris' entrance. "Come in, and I'll show you what else we have done. I hope you like it."

The moment Morris walked into the lounge he saw his apartment open up into the most magnificent home he had ever hoped to own. He was rendered speechless; a modest collection of rich wooden furniture was strategically placed around the rooms, carpets lay on the floor, genteel pictures hung on the walls, ornaments and exotic statuettes stood on side tables; there were no echoes of footfalls and voices bouncing around the room. A vase filled with brightly coloured flowers even graced the mantelpiece.

"You did all this? While I was away? How…?" he trailed off.

"Do you like it?" Rose Bertha asked apprehensively, but she already knew the answer.

"How much did this all cost?" Morris was suddenly suspicious.

"Do you like what Rose Bertha has done, Morris?" Mrs Friedman asked more forcefully, demanding his attention.

"Yes, yes, of course! This is incredible," Morris assured her. "I thought I was in some other person's apartment. I can't believe what I am looking at."

Morris was honestly impressed, and when Rose handed him a pile of handwritten receipts and told him the final tally, Morris stared at her in disbelief; the cost was well below the budget he had given her. Not believing Rose Bertha, he quickly flicked through the receipts, and, with his unusual gift for numbers, mentally added up not only the total prices but the cost of each item.

As the ladies walked him through his new home, he marvelled at Rose Bertha's ability to turn a bare and empty flat into a luxurious, high-class establishment at such little cost, and so quickly. The fact that they bought second hand and slightly damaged furniture did not worry Morris in the slightest. In fact, it made his new home look as if he had lived there for a long time. When they got to his bedroom, however, there was no bed in place.

"We didn't buy you a bed, Morris, because you told us you already have one at your warehouse," Mrs Friedman announced. "We can arrange for a transport company to collect it tomorrow and bring it up here."

"Oh, no, please don't worry. That will not be necessary." Morris was suddenly uncomfortable. He desperately searched for a reasonable excuse to prevent anyone from ever seeing his mattress again. "I err... I agreed to sell it to one of my suppliers once this apartment was ready, so, yes, we will have to buy a brand new bed," Morris grinned sheepishly. "We may as well organise an immediate purchase. Something warm and comfortable. I had a bed in Paris that was heavenly."

Mrs Friedman flashed a wink at her daughter as Morris took in the dimensions of the bedroom.

"What about linen, Morris? Sheets, pillows, blankets? Do you still have those?"

"No, no, I'll need all of that too," he advised her nonchalantly, pacing from one wall to another. "We may as well do a proper job of it. Perhaps one of those extra large beds will fit comfortably into this room."

Rose Bertha smiled knowingly, "I know just the bed you would like, but they are not cheap."

"How much?" Morris grunted gruffly; he always took money seriously, no matter what the cause for spending it might be.

"I think what I have saved you will allow us to purchase the bed and bedding and still come in under your budget," Rose Bertha almost chanted as she looked around the room once more.

"Good!" Morris nodded his approval before walking back into the living area to admire the astonishing transformation. He forgot to say thank you; his mind was already on the next issue. In fact, he was already planning and scheming about his business, his brothers, and the stock in foreign storerooms. He was also mindful of the fact that he was never going to sleep in a warehouse again, let alone on a lumpy mattress barely two inches thick and smelling like a wet horse.

After he had inspected and admired his new home for the second time, it dawned on Morris that the Friedman ladies had done a marvellous job. Not only was it completed magically under budget and while he was away, but the eclectic, mismatched yet somehow regal décor appealed to him. Having come from nothing he would have been blissfully happy with just the basic furniture, but what he had now, a complete and almost decadent home, was totally unexpected. Above all, it was his, and his alone.

Suddenly he came to his senses, "I really must thank you, ladies, for what you have done. It is magnificent, and I know I will be very happy here. I will be relocating here immediately," he smiled broadly.

"Oh," Rose Bertha objected, "your bed won't be delivered for a good week or two."

Morris churned this over in his head; this would not do. "I shall sleep on the sofa until then. I cannot let this beautiful home remain vacant a second longer."

When Mrs Friedman and Ruth took their leave, they headed directly for the tea room on the corner, just as they had done the day before Morris left for Paris.

"That boy is a handful," Mrs Friedman confessed.

"He's not a boy, Mother. He may look like a boy, and at times even act like one, but I think he is an extremely intelligent man."

"He is different; I will admit that," Mrs Friedman mulled. "He is a man of the world, well travelled, and holds his own with older, very wise men in the community when it comes to business. Put him in a home, though, and he is just a child. I'll bet he has no idea how to cook a meal."

"Well I don't like his moods, and he can be quite arrogant," Rose Bertha grimaced as they entered the quaint tea shop and took a seat at a vacant table.

"It's obvious he needs a woman in his life." Mrs Friedman set her agenda in motion as she caught the eye of the shop owner.

"No woman could handle him!" Rose Bertha coughed in surprise.

"Oh, you could. You underestimate yourself, my dear. If I can handle your father, you can handle a boy like Morris. Besides, he seems quite well-to-do; he is already an international businessman and appears much respected by your father and Mr Goldberg. If Yoni Goldberg holds Morris in high regard, that's certainly something to be taken into consideration."

"He has poor taste, Mother," Rose scoffed. "He is short, has a temper, and really needs some finesse instilled into him."

"Of course he does. He is young," Mrs Friedman casually objected, "but he has manners and good etiquette. You've seen him at the dinner table? I couldn't fault his table manners. It is obvious his parents brought him up well. I like him, oddly enough. I think we should set you and him up for marriage."

"Mother!" Rose exclaimed, catching the attention of other patrons in the tea room, then quickly lowered her voice to a whisper, "I could never marry a man like him. Besides, he doesn't find me attractive."

"Oh, I'm not so sure about that. I caught Morris stealing a good look at your breasts a few times. Now come along Darling, let's have some tea and then go and choose your marital bed."

Rose stared at her mother in horror and total disbelief. What bothered her more than her mother's outspoken and flippant way of discussing personal matters was that once she began scheming and matchmaking she very seldom failed to achieve her objective. A wave of uncertainty washed over Rose; she was not ready to marry, and certainly, a man like Morris was not her preferred choice of husband.

Chapter Fifteen

Bulawayo, Rhodesia 1900

David strode down Selbourne Avenue towards Suburbs. It was starting to get dark, and he was in a hurry, but he didn't want to arrive sweaty and flustered. He heard a horse-drawn buggy approaching from behind him and glanced over his shoulder, recognising the driver as a customer of his.

"Good evening, Mr Langbourne," the driver called out, "care for a lift? I'm going your way."

"Thank you, sir," David smiled his appreciation, and at a gentle jog swung himself onto the seat beside the man without the buggy even slowing down.

"I hear your brothers are caught up in that Mafeking siege. So sorry to hear that."

"It was my brother, Louis, and me," David replied amiably. "We escaped from Mafeking and returned to town just a few hours ago."

"Good grief, Man!" the driver was startled. "What's going on down there? It's all over the news and sounds awful."

"It's not good, I agree, but Colonel Baden-Powell is doing a sterling job holding the Boers at bay."

The view from the buggy was quite enchanting. The rows of trees planted along Selbourne Avenue were still young, and David could see over the tops of them quite comfortably. Bulawayo was developing rapidly, and he noticed many houses in various stages of construction. The dusk air was cool, and a sense of freedom and happiness washed over him. David realised that he was truly contented. He was with his brothers again, and they were all safe. Business was sound, and he was about to wrap his arms around the only love of his life. It seemed as if only a few minutes had passed before they were in Suburbs and he needed to alight. David suddenly realised his driver had been talking to him and he had not heard a word.

"Oh, I beg your pardon," he suddenly came back to the present. "My mind is occupied by a thousand things, and I have so been enjoying the view from up here. I have to get out now. Thank you." David couldn't remember the gentlemen's name, so added, "I tell you what: my brother, Harry, has arranged that we meet at the Charter Hotel tomorrow evening at five o'clock, in the bar, to talk to some of the community about our experiences. Please come on down and I'll buy you a beer. We can chat more then."

"Splendid," his voluntary chauffeur said as he pulled on the reigns to stop the cart. "Welcome back to Rhodesia, young man. I look forward to hearing about your experiences tomorrow."

Hopping off the buggy and waving the kind gentlemen off, David made his way to the Rubinsteins' residence. Because Suburbs was such a new residential area, there were few fences or hedges demarcating an owner's property. Being anxious to knock on Hanna's front door David cut some corners, walking through a couple of gardens before arriving at the Rubinsteins' front door. Soft lights glowed dimly behind the drawn curtains. David took a deep breath, tucked in his shirt, and rehearsed in his mind what his opening line would be before knocking firmly on the wooden door. A moment later he heard a low grumbling and a man's footsteps on the wooden floor. When the door opened, it was Mr Rubinstein.

"Good Lord, David," he exclaimed. The word 'David' rebounded through the house.

Before David could respond, a high-pitched shriek burst forth from inside. Hanna came bundling down the passage, bumped her father to the side, and flung herself into David's arms. She hugged him hard and wouldn't let go, her wild screeching and confused words turning into uncontrollable sobs. David wasn't expecting this reception at all and suddenly felt very self-conscious. He relished having Hanna in his arms, pressed tightly against his body, and truly didn't want to let her go, but both her parents were now standing at the door watching this spectacle with great curiosity. Mrs Rubinstein began to cry in sympathy with her daughter which made David all the more uncomfortable.

"Come in," Mr Rubinstein attempted to salvage the dignity of all concerned. "When did you get in, David?"

"A couple of hours ago, Mr Rubinstein." David reluctantly tried to disengage himself from Hanna, who now had a positive torrent of tears streaming down her face. Before he could say any more Mrs Rubinstein forced her way through the doorway, she too bumping her hapless husband to one side and enveloped David in a monstrous hug.

After the heady excitement had subsided, and Hanna had composed herself as much as she was able to in the circumstances, the four sat at the dining table and enjoyed the evening dinner. David, although having eaten barely an hour previously, had no trouble enjoying yet another meal.

The conversation was convivial, and David relayed many of the events he and Louis had experienced in Mafeking. Under the table Hanna reached her foot over to David's and kept it pressed against his, smiling shyly at him each time he looked at her, which was often. When dinner was over Mrs Rubinstein made a pot of tea, and they adjourned to the lounge. Soon afterwards she asked her husband to help her hang a picture in their bedroom, thereby tactfully giving the two young people some privacy. The move was not lost on Hanna, who gave her mother a grateful smile.

"Don't you ever, ever leave me again, do you hear?" Hanna scolded David teasingly, but she was serious as she held his hand and squeezed it tightly. "I died a thousand deaths not knowing where you were. It was horrible, David, truly horrible."

"I know, and I am so sorry. The Boers cut off all communication before they surrounded Mafeking. I was so frustrated that I couldn't let you know what was happening. It drove me nearly demented, and I pined for you."

"Well, I will never let that happen again. I'm going to make sure you stay by my side forever more."

"And I want you to be with me forever. I have had a lot of time to think about you while captured in Mafeking, and I have this overwhelming desire to ask you to be my wife." David slid off his seat and onto one knee.

"Will you marry me, my sweet Hanna?"

She nodded her acceptance through a stream of tears, and, somewhere through the sobs, David heard a 'Yes! Oh yes.' Hanna bent forward slightly to hug him and cried on his shoulder.

"Wait," David extracted himself from her embrace, "I need to ask your father's permission."

Hanna stared at David through a blur of tears, then without warning called loudly for her father.

"Wait!" David hissed in a panic, "I need to prepare myself. I don't know what words to use."

"Father!" Hanna called again, ignoring David's protests. Nervously he struggled to his feet just as Mr and Mrs Rubinstein came into the room.

"What?" Mr Rubinstein asked, confused by Hanna's tone and the copious tears that smeared her cheeks.

"David wants to ask you something," she smiled as she sat daintily on the sofa.

"I, ah... Well, I just wanted to know, I mean ..." David ran a finger around his collar, "I would like to ask you for your daughter's hand in marriage," David finally managed to say, blushing uncontrollably.

Hanna's father stepped over to David without hesitation and extended his hand, "Of course, David, of course. We would be honoured and delighted to welcome you into our family."

David breathed a sigh of relief and was instantly smothered by his future mother-in-law as she hugged him and cried on his shoulder before she repeated the performance on Hanna's shoulder.

The conversation that followed naturally focussed on the wedding plans, and it soon emerged, much to the irritation of Hanna, that her parents insisted their wedding was to be held in England as most of their immediate relatives lived there. They had been planning a trip to England as it was, but the Boer War and the sabotaging of the rail network had put paid to those plans.

"Can't we get married in Bulawayo?" Hanna pleaded. "Who knows how long this horrid war will last?"

"I don't think it will last too long, Hanna," David sided with her parents. "The Brits are pouring into South Africa, hundreds of thousands of troops. I think it will be just a couple of months now. In any case, I would like to return to Ireland and introduce you to my family. Morris said I have to wait five years before I can return to England, but I would really like to go back sooner than that. A wedding there would be such a good excuse for us to go home."

Reluctantly Hanna agreed, and, after an evening of tumultuous emotions, David bid the family goodnight and walked back into town, grinning like a Cheshire cat. Harry had left the back door to the warehouse unlocked and one candle lit, so David quietly let himself in. His brothers were sound asleep in their bedrolls on the floor, but the enjoyment of the day was too much for David to keep to himself; he had to share his news.

"Louis, Harry, wake up," he demanded.

His brothers stirred, and both rolled onto their elbows.

"Hanna and I got engaged this evening," David announced proudly.

"What?" Harry mumbled.

"I'm not surprised," Louis grinned, "not surprised in the least. Congratulations Brother."

Harry got to his feet and stepped over to his desk, opened a drawer and retrieved a bottle of Scotch whisky. He pulled the cork off and held the bottle aloft. "A toast to my brother, and my future sister-in-law."

"Why, thank you, Brother Harry," David beamed, "but why are you hiding whisky in your drawer?"

Harry took a swig of the liquor and grimaced as he passed the bottle to David. "I hate this stuff, but a customer gave it to me last month as a 'Thank you' for giving him a healthy discount. I thought this was a fitting occasion to open the bottle. I've been expecting the news."

David took the bottle and drained a mouthful of the expensive liquid before hissing through his teeth as the alcohol burned its way down his throat. "Don't tell Morris you gave someone a discount!" he joked before passing the bottle on to Louis.

At that moment David was sure he was the happiest man in the world. He was engaged to the sweetest, most beautiful girl, and was sharing his engagement with his two young brothers in the security of his warehouse, in the magnificent, peaceful country of Rhodesia.

It couldn't get better than that.

* * *

TUESDAY 13TH FEBRUARY 1900

MORRIS LANGBOURNE
C/O
MR Y GOLDBERG
LLOYDS LONDON

EAGLE AND GIRAFFE ESCAPED TIN STOP SAFE IN
LANGBRO STOP EAGLE ENGAGED TO HANNA RUBINSTEIN STOP
WILL MARRY IN ENGLAND WHEN WAR OVER STOP
NEED STOCK URGENT STOP CAN YOU SEND VIA PORTUGUESE
EAST AFRICAN PORT STOP
BADGER

Chapter Sixteen

Finsbury Pavement : 1900

Morris stood with his back to the window, hands in his trouser pockets, and admired his new home. He had to admit that Rose Bertha had done a sterling job, and, while perhaps done inexpensively, he truly felt himself to be living an upper-class life; Morris could not have been happier. If he were to invite Yoni Goldberg over for a meal, perhaps a business lunch, he was confident Yoni would not feel out of place. He was only twenty-five years old and already a force in the business world. He recognised that his business activities in South Africa and Rhodesia were the reason for his success.

The moment that thought crossed his mind Morris' attention switched from the luxury and warmth of his home back to his family business, and a scowl suddenly creased his brow. He stepped quickly to his desk, sat on the squeaky chair and opened the small drawer on his right, extracting a leather-bound ledger. He flicked to the last page with entries and ran his finger down the columns, a cloud of concern colouring his thoughts. In his personal capacity, he was very low on cash. The next rent cheque might even be a problem. As far as the business was concerned, however, Bulawayo was doing exceptionally well under Harry's management.

What frustrated Morris, almost to the point of anger, was that Langbourne Brothers in Bulawayo was doing very well - on paper. As far as actual cash flow was concerned, however, there was very little usable currency going into their bank account. They were owed a significant amount of credit, and the Marshall-Hole Currency they had accumulated was not much good to him in England. He would have liked to declare a dividend so that he could put some real money into his personal account, but that was impossible until the situation in Rhodesia, or in fact all of Southern Africa, normalised. He was comforted, though, with the knowledge that David was on his way to Port Elizabeth to ship his first international order to Johannesburg. It was going to make a massive difference to their sales and stock levels, and would ultimately increase their profitability dramatically.

Louis was now active in Johannesburg and ready to receive what David sent him, so all Morris' plans were running like clockwork. His immediate problem was that he had new purchases on hold around England, Scotland, Hong Kong, and now, Paris. His purchases from Paris were going to set Langbourne Brothers apart from everyone else, of that Morris was certain.

The problem was that he could not release those orders until he had the cash in the bank to pay for them, and some of his suppliers were putting him under a lot of pressure to get the orders into production. The French, especially, were persistent to the point of being irritating. Some Parisian factories had representatives in London who would call on Morris a little too regularly and forcefully for his comfort, and, on one occasion, Morris exchanged some words that would not be considered very polite in gentlemanly circles. Nevertheless, that was what business was like when dealing with Morris, and he secretly relished everything about it, including the outbursts and the reasons for them.

Yoni had invited Morris to a lunch meeting at the London Chamber of Commerce on Eastcheap Road, and it would take him about twenty minutes to walk there. He was looking forward to the meeting as he was keen to expand his network of business colleagues, and, of course, to meet with the man he admired immensely, Yoni Goldberg. Morris checked his fob watch and saw that, as was his wont, he had forgotten to wind it that morning. He unhooked the metal chain from his belt and unceremoniously tossed the watch into the second drawer in his desk. A quick glance out of the window reminded him to take an umbrella. Without further delay, he collected his jacket, Derby hat and umbrella from their hooks in the hallway and hurried off to his lunch appointment.

The luncheon was a very formal affair, some gentlemen even wearing top hat and tails. Yoni, wearing his customary bowler hat and knee-length pure wool black overcoat, greeted Morris outside the building and ushered him in. The dining area was abuzz with business elite, some smoking pipes with importance and others passionately engrossed in conversation, some nurturing a crystal glass with a shot of whisky or enjoying a light-hearted moment with a colleague or friend.

Morris was significantly shorter and younger than anyone else present and attracted some curious stares, but these were lost on Morris, who had never noticed such things. Because he was the guest of Yoni Goldberg, however, a man of some distinction in the business community, Morris was accepted as an equal when introduced. Morris revelled in the company of these gentlemen and contributed to the conversation with ideas and solutions to problems that had many raising their eyebrows in amazement. Yoni, on the other hand, didn't participate much. He preferred to watch Morris engage with these prominent men and observe their reactions; he was proud of Morris, just as a father would be proud of his son.

When lunch was served, Morris and Yoni sat together at a table for ten and continued to enjoy the company of those seated with them. When a local councillor asked Morris about his time in Africa, the conversation remained on that subject for the duration of the luncheon. It never went off topic, and Morris comfortably held the floor. He advocated for more business and investment to take hold in Rhodesia, as the opportunities would be immense once the Boer War ended. When the meeting broke up, the councillor suggested that if Yoni were to propose Morris as a member of the Chamber, he would second the application, such was his regard for the young businessman.

As they walked back to Lloyds of London Morris suggested they swing past his flat so that he could show Yoni where he lived, and what Rose Bertha had done for him. In reality, he couldn't wait to show off his new living arrangements. Yoni agreed because it was on the way. As Morris had hoped, Yoni was impressed with what he observed, or at least he appeared to be. He complimented the paintings (although he tactfully didn't mention that he would never allow them in his home), but overall he approved of what Morris, through Rose Bertha, had achieved.

"I think this is lovely, Morris," Yoni nodded his genuine approval.

"Rose Bertha did a wonderful job."

"Well, Mrs Friedman had something to do with it too," Morris grouched. "I find her to be a most unusual woman."

"How so?" Yoni looked surprised.

"Oh, I don't know. She can be quite manipulative, I think."

"I don't think so," Yoni shrugged off the suggestion, although he knew Morris to be absolutely correct. "You know what this place needs?" Yoni waved his arms openly at the flat.

"What?" Morris cast an inquisitive eye over his home. He couldn't think of anything else he could possibly want.

"A woman's touch. A place like this should be shared with a lovely woman. Have you considered getting married, Morris? You are at that age now, you know."

"Me? Married?" Morris exclaimed in horror. "No, I'm too busy to be worried about a wife."

"Not at all," Yoni smiled heartily, "It is when you are busy that you need a loving wife to care for you. She would keep your home, and look after you, listen to your worries and provide nourishing meals."

"You think so?" Morris looked at Yoni curiously. Because he deeply respected this man he tended to value his opinion, and thus would listen to him a little more seriously than he would anyone else (apart from David that was, and even his brother was now engaged to be married).

"Of course, Morris," Yoni slapped him firmly on the shoulder. "Women are essential to us men. What happens if you fall ill? Who will care for you? You have no-one here, Morris. If you got sick and died nobody would know until Mr Edwards in the property section came looking for his monthly rent cheque," he chuckled, making light of a grave matter.

"Heavens," Morris suddenly looked concerned, "I had never thought of that. In fact, women never even cross my mind," Morris lied as he thought back to the beautiful ladies in Paris. "Well, now that you mention it, perhaps you are right." He began to smile.

"Good," Yoni encouraged.

"I will return to Paris soon and see if I can find a lady who would care to marry me. There appeared to be many beautiful women there. Thank you for the suggestion, Mr Goldberg."

"Paris?" Yoni exclaimed in surprise. "Why Paris, Morris? It is so far away, and I believe the French girls don't like to leave their country of birth. They speak a different language too. I think you should look for a lovely lady right here in London."

"You might be right, Mr Goldberg," Morris had to agree, "I will start to look out for a suitable woman then."

"Actually," Yoni tugged at his bushy beard, seemingly lost in thought, "what about Rose Bertha? She is a lovely young lady, and very talented. She comes from a very well-to-do family, a family you already know."

"Rose Bertha?" Morris exclaimed in disbelief. "No, she, well…"

"I think she would be an excellent choice," Yoni cut him off, smiling broadly at his suggestion.

"You think so?" Morris was confused; he had never thought of Rose Bertha as a wife, living in his home, with him!

"She's a beautiful girl, Morris," Yoni shrugged his shoulders in mock resignation.

Morris pulled up some memories of Rose Bertha in his mind; she was not exactly attractive, but she did have a nice body, her breasts, particularly, were curiously interesting and mysterious to him, and after all, she had had more to do with his home than he had. She was polite, dressed exceptionally well, wore a particularly agreeable fragrance, and had a very kindly disposition. She would make an admirable wife.

"I don't think she'll marry me," Morris thought aloud.

"I had lunch with Mr Friedman on Monday, and he likes you very much. He did say to me that if you asked him for Rose Bertha's hand in marriage, he would find it impossible to say no."

"He did?" Morris exclaimed, startled.

"Indeed! He would love to have you as a son-in-law. I think you should think about it Morris," Goldberg laughed, "a perfect match."

"It is?" Morris questioned Yoni and himself. "Well, perhaps I should give it some consideration."

"Do that Morris. Mr Friedman would make an excellent father-in-law."

As Yoni left a somewhat confused Morris to walk back to his office, he was frowning. He believed he was right; Rose Bertha would make a wonderful wife for Morris and Mr Friedman, an excellent father-in-law. However, he knew that Morris was correct about Mrs Friedman; it was she who had put the idea to him of Morris and Rose Bertha getting married, and she had convinced him to plant that idea into Morris' head, not her husband. Yoni started to smile, '*You are right, Morris, she is a very manipulative woman,'* he thought as he chuckled to himself.

Morris' proposal to Rose Bertha was not a particularly romantic affair. He had been invited around to the Friedmans' home for dinner on three occasions, each time to secretly impress upon him what an excellent cook and homemaker Rose Bertha was. Morris had to agree that she was an exceptional person, and the more he saw of her in this new light, the more he began to appreciate her. At the end of each meal, Mr and Mrs Friedman would tactfully leave Morris and Rose to chat in the drawing room, which he did for a respectable length of time. He left soon after, with profuse thanks for the meal and hospitality, leaving Mrs Friedman and her daughter suitably frustrated, and Mr Friedman none the wiser.

It was only on the fourth visit that Morris found the courage, and made the commitment, to broach the subject of marriage as he and Rose Bertha sat congenially in the drawing room as had become their custom.

"It has been suggested," Morris stated matter-of-factly, "that I am at the age that I should consider getting married."

"That would be a sensible idea," Rose replied, nonchalantly.

"Has marriage ever crossed your mind?" Morris tentatively questioned.

"No, not really," Rose pondered thoughtfully. "It has been said, though, that I am at the right age to look for a husband too."

"Perhaps we should consider getting married," Morris suggested awkwardly.

"Is that a proposal, Morris?" Rose feigned surprise.

"Oh...," Morris suddenly became flustered, and he felt a hot flush burn in his cheeks, "that is, of course... what I meant..."

"If it is," Rose Bertha quickly interrupted when she saw the conversation going haywire, "then I accept."

"Oh!" Morris looked perplexed. He realised he had indeed proposed, and she had accepted. "Well, then I should ask your father for your hand in marriage, I suppose."

"That might be a good idea," she said, a coy smile spreading across her face.

"Good, good," Morris repeated in a slight daze. "Well, if you would please excuse me, I had better find him."

"He is in the library," she prompted.

"Good show." Morris stood and ambled down the hall while Rose went into the kitchen to tell her mother what had happened.

"Excuse me, Mr Friedman, may I have a moment?" Morris poked his head around the door.

"Certainly, come on in. How may I help?"

"I'd like to ask you for your daughter's hand in marriage, if I may."

"Oh," Friedman was caught off guard, he was not expecting this at just this moment. "Well, yes, of course. Indeed, we'd be delighted," he stood and shook Morris' hand. "I think we ought to tell the ladies."

Just then Mrs Friedman and Rose entered the library, right on cue, and both of them were smiling broadly. His future mother-in-law gave Morris a very tight hug and instructed her husband to open a rather expensive bottle of French Bordeaux for the occasion.

"It will be wonderful to have you in the family, Morris," Mrs Friedman gushed. "Now, give your bride-to-be a kiss."

"A kiss?" Morris was shocked! He had never kissed a girl, and certainly never even considered doing so in front of her parents.

"Go on, don't be shy," she encouraged, pushing Morris closer to Rose. "You are family now."

A wave of uncertainty washed over Morris as he looked at Rose Bertha. She smiled serenely at him, her lips so inviting, yet so foreign. Suddenly he took her arm and gave her a peck on the back of her hand.

Rose Bertha's and Mrs Friedman's eyes locked uncomfortably, Mrs Friedman gently shaking her head in disbelief. *'Oh dear, my poor, poor daughter, this boy has got so much to learn'*, she thought to herself. Rose was thinking the same thing.

Chapter Seventeen

Bechuanaland and Rhodesia 1900

Everyone throughout the world, it seemed, was talking about the Siege of Mafeking. It was in every newspaper, discussed at meals, in the pubs and at Sunday picnics. Prayers were said in churches, politicians argued, professionals strategised. Colonel Baden-Powell and his handful of loyal soldiers fought tooth-and-nail against the entrenched Boer army. The conflict became progressively worse, but each day Baden-Powell would find a new way to fend off the attackers, even occasionally going on the offensive, gaining ground, and taking prisoners.

He lost men too, good men bravely killed in combat, or who sadly lost their lives in freak incidents and illness. Hunger was rife, horses were slaughtered to provide meat, and locusts, dried and ground into a rough powder, were added to the dwindling supply of flour in ever increasing ratios. But Baden-Powell held his ground, and the world held its breath, urging him in their thoughts and prayers to hold out for a little longer while the British mounted their offensive.

On the 200th day of the siege, the Boer commander sent Baden-Powell a note, asking if he would like to field a team for a friendly game of cricket the following Sunday. Legend had it that Baden-Powell politely declined, saying, "No thanks, we are in the middle of a game already, and we are currently 200 not out." The humour may have been lost on the Boer commander, but the world went into raptures, hailing Baden-Powell as a hero, and applauding his quick-witted response under such conditions of adversity.

When Ladysmith was relieved by General Buller in Natal, Baden-Powell had no way of knowing, and kept fighting with all he had, while casualties were mounting at an alarming rate on both sides. News of the eminent reporter, Winston Churchill, emerged that he had escaped his captivity in Pretoria, which bolstered the resolve of the British. He made his way to the Cape and joined the northward march of the Commonwealth armies, reporting on the state of their victories along the way. Yet again, Baden-Powell had no way of knowing of the advance and kept fighting for his people and the trapped residents. Knowing there was a printer still operational in Mafeking, Baden-Powell made full use of his services and initiated a newspaper called "The Mafeking Mail : Special Siege Slip" which channelled news articles of the garrison and community. In the interests of keeping morale high, it also contained adverts for fairs, sporting and other events.

The united armies of the British Empire, Australia, Canada, and India amongst others, marched their way up from the Cape, through the Orange Free State and into the Transvaal, forcing the Boers into retreat. Kimberley's siege was lifted, and among the residents was none other than Cecil John Rhodes. A relief force was rapidly assembled to go to Baden-Powell's aid. Colonel Plumer got word by pigeon carrier that an army was advancing and immediately broke camp to march south and join them. After seven months of siege, the Mafeking residents heard fierce fighting off to the west, and plumes of smoke in the distance signalled that help was finally at hand.

Baden-Powell had held Mafeking for over seven months, 217 days to be precise, and the world burst into wild celebration when news of the relief reached the international press. Parties were thrown throughout England, and Colonel Baden-Powell was instantly branded a hero. So jubilant were the people of England that a new fashionable word for "a great rejoicing" was coined: "maffick".

Barely two weeks later the British occupied Johannesburg, and a few days after that, the capital Pretoria was claimed, sending the remaining Boers on the run and into hiding; many returned to their devastated farms in an utterly despondent state.

Elsewhere in the British Empire there was much celebrating, and none more so than David and his beautiful Hanna. Their time had come, and preparations began in earnest to depart for England. It soon became apparent that, as eager as David and the Rubinstein family were to get to England, matters had to be dealt with appropriately on both sides. Sadly, their timings differed considerably. David had to get to Port Elizabeth and secure the transfer of their much-needed stock, and Mr Rubinstein had commitments at work. Furthermore, they had to wait for the various rail lines that had been damaged in the Boer War to be repaired and made serviceable again.

The Mafeking, Johannesburg and Cape Town lines were repaired relatively quickly, but there were delays on the Port Elizabeth and East London lines, so it was decided, mostly through telegraphic exchanges between David and Morris, that the brothers' departures from Bulawayo would be staggered. Louis would leave for Johannesburg first and establish Langbourne Coetsee with Danie as initially planned, and then David would go to Port Elizabeth as soon as practical.

Mrs Rubinstein convinced her family not to wait for David, as she wanted to attend to Hanna's wedding dress, find a venue for the event, and deal with the almost overwhelming arrangements that needed to be made for such an auspicious occasion. The moment her husband was able to leave his office they would depart, and David would follow as soon as possible. Current indications were that he would be no more than a fortnight behind them.

Louis left on the same train as the Rubinsteins, a host of emotions yet again evident in all parties on the platform. Louis changed trains in Kimberley and headed for Johannesburg while the Rubinstein family continued to Cape Town and, the day after arriving there, boarded the "Tintagel Castle" owned by the new Union-Castle Mail Steamship Company, reserving a first-class cabin for the grand occasion.

David had a three-week delay, but, eventually, his time came, and with fond farewells, he left Harry once more in charge of the Bulawayo business.

"You have done well." David slapped his brother on the shoulder and gave it a hearty squeeze, "I am very proud of you, and I will certainly tell Morris of my opinion. He will be extremely pleased, of that I am sure."

"Oh, it's nothing," Harry humbly replied, "I have a good team, and I do it for the family. I'm happy here, although I would like to visit the family in Ireland sometime."

"Yes," David agreed, "Morris' idea of rotating only every five years is a bit harsh. I'll be having a word with him about it. I think we need to return once a year, for a holiday at least, as well as rotate. Heavens, we can afford to travel now."

"That would be a most welcome arrangement," Harry grinned. "I wish you and Hanna all the best, and please send my love to the family. Especially Sarah," he added quickly. It was no secret that Harry and Sarah had a very close bond.

"I will be sure to do that," David promised as the horn sounded and the conductor summoned all passengers aboard. "Look after the fort for me," David called to his young brother and threw him a pseudo salute. Harry chuckled, and threw one back at him. He pushed his thumbs into his suspenders and watched the train slide out of view.

David settled into his compartment and allowed a thousand thoughts to lose themselves in the calm Rhodesian scenery. Presently he decided to visit the dining car to see if anyone he knew was also travelling on the train. The chances of that were very good, he thought, and he needed some stimulating conversation to take his mind off the long journey ahead. On entering the plush carriage he was disappointed not to see an acquaintance, so found the last empty table and took a seat. Immediately an African waiter in crisp white western clothing served him and David, in his best siNdebele, struck up a jovial conversation, ordering a meal in the process. As he lent back in the leather seat, an older gentleman approached and asked David if he would mind if he joined him.

"By all means," David invited. Knowing socialising on these lengthy rail journeys was essential, David was sure most passengers agreed with his sentiments.

"It seems all the tables are taken. Colenbrander is my name, Johan Colenbrander."

"Pleased to meet you." David tried to get to his feet as he shook his hand, but the seat, being bolted firmly to the floor, stopped him in an awkward position. "I'm David Langbourne."

"Oh yes, I know of you. You escaped Mafeking." He gave a broad smile.

Johan Colenbrander was a handsome man, tall with copious dark, wavy hair, thick arms and broad shoulders. He was a physically powerful man in every respect, still so despite his age. His face was well weathered, and there was a large, prominent scar running down the right side of his face. It stretched from his hairline past his eye and across both his upper and lower lips. His eyes were piercing, and David could tell that this man had some fascinating stories to tell. Deep in his eyes, David could see sadness and bitterness lurking, even though he was smiling.

Since David was a natural conversationalist, being able to adapt to any social situation, he struck up the conversation at once. "I've seen you around Bulawayo," he said. "I recognise you from somewhere."

"I've been into your shop on a couple of occasions. Your brother, Harry, I believe his name is, handled my custom very well."

"That is very good to know," David beamed.

"I was so impressed with his service and concerns for my needs that I gave him a bottle of whisky as a token of my thanks. I hope he shared it with you," Johann joked.

"Hah!" David exclaimed, and lightly slapped the top of the table, "He opened the bottle the day I returned from Mafeking, and in celebration of the announcement of my engagement to be married."

"Oh, you are to be married? Congratulations."

"Thank you Mr Colenbrander," David allowed his happiness to show. "My Hanna is the most beautiful and sweetest girl in the world. She is sailing to Southampton right now, and I will be joining her shortly."

Johan looked very pensive, almost sad. "My wife was like that too. She passed away recently."

"Oh, I'm sorry," David murmured, suddenly feeling very sorry for the man.

"It's all right. You were not to know. Mollie was a most remarkable woman. She could hold her own in any situation and could shoot a gun better than most men. She was braver than a lion and cared for everyone she came into contact with. Sadly she had a heart condition for many years and told no-one. Her doctor was sworn to secrecy until she passed away. She went to lie down not long ago, and her heart just gave up." Johan wiped a tear from the corner of his eye, trying to hide his emotions.

"I would have liked to have known her." There was genuine concern in David's voice. He thought it might be appropriate to swing the conversation onto a different track for a while, so took a deep breath and leaned back in his seat again. "So, what do you do up in Rhodesia?"

"Oh, I was commissioned by Mr Cecil John Rhodes to be his interpreter.

I sat with him when he sat on that anthill and negotiated a truce with the Matabele chiefs at the end of the rebellion."

"That's where I have seen you," David sat bolt upright, "and I have met your late wife. Indeed, she was a beautiful lady. Didn't she squirrel away some pistols to you and your negotiating team when you were supposed to be unarmed?"

"Shhh…" Johan hissed with a finger to his lips, but a smile hovered about his mouth. "Rhodes had forbidden weapons, but Molly insisted, just in case, you know. Rhodes was none the wiser, and never shall be!"

David chuckled. "Yes, she was a character. Forgive me for the asking, but did you get that scar fighting the Matabele?"

This time Johann laughed. "No, I got that back when I was a young whippersnapper in Zululand: 1881, I believe. I got tangled up in the Zulu War and was hunting this ferocious warrior chief. I was on my horse and about to run him down when he suddenly turned and threw his axe at me. I had taken my eyes off him for just a second to control my horse, and when I looked up, I had no time to dodge his projectile and bang, right in my face. I fell off my horse, hurt my arm in the process, and before I knew it the man was attacking me with his spear!"

"Good grief," David was mesmerised by the story. "How did you escape?"

"I was lucky. We had a few fisticuffs, and I can tell you, that man was the toughest, strongest warrior I have ever fought. He stabbed me four or five times, sliced my skull in three or four places." Johan studied his arms and hands, and rubbed his neck, "Lacerated my fingers, speared the back of my neck, stabbed… I was a disaster, but I eventually managed to turn his spear on him and kill him."

"You killed him?" David was horrified at what he had heard.

"Yes," Johan looked surprised, "Yes, of course. I've killed hundreds of Zulu warriors in my time. You sound shocked; you've been through some wars yourself, so the reality of wartime deaths is not unknown to you."

"I've been surrounded by three wars so far - two Matabele Rebellions and the Siege of Mafeking, but never did I fight in them. I have never pointed a gun at another human. I don't imagine I could ever take another man's life."

"If you fight in a war, it's inevitable. You have to." Johan sighed.

"I'm afraid I could never be a soldier," David admitted.

"My soldiering days are not over." Johan stared out into the distance as the scenery sped by in a blur. "I have a debt to settle with the Boers. They took my land and my businesses in Zululand and killed my friends, one of whom was the Zulu Chief Zibebu. I'm going to hunt them down and capture them, but if they fight back, they will die."

David looked at Johannes in disbelief. "Mr Colenbrander, the Boer War is over."

"Have you not heard?" Johan's eyes pierced David's with icy venom. "The conventional war is over, yes, but the remnants of the Boer army are regrouping and entering a guerrilla phase of warfare. They attack at night, sabotage railways, industry and government institutions. After they attack, some return to their farms and claim to be docile farmers, until their superiors rally them again. People like me have been asked to volunteer our services to capture these men."

A cold fear gripped David's heart, "I… I didn't know," he stammered in disbelief, "but…"

Colenbrander saw that the conversation was upsetting his companion "Never fear, Mr Langbourne," he hastened to add when he saw the fear in David's eyes, "you shouldn't come across any danger in the south. They are mostly in the north, and that is where we will concentrate our efforts. Now, let's change the subject to something lighter. Do you see that gentleman sitting over there?"

David looked over his shoulder and saw a man with fair hair in a light suit, talking to a gentleman with a manicured moustache.

"His name is Fitzpatrick, Percy Fitzpatrick. When he has finished his conversation with that gentleman, I will ask him to join us if you don't mind."

David nodded his acceptance, his mind reeling over the possibility of a new war erupting while his goods were being railed up to Johannesburg and then on to Bulawayo. He was unable to concentrate on the conversation; he needed to get to Port Elizabeth quickly, and then catch the ship out of Cape Town as soon as possible after that.

"You will enjoy Mr FitzPatrick's company. He was a wagon driver in his youth, working the routes from Portuguese East Africa, over the highlands and into Rhodesia. It is an incredibly demanding job; wild animals, swamps, sickness, and the sheer height of those mountains is indescribable. He has some wonderful stories to tell. You must ask him about a dog he once had called Jock. That dog was a legend; everyone knew Jock..."

Johan's voice droned on, but David struggled to follow the conversation. Percy Fitzpatrick did eventually join them and was a welcome distraction for David. He found Fitzpatrick very easy to listen to, and some of the anecdotes of his wagon driving days were indeed spellbinding. His stories reminded David of the time he presided over eighteen wagons from Johannesburg to the Limpopo. David didn't have mountains to traverse, but all the other perils had presented themselves, including the illness which he felt he had never fully recovered from.

"When I was driving wagons from Delagoa Bay," Fitzpatrick continued, "we would take time out every so often to hunt for antelope." He paused to light a cigar. "That was a welcome break from a hard drive. My Jock was an exceptional hunting dog, and he saved my life many times. We had an accident one day while we were hunting. I fired a shot at a Tragelaphus strepsiceros, a kudu cow, and she appeared to stumble, although I didn't hit her, nor injure her, but Jock thought I had. He went to bring her down, and she gave him such a kick under his chin he was knocked senseless. From that day forward he lost his hearing completely - stone deaf forever more."

"Good gracious!" David was enthralled at Percy's storytelling. "What was that word you said earlier, trage-something?"

"Tragelaphus strepsiceros, it's the scientific name for a kudu," Percy said nonchalantly.

"Percy tries to impress people with his vocabulary," Johan winked at David with a wry smile, "I think he hopes to publish a book one day."

"Perhaps," Percy smirked in return, "but what I am trying to do is learn all these scientific names of the wildlife in Africa, a personal ambition of mine. At least it makes me sound intelligent." He laughed at himself, and his companions joined in.

"So," David scratched his head, "why do scientists want to complicate something that is already quite acceptable?"

"Because, my boy," Percy dragged on his cigar and blew billows of white smoke at the ceiling, "it seems that many animals, birds and insects for that matter, are related somehow. All a bit complicated I'm afraid, but the first name denotes the genus, and the second identifies the type of genus. For instance," he paused again, leaned forward and flicked some ash into an ashtray, "there are many types of Tragelaphus, the Tragelaphus scriptus is the common bushbuck, the Tragelaphus strepsiceros is the kudu."

"I think these scientists are absolutely mad, especially when they use a dead language to complicate an already complicated matter," Johan muttered, patting his jacket pocket as he searched for a cigarette.

"No, no my good friend, not in the least," Percy objected vehemently. "It's all for very good reason. Did you know when the scientists came out to Africa and classified all the animals they could find, the very last one was the nyala?

"A most peculiar antelope, the male is so different to the female that they could well be a completely different species. The female is small, timid and light brown in colour, but her male counterpart is large, dark grey, and has unusual bright yellow legs as if wearing the most comical socks. However, the scientific fundis surprisingly found the nyala is related to the kudu! A scientific name clarifies this mismatch beyond doubt. Incidentally, when they discovered that this antelope was related to the Tragelaphus genus, and as it was the very last to be classified, the scientists allowed the second part of the name to be decided by their faithful Zulu guide. When they asked him what he would like to name it, he declared Tragelaphus angasii, and so it is today," he stated proudly, showing off his knowledge of the Latin vocabulary.

David and Johan looked at each other blankly. They both began to chuckle, and soon were laughing heartily.

"What did I say?" Percy looked offended.

"Angasii?" David said through his laughter.

Johan caught his breath, "angasii, or angazi, is the Zulu word for 'I have no idea!' ", and promptly burst into laughter again.

The evening progressed along that happy vein, keeping the travellers amused and their minds off the monotony of the journey - which was precisely the distraction David had been hoping for. Nevertheless, David, however, did not sleep well in his compartment later that night despite the soothing sound of the wheels clanking over the iron railway line joints. Early the next morning when the train pulled into Mafeking, blowing steam and objecting belligerently, David was fully awake, a nagging concern about the country's political situation settling deep in his stomach. He parted company with the men he had met the night before, and, needing to wait six hours for his connecting train, decided to look around the settlement and perhaps visit Julian Weil, or even Colonel Baden-Powell if he was still there. Unfortunately, neither of them were; Weil had gone to the Cape, and Baden-Powell had been assigned to another part of the country to ensure, and secure, a British victory. David, thus, was forced to wander aimlessly around the town, looking at the astonishing damage that had occurred during the four months after his escape.

The town offered everywhere the spectacle of disaster. Roofs were missing from buildings, and walls were peppered with holes so big a person's fist would easily fit inside. Some were even big enough to crawl through. The trenches that had saved many a citizen's life no longer had defined edges but were worn from the constant hurried sliding of people diving over the edge for cover in the nick of time. No panes of glass could be found intact, and lamp posts were bent, dented or entirely ripped out of the ground. Even the shady tree that David and Louis had sat under was now just a shattered stump. He shivered when he saw the splintered timber.

David stood at the front of a residential house, hands in pockets and shook his head in disbelief as he stared at its front door; a good one half of the door, from top to bottom, was simply missing. He heard a whimper coming from his left and strode around the corner to see what it was. There was a rather attractive young lady in a blue bonnet wearing a beautiful flowing dress, holding a bible and sobbing gently.

"Are you alright, Miss?" David asked gently, taking his hands out of his trouser pockets. "May I help you?"

"Oh, hello," she immediately smiled and wiped a small tear from her cheek, "Please do not worry. I'm fine, actually."

"Is this your house?" David asked politely as he waved at the almost destroyed building.

"It's our headquarters. I'm with The Salvation Army. A bit of a mess, isn't it?" She tossed her head slightly in the direction of the ruined structure.

"Yes," David spoke slowly as he took another look about him. "Quite a mess. Were you here the whole time? I don't remember seeing you before."

"No, we were evacuated on the last train out. I've just been sent back to rebuild our headquarters and resume my duties. My name is Captain Daisy Quarterman."

"David Langbourne," he introduced himself to the beautiful girl and began to extend his hand, but quickly withdrew it awkwardly, not quite sure what the correct etiquette was when introducing oneself to a young lady, particularly one with a military title. "You're lucky you got out. I was here for the early part of it, but I escaped," David confessed. "However, now that I am passing through, I shudder to think what the last part of the siege must have been like for the residents and soldiers that remained. This is shocking."

"Look," Daisy thrust her bible at David, "I've just found my bible in the rubble. There's a bullet hole right through it. I left it here in the rush to evacuate."

"Good grief," David marvelled at the sight. It made him wonder at the destructive force behind a bullet, such that it could penetrate a book as thick and dense as a bible, and he pondered what it would do to human flesh and bone.

"I was due to be married," Daisy said, "but the war put that on hold. Wars are terrible things, aren't they?" She spoke sadly as she looked all about her.

"Are you going to get married now that the war is over?"

"Yes, indeed, to a wonderful man called Walter Scott," she beamed proudly, "also of The Salvation Army."

David chuckled. "Congratulations, and I too am about to be married, to a beautiful lady called Hanna Rubinstein. I am, in fact, on my way to England for that very occasion."

"Congratulations are in order for you too, then! Well, Mr Langbourne, I do believe you have cheered up my day most satisfactorily."

Just then the sound of the train's whistle reverberated over the derelict town.

"I have to be on my way, Miss Quarterman, I mean, Captain. I have so enjoyed our encounter, and hope we may cross paths again when you are Captain Scott," he grinned, bowing his head in respect.

Likewise Mr Langbourne," Daisy smiled, and gave a mock curtsy in response.

With both of them smiling happily, David turned on his heel and headed directly for the station. He knew that, if he had not met Daisy

Quarterman, he would have departed this devastated town in a very mournful frame of mind, but somehow she had reminded him that good things could still come after a war.

As the train pulled gently away from the station, David reclined in his seat and watched the harsh, yet beautiful, African bush slide effortlessly past him. His mind was at ease. Rhodesia was a stable and progressive country, their business was well established and very prosperous, and his two younger brothers were performing far above expectations. David's thoughts turned to his family. He would soon be in London with Morris again, and later reunite with the family he loved so dearly in Ireland, a family he had not seen in almost a decade. And, of course, he would soon have Hanna, the girl he was wholly in love with and about to marry, safe in his arms again.

David smiled contentedly and offered a silent thank you to the passing African landscape. He owed his happiness to Africa, and by Jove, he was a very happy man!

TO BE CONTINUED...

ACKNOWLEDGEMENTS

Without good friends and well-meaning people whom I have crossed paths with in my journey to tell these stories, I would never have put pen to paper.

As always, I am very grateful for Cindy Kramer in Cape Town, my mentor, who vets everything I write, and gives me honest and frank feedback. She gives me a great deal of confidence to let my writing lose into the world.

A special thanks must go to my loving wife, Sharon, who not only encourages me to write and tell my stories, but, as must be with all author's spouses, becomes very lonely when the creative juices begin to flow, and unintentionally, the author's world becomes overwhelmingly focussed and insular.

My thanks to my Editor, Mike Kantey, in Plettenberg Bay, South Africa. Not only do I value his literary experience and skills, but, his inspiring knowledge of the Xhosa language and South African political, historical and cultural spheres.

In my previous books I have acknowledged my sincere thanks to a number of relatives of the family, and even now, in the 4th book in the series, I have had to consult my research with them continually. My thanks, again, to Pam Sussman Landau (Canada), John S Landau (USA), David Landau (UK), Steve Landau (USA) and Nancy Rich Wiseman (USA). Further grateful thanks goes to Steve Landau for putting his editing and proofreading experience to the final draft.

A very special thanks to Richard Landau (South Africa) and his daughter, Laura Landau (USA) who recently discovered a hand-written letter dated over 100 years ago, which will allow me to write another exciting, and hitherto unknown episode, in the Langbourne adventure!

I'd like to recognise the members of 'The Saturday Chapter' (North Lakes, Brisbane), a small group of authors who readily share their advice, blunt honesty, experiences and laughter. Through them, my exposure into the world of writing has truly opened up.

It is difficult to give thanks to someone who has long since passed, but I do recognise my late grandfather, Archie, and my late father, John, for the memories they passed down to me before they died. As with many people I have spoken to while writing this series, I regret not asking Dad and Grandpa more when I had the chance. Therefore, I appeal to those of you who are reading this to talk to your living relatives, and find out all you can about your heritage. It is hard to explain how rewarding it can be. There are stories out there that are becoming lost in the haze of time, stories that need to be remembered, and stories that need to be told. It is up to us to keep the memories of our courageous forefathers alive for future generations.

Last but not least, I'd like to thank my readers for their support and feedback. It is because of you that I keep writing.

RESEARCH MATERIAL

Books and material consulted in the research the Langbourne Series:
(Listed by date of publication.)

Rhodesia Past and Present - SJ Du Toit (1897)
Three Years in Savage Africa - Lionel Decel (1898)
'96 Rebellions - BSAC Reports (1898)
On the South African Frontier - William Harvey Brown (1899)
Sketches in Mafeking and East Africa - RSS Baden-Powell (1907)
Jock of the Bushveld - P Fitzpatrick (1907)
Southern Rhodesia - Fergus W Ferguson (1909) (Rare Book)
Old Rhodesian Days - Hugh Marshal Hole (1928)
Commando - Deneys Reitz (1929)
The Monuments of Southern Rhodesia - RJ Fothergill (1953)
The White Whirlwind - TV Bulpin (1961)
Encyclopaedia Rhodesia - The College Press (1973)
A Guide to the Rock Art of Rhodesia - CK Cooke (1974)
Rhodesia Before 1920 - National Gallery of Rhodesia &
National Historical Association of Rhodesia (c.1975)
The Boer War - Thomas Pakenham (1979)
Running the Gauntlet - George Mossop (1990) (1930)
Girl in a Blue Bonnet - Dot Scott (2007)

And

Records, journals, documents, letters, interviews and photos of the
descendants of the Landau Family

ABOUT THE AUTHOR

Alan Landau was born in Salisbury, Rhodesia (now Harare, Zimbabwe) in 1959. In 1978 he joined the British South Africa Police (formally the BSAC). At that time Rhodesia was entangled in a civil war that ended in 1980. After serving in the new Zimbabwe Republic Police for a short time, Alan retired to enter the commercial world.

Alan worked in Zimbabwe's widely known tobacco industry for five years before joining his father and ultimately taking over the family business when his father retired to the UK. Later on, Alan was involved in the travel, tourism, hotel, property, financial, and retail sectors. His service to his community took the form of Rotary International with a committed focus on the Rotary Youth Exchange Program.

Having migrated to Brisbane, Australia, in 2001, Alan bought a franchise in the retail sector, which he successfully ran with his late wife and two children. In 2012 he sold the business and went into semi-retirement. He now pursues his hobbies of writing, travelling, wildlife safaris and ornithology with his wife, Sharon.

More about the author can be found as follows:
Web: www.landaubooks.com
Twitter: @landaubooks
Facebook: www.facebook.com/landaubooks
Instagram: landaubooks

The Langbourne Series

Based on a true story, the Langbourne series follows the lives of four intrepid brothers who journey to Africa in 1891. Without parents, friends, or family, they disembark the ship at Port Elizabeth and set their minds to making enough money to support their destitute family in Ireland. But Mother Africa has ideas of her own.

A Landau Books Publication
www.landaubooks.com

"To Brave Men"
by
Alan P Landau

Based on the true story of the Shangani Patrol, delve into this enthralling narrative as the haunting tale of the ill-fated Shangani Patrol unfurls with gripping intensity.

Embark on a journey alongside the audacious Fred Burnham, whose adventurous spirit knows no bounds.

Meet Major Allan Wilson, a valiant officer navigating the harrowing perils of war with unwavering courage.

Discover King Lobengula, a complex figure embodying both ruthless tyranny and diplomatic finesse, leaving an indelible mark on his people.

Witness the loyalty of Mjaan, Lobengula's steadfast Induna, tested to his limits.

Set in 1893, against the backdrop of a war-torn southern African landscape, the remarkable bravery of these men echoes through time, reshaping the course of history. Immerse yourself in a world of bravery, sacrifice, and unbreakable human resolve in this captivating and unforgettable tale.

"Of Sand and Stars"
by
Brenda Kate

In the vast Australian outback, FBI agent Mandy Richardson and an enigmatic Australian astronomer kindle a forbidden romance while unravelling a sinister plot. Their combined knowledge uncovers a scheme for mass destruction, forcing them to navigate dangers and reconcile loyalties. Racing against time and torn between duty and desire, they must conquer ruthless adversaries and protect humanity. Prepare for a thrilling journey where love defies rules and survival hangs in the balance.

Another Landau Books Publication
www.landaubooks.com

www.ingramcontent.com/pod-product-compliance
Lightning Source LLC
Chambersburg PA
CBHW021010120726
47905CB00009B/2939